3 QUEENS
An Unforgettable Urban Romance

A NOVEL BY

PORSCHA STERLING

This PORSCHA STERLING novel is published by

Royalty Publishing House, Inc.
P.O. Box 924043
Norcross, GA 30010

Cover Designer: Marion Designs

JOIN MY MAILING LIST!

Join my mailing list to stay up to date on my blog posts, news and my new releases. I also run many contests that are only mentioned to my mailing list subscribers.

Click this link to join or text PORSCHA to 25827

To submit a manuscript for my review, go here or visit www. royaltypublishinghouse.com and visit the 'submissions' tab.

Many Thanks to...

My BIG, little men, **Alphonzo** *&* **Kingston.**
Leo, you are the most patient man alive. Love it and I love you. #Thankful

Michelle, *you are my right hand and I'm so grateful for you.*

Thank you to the authors signed to **Royalty Publishing House**...*I couldn't run a company, read, write and stay fly like I do if you guys weren't the best team ever.* **#TeamRoyaltyForever**

Thank you to **my readers** *who have stuck with me since the beginning because they know Porscha and #Royalty only delivers #dopebooks.*

PROLOGUE

ossing the short and sweaty bangs of her bob to the side, Kaylen bit her lip and attempted to focus on the job at hand. She only had a few more minutes before Salem returned, and she already knew that he would be poised, and ready to kick her ass.

Using all of the strength that God gave her, Kaylen grunted loudly and once again tried for seemingly the millionth time to use the small and severely bent hairpin to pick at her chains. Tears welled up in her eyes, and she blinked them back quickly as they began to blur her vision.

She jabbed at the small metal into the lock and began to think back through the past few months. How did she get here? When did her life begin to take such a drastic turn and how did she not see it coming?

It could be worse; she thought to herself. Brushing a drop of sweat off her brow, she looked at the blood soaked panties that clung to her bruised skin. *But how could it....how could it get any worse than it was at this very moment?* She prayed to God that she would never know.

With that thought, she bit her bottom lip and took one last jab at the lock. She then yelped out in pain as she felt a slap that immediately made her see the moon and stars.

"Bitch! What the fuck do you think you are doing?" Salem had returned. Kaylen hadn't even heard him approach, and from the ringing in her ears, it would be a while before she was able to hear anything else again.

She lifted her face and tried to stare at him through her pulsating eyes, which were already beginning to swell.

"Didn't I tell you what I would do if you tried to escape again? What you thought, I was playing?" Salem spat. His brows were curled in a way that made his face look somewhat deranged.

Salem paced back and forth while rubbing his hands through his ragged dreadlocks. Kaylen shivered as she looked at him. He was obviously trying to plot her punishment.

Suddenly, Salem turned sharply towards Kaylen and ran over to her. He grabbed her by her neck, and began punching her square in the face and as hard as he could.

As blood filled her mouth, Kaylen began to feel as if she was being disconnected from her body. The last thing she saw as she slipped into unconsciousness was Salem pull out his hunting knife.

I guess it's about to get worse; she thought as she fell back on the filthy floor.

KAYLEN

6 MONTHS EARLIER

*I*t all started on a hot, Tuesday afternoon.

"Miss....excuse, me. Excuse me!"

Without turning to look, Kaylen rolled her eyes at what she knew to be desperation staring at her with lustful eyes.

This was nothing new. Although Kaylen had never been someone that others would immediately call "pretty," she never had problems in the men department. She had her mama and LA Fitness to thank for that.

Without slowing her stride, Kaylen glanced at the brother standing to her right and sucked her teeth. In two seconds, she was confident in her initial decision to keep walking. She could easily see that this man could not handle her.

Kaylen liked nice things, and she made sure that she worked to get what she wanted. A brother on the corner trying to holler at her while standing at the Marta bus stop was not the business. Kaylen clutched her Louis Vuitton bag, and continued on to her Lexus that was parked curbside. She checked out her French manicure to ensure that it was dry before dipping her fingers into her purse to retrieve her keys.

"Oh...I get it," he said to himself. His stare continued to follow Kaylen as she deactivated her alarm and neared her vehicle.

Yeah, that's what I thought; Kaylen thought as she opened her door. With a small smirk on her face, she dropped her purse into the passenger seat and slid into her car.

Lesson learned, I guess; she thought as she quickly eyed her admirer while he looked at her with a face of defeat. He now knew he had no chance.

Kaylen was not rich by any means, but she knew how to survive. And she was not content if she could not look good doing it. None of her classmates knew from looking at her that she had to work a day in her life. Kaylen always carried herself like she was born with a platinum spoon and a custom-made Benz to go along with her crib and diapers. That definitely had not been the case, but you wouldn't be able to tell that she hadn't.

Kaylen took a quick look at the clock on the dash as she slowly brought the car to a stop at the traffic light.

Damn, guess I have to stop by Chequers later...no time to eat. Sucking her teeth, Kaylen took a sharp left heading in the direction of her condo to prepare for work. Working is what kept her in that luxury condo in Buckhead with a closet full of expensive, name-brand clothing. Working is what made sure that she was able to afford her Lexus convertible, Mercedes Benz, and it's what paid for her tuition at Emory's College of Medicine.

She had always been taught by her father that not a damn thing would be given to her if she didn't work for it. He knew that there would be a day when she would have to take care of herself, so he taught her the only thing that he knew how to do. He taught her how to cook. From her earliest memory, she could remember sitting in the kitchen with her father as he cooked large orders for people he called his "friends." Eventually, Kaylen got to the point where she was able to make orders on her own while he just sat behind her, watching. And although her father always gave her everything she wanted, she eventually learned that what he'd told her was the truth. After he had passed away, not a thing was given to her. Not a *damn* thing that she hadn't worked for. So she had to use the only skill that he had given her. She became a cook, and she made plenty money doing it.

4

As Kaylen pulled into her garage, she felt her cell phone vibrating against her thigh for the third time since she had sat down in her car. Annoyed, she pressed the button on her steering wheel to answer the call.

"Speak on it," Kaylen said as she hit the button to lower her garage door.

"Kay, what's going on whichu? You already know what today is," Levi said, sounding noticeably irritated.

"Yes, I already know. Meet you in two hours."

"Two hours...damn, you must not want this money. We got a lot of people waiting on...."

"Later, L." Kaylen pressed the button to end the call and hopped out the car. Levi knew she didn't repeat herself, and she definitely didn't explain herself. He needed her, and she knew it. That's the way it had always been with him. At one point, she and Levi had a little bit of something that someone somewhere would probably call "puppy love," but that was long gone, and now they were strictly business.

Kaylen sighed and grabbed her purse out of the passenger seat. She didn't want to think on those things right now. Right now, the only thing on her mind was taking a quick soak in the tub and getting her mind right for what she knew would be a large order and a long day of work.

Kaylen unlocked her garage door, and walked swiftly into her townhome to deactivate her alarm. She sat her purse down on the bar countertop and walked towards the alarm pad. As she pressed her thumb against the metal pad, the beeping ceased, and she heard the heavy thumps of her puppy's paws running down the stairs.

"Hi Tiny! How's mama's little boy?" Kaylen said running her hands over the top of her Rottweiler's smooth head. As the dog panted with excitement, Kaylen ruffled his ears then walked towards the pantry to find him a treat. She tossed the treat in Tiny's bowl and walked up the stairs to her bedroom. As she walked towards the bedroom, she began taking off her clothes and dropping them on the floor behind her. *Joys of living alone*, Kaylen thought as she tossed her shirt over her head, allowing it to land on the top of the stairway.

She walked into her master bedroom and sat down on her California King-size bed. She did not have on a stitch of clothing, except for her shoes, and her skin appreciated her posh Charlotte Thomas linen. Leaning over, Kaylen began to undo her heels when her phone rang. She shook off her red bottoms, then sprang up from her bed, and hustled over to the entrance of the bedroom where she had left her jeans. Rummaging through the pockets, she was able to locate her phone right before the last ring.

"Hello?" Kaylen said hesitantly. She didn't normally answer numbers that she didn't know.

"Hey, baby. How are you?" The deep baritone on the other line made an immediate smile tease the sides of Kaylen's lips.

"Everything's great....how are you, Caleb?" Kaylen asked as she resumed her position on the bed. Caleb was.......well; Kaylen was not quite sure what Caleb was, but she was sure of what she wanted him to be. She and Caleb had been seeing each other for over three years off and on. Although nothing had ever been made official between them, Kaylen always kept hope alive that it would. He was six feet, four inches tall, and a smooth espresso brown. Caleb had a short cut and impeccable taste when it came to everything. He was always dressed to impress, his home had décor that hinted to the assistance of an interior decorator, and he had the most charming personality.

Kaylen loved to be around him and would love for him to be her man, but he had one major flaw....he was a huge cheater. Caleb couldn't stay faithful to save his life, and he didn't believe in committing. The fact that he even had a new number clued Kaylen in on the fact that he must have had a run-in with one of his women who didn't readily accept "her place" in his life. But Caleb was not a bad guy at all.

Actually, his outlook on women and how he felt about relationships, sharply contrasted how he treated her. He treated her like a Queen when they were together, but his opinion of women was that they were unnecessary and needy. That was why she could never get it to work with Caleb. Although he treated her right, he never wanted anything more, not to mention that she did not hear from him on a consistent basis at all. This was her first call from Caleb in three months. It was always like that with him and probably always would be. However, every time he called, they would pick up like he had never left.

"I'm well, Kaylen. Was just thinking about you and decided to give you a call. I actually still have the red panties that you left the last time you were over here."

Kaylen wasn't certain, but she thought that she could hear him smiling through the phone. She closed her eyes, and pictured him rubbing the panties on his crotch as he spoke to her. The thought made Kaylen get wet instantly. She took in a deep breath and exhaled slowly, pulling in the scent of her vanilla candle on her nightstand. Kaylen was conflicted and didn't know what to do.

She and Caleb had crazy chemistry. When he was around, she felt at ease, safe, and constantly aroused. He was the only man that she had sex with on the first night. Kaylen met Caleb on her way to class one day. He was a stand-in professor for her anatomy class. Although he had a medical degree and was qualified to teach the material, this was not a day where a lecture was necessary because they were in the lab. Kaylen came to class extremely nervous because it was the first day that they would have to work with cadavers. She had only seen one dead body in her life, and that had been what seemed like the beginning of the end for Kaylen.

When Kaylen walked into the lab, the first thing that she noticed was the putrid smell. She immediately covered her nose and mouth with her hand, and ran up the stairs and out of the building. She had just made it to the lawn in time to throw up every item that she had for breakfast that day. As she heaved into the grass, other medical students passed by her. The senior students understood her plight since they had been in her shoes before. Her arriving classmates looked on with their own eyes filled with the same anxiety and trepidation that she had felt. Once she finished, Kaylen looked up with her hands placed squarely on her knees as she tried to catch her breath. And that's when she noticed Caleb walking her way.

"I'm guessing you have lab today...am I right? First time dealing with the bodies, huh?" Caleb said as he grabbed her backpack from off the sidewalk. Kaylen was too winded to speak just yet, so instead she shook her head quickly as she confirmed his suspicions.

"Don't worry. You will adjust to the smell soon. I'm headed your way...let's go," That chance meeting had been the beginning of what Kaylen had hoped was meant to be. And here she was: three years, many booty calls, followed by unanswered calls, and lots of other women later. Still, Kaylen and Caleb were nothing more than friends with benefits. No matter how much Kaylen wanted more from him, Caleb was sure to resist.

"I'm just as fine now as I was the last time we spoke, Caleb...three whole months ago," Kaylen said jerking out of the trance that Caleb's voice had placed her in. She had to fight his advances as much as possible. She needed to be able to stand her ground.

"Well, can I see you? I would love to take you out for some fun. I have to leave out in the morning, but I have some time tonight."

Kaylen rolled her eyes and fell backwards on her bed. She could see right through his bullshit. *Does he really think that, after all this time, I can't cut through the crap and see that """ I have to leave in the morning" really means "No trying to sleep over after I have my way with you??" No, thanks!*

"Unfortunately, Caleb, I have other plans. We will have to meet up some other time when you aren't in such a rush. Gotta go...Kisses, Caleb. "With that, Kaylen hung up the phone before he could respond. She had to get ready for work anyways, and that made it all the easier to brush Caleb off.

Kaylen tossed her phone onto the bed before getting up, and walking over to her bathroom. As she walked over to her claw foot tub, she ran her nails along the edge of the granite countertop that made up the base for her sink. Everything in Kaylen's home had been hand-picked when she moved in. Although Kaylen liked to take the credit for how immaculate the place looked and how well it was deco-rated, all credit went to her best friend, Alexis.

When Kaylen first bought her condo: she knew she wanted it, but she didn't know what to do with it. Even though she lived a life of luxury when her father was alive, the life she had lived shortly after his passing made her memories of what it was like to have nice things seem so far away. Kaylen's idea of "nice décor" included a small sofa, a television, and a bed in the master bedroom. Alexis had been the one behind turning the condo into the beautiful place that it was now. The décor made her feel a little less than whole, so she decided to buy Tiny to keep her company. After that, Kaylen and her home were complete.

Kaylen started the water in her tub, and poured in the lavender bath elixir that Caleb had bought for her a while ago. The smell of the lavender put her completely at ease, and she loved it because of that. Since she had work to do later on, she needed to calm her nerves and get in the correct frame of mind. Kaylen placed her foot into the tub slowly, gauging the temperature of the water. The water was just right, so she slid the rest of her body into the tub and laid back into a total recline.

This is the life, she thought closing her eyes. She slowly breathed in the scent of the lavender, and held the breath for a minute before exhaling. The steam rising from the water made tiny beads of sweat sprout on her forehead, but that was exactly how she liked it. Kaylen was just about to drift off to sleep when she heard her phone ringing. From the ringtone, she knew it was Levi calling her again. Sighing, Kaylen lifted one of her legs up from the tub, and rested it on the knee of the opposite leg as she waited for the ringing to cease.

Guess this bath will be shorter than I would like, Kaylen groaned although she made no attempt to rush. She needed this time.

"I'm on my way. Where am I headed?" Kaylen asked as she bit at her nails. It was a nasty habit, but it was one that carried on from her youth. Nail biting had always been a habit of Kaylen's during extremely tense times or periods of indecisiveness. Her mother had always tried to cure her of the old habit; but to no avail, and when Kaylen began to live with her aunt the behavior did nothing but increased.

"Meet me at the normal spot," Levi replied. Kaylen noticed that he had a lot of noise in the background.

"You not there yet?" She asked for no particular reason other than curiosity. Levi always seemed to be everywhere way ahead of time. She figured it was just a personality trait of his. He didn't trust many people, so he showed up early to survey the scene everywhere that he went.

"Not yet. I had some business to take care of first. I will be there before you," Levi said, his voice a little above a whisper. He had a knack for speaking very quietly, and Kaylen hated it.

"Ok, well I will be there soon," Kaylen said, hanging up the call. Kaylen had about a thirty minute drive before she would arrive on the other side of town to the meeting place. Levi picked that particular place for them years ago when they first began working together. Stopping at a red light, Kaylen glanced down in her middle console and picked through her CDs. Although she had satellite radio and loved the variety that it provided every now and then, she needed to be able to listen to something that got her in a zone.

She pulled out her Rick Ross CD and pushed it into one of the open slots in her ten-slot CD changer. No one that knew Kaylen would ever guess that, among her John Legend, Alicia Keys, and Miguel albums, she had a few Rick Ross CDs stashed. She used to spend her summers in Miami on vacations with her parents, and had met the rapper on occasions before he became the boss he is now. Ever since then, she was in love with his music because it got her right.

As Kaylen pulled up to the small shack in the middle of one of Atlanta's most despondent neighborhoods, she noticed that Levi had remained true to his word and was already there. Kaylen pulled her Toyota Corolla up next to his Dodge truck and turned off the car. When it was time for work, she left the Lexus and the Benz at home. Her Corolla was the first car that she had ever bought for herself back when she was just a teen, and barely able to drive. Levi had taught her how to perfect her driving while in her Corolla, and although she had later upgraded, she kept the car for work, and also to remember where she came from and who she really was.

Kaylen opened up the door to Levi's truck and climbed into the passenger seat. He turned towards her, and his face softened for a minute. He hurried to change back into his normal blank expression, but it was too late. Kaylen had already taken notice of the way that he looked at her. She and Levi had decided a long time ago that they would no longer mix business with pleasure, and since making that decision, they had stuck with it. Kaylen knew that she would always love Levi. He'd saved her life back when she was nothing more than a troubled teen, but she knew that it was best for them to remain friends and business partners only. Levi had reluctantly agreed, but he went along with her wishes.

"Ok...I'm ready to pull out." Kaylen said looking briefly at Levi before pulling out her phone to place it on silent. Levi stared at her for a split second before turning the key in the ignition.

"Alright, then we out," he said under his breath before backing out. Kaylen leaned her head on the headrest and stared out the window. She never knew exactly where they were headed when it was time to work; that part was Levi's job. She only rode along, and did what she was supposed to once they arrived at the location.

Well, here we go again, Kaylen thought before retreating into her thoughts as she watched the trees pass her by.

ALEXIS

"*D*amn, K, pick up the phone!" Alexis huffed as she listened to the ringing on the line. This had to be the fourth time in a row that she called Kaylen and got no answer, no text message, *nothing*. Alexis, Jaz, and Kaylen had plans to go out in less than a few hours, and Alexis needed to speak with Kaylen before they went. Annoyed and frustrated, Alexis flung herself onto her bed, and began to think about what she had just heard.

Apparently, Jazmyn's boyfriend had just kicked her out. She got caught cheating *again*. The big deal wasn't even that she had got caught cheating; it was *how* she got caught cheating. The cheating part really was not a surprise at all. Jazmyn was her girl, but she really couldn't help herself. Men often tripped over her and offered to give her everything she wanted, but she could never turn down the next dick making at least six figures that came her way.

Sometimes, Alexis thought that it was more of a game to Jazmyn than anything. She didn't need the men for their money; however, she wasn't content until she was able to "conquer" the next big spender. What made it worse is that whenever her boyfriend at the time would break up with her, Jazmyn always acted like it wasn't her fault, and she didn't know how he could do her like that.

Alexis and Kaylen had been sure that Raymond would be different since Jazmyn had managed to stay with him for a whole year, but once again, they were wrong. He'd had a long run, but Jazmyn had made sure this time that she proved to her friends that he was no different from the rest when it came to her inability to remain faithful. Alexis looked over at her phone and sighed deeply with great annoyance. She wanted to warn Kaylen that they would be on "girlfriend" duty tonight, but since she wasn't answering the phone, that was out of the cards for the moment.

Alexis decided to forget about Kaylen for now, and walked over to her closet to find something to wear for the night. She looked in her lavish closet, and walked towards a section in the back that was tucked in a small nook in the corner. This was her special section of clothing that had a specific purpose of being worn only when she was going out with the girls. This section was where she kept her "freakum dresses" and her "tease-me shirts" with her signature plunging necklines.

Showing a little skin was nothing that Alexis had ever been afraid of; she just made sure she did it with class. She always adhered to her mother's rule of picking one part to show at a time. You never have your breasts *and* legs out. You pick one and cover the other. *That's how a lady does it.*

Alexis finally decided to settle on a new Chanel two piece jumpsuit that she had just bought while on vacation in New York the month before. She knew that this would fit her curves just right, and would draw exactly the kind of attention she wanted. Alexis was thick in all the right places and being that way came with lots of perks in the men department.

She had never desired to be a size two or a size seven. She was a happy size twelve and Marc, Alexis' husband of five years, loved it. Although he came from a family of small, tiny women, he had always said that there was something about a woman with curves that made him react in a way that he never could otherwise.

Alexis rubbed the soft fabric on her Chanel jumpsuit and thought about her husband. Marc was away, yet again, on business and had left her alone. Alexis missed him, but did not mind his being away at that moment. His absence gave her time to be with her girls, and apparently, at least one of them needed her.

Alexis was interrupted from her thoughts of Marc when her cell rang. She ran over and jumped on her bed to reach across and pick up her phone. Glancing at the screen, she saw it was Kaylen. *About damn time.*

"Hello, Ma'am...glad to see you're alive and well!" Alexis said as she rolled her eyes and twisted one of her long auburn strands of hair around her forefinger.

"Oh, calm down, Lexi! I had my phone on vibrate and didn't know you were calling. What's going on that's so important anyways?"

Alexis pulled the phone away from her ear and looked at it incredulously before answering. Kaylen had a lot of attitude for someone who was obviously in the wrong, but this was not the time to get into an argument over nothing.

"Well, I was just calling to tell you about your girl, Jaz. Her and Ray are having "issues" if you know what I mean."

"Oh...yep, I got you." Kaylen said only slightly distracted, but even still, a little annoyed. Kaylen and Alexis loved their friend, but both were a little disappointed that they would be on damage control duty tonight. When Jazmyn had relationship issues, she was such an easy target for any man who looked like he may have a lil' bit of cash, leaving her girls to watch out for her grown ass. Kaylen had just gotten off of work and was hoping to relax tonight with a few drinks. Well that wouldn't be happening.

"Alright, Kay. See you in a lil' bit." Alexis hung up the phone as she walked back into her closet. She dropped her phone onto the vanity, and looked back at her Chanel jumpsuit that lay on the white chaise lounge in the middle area of her closet. She thought for a second, then grabbed up the hanger off the lounge.

Naw, I'm feeling like Prada tonight.

14

"Hey baby! How is work going?" Alexis asked as she placed her Bluetooth in her ear. She removed the towel from her head and ran her hands through her shoulder-length naturally curly hair. Although Alexis loved her natural hair, it did prove to take a lot of tender love and care whenever she washed it. She checked the Bluetooth again to make sure it was secure before walking over to grab her hair-dryer.

"Great, Lexi. I've been able to secure some pretty good deals that should bring in a lot of money in the long-run. I really would have liked it if you were able to come here with me. Yesterday, I took a few of the clients and their wives out to dinner. It really made me miss you, Lexi." Marc paused, and Alexis knew that he was trying to find a way to ask her if she would fly out to be with him for the remainder of his trip. Although she loved Marc, she needed her breaks and the time to herself that she was able to get because of his business schedule. She knew that there would come a day when he didn't travel so much, and she would be ready for that when the time came, but as for now, she needed to be able to be alone sometimes.

"Well baby, guess what I'm getting into tonight?" Alexis changed the subject quickly in order to avoid going down the same old road with Marc that he tried to drag her down during each phone call. She loved her husband and longed to be with him, but she wasn't prepared for what she knew would accompany their time alone. Marc gave a long sigh before answering. He knew his wife and knew exactly what she was up to, but he also knew to just go along with it.

"I'm not sure, Lexi. Why don't you tell me?"

"Well...I'm finally getting a chance to go out with the girls. It's been a long time since Kaylen's been able to dodge schoolwork long enough to do anything with us," Alexis said as she began to blow dry her hair. She placed it on low so that she could continue her conversation with Marc, and started what was usually a fairly quick process of straightening out her curls.

"That's good to hear. Just make sure that you pay attention to your surroundings. You know I love you. I will let you go ahead and get ready. Give me a call when you get in, so I know you made it home safely."

"I love you too, Marc," Alexis said as she looked at her reflection. She couldn't shake the feeling that she was not doing the right thing and that she should be with her husband. She wanted to be with him, but they had issues of a peculiar nature. There were just things that needed to be ironed out in their relationship, and Alexis wasn't quite sure how to go about it. Marc was a great listener, and he was very sensitive to her feelings and what she thought, but Alexis truly was perplexed about how to speak to her husband regarding some of the more sensitive issues that were bothering her.

Lord, help me find a way. Alexis prayed to herself. She had never been religious and wasn't from a family that went to church other than on Holidays, but she knew that there was a higher power that had to be listening to her from time to time.

Alexis finished blow-drying her hair, and picked up her jar of coconut oil. She poured a little into her hand and ran her fingers through her hair. She was just about to pick up her brush when she heard a door close shut. Alexis tightened the towel around her, and ran to look outside of her bedroom door in the direction of the noise.

"Did I startle you, Sister?" Alexis groaned loudly as she looked at Vanessa walking towards her. *Glide* would have been a more appropriate word to describe the way that Vanessa sauntered across the room.

Vanessa was Alexis' younger sister, and also Alexis' great pain in the ass. Vanessa and Alexis had always had a love-hate relationship from as far back as they could remember...it probably began around the time that Vanessa was born because Alexis really could not remember a time that she was ever able to live peacefully with Vanessa around. They had their moments of tranquility, but it was often quickly followed by drama and confusion; two things that seemed to follow Vanessa wherever she went, and also two things that Alexis hated and would rather avoid. Alexis had spent most of her teenage life looking after her younger sister and protecting her in an effort to hide a lot of her troubling ways from their parents. The result had been Alexis taking the blame for a lot of the wrong-doing that she had taken no part in.

"Yes, you did, and now I know that I need to either get my locks changed, or collect your key. How did you get a key to my place, anyways?"

"Marc told me where you keep the spare, so I decided to let myself in," Vanessa finished as she walked past Alexis and into her room. Alexis watched as her sister walked over to her bed, and gently sat down on top of it. Vanessa was beautiful in every way. She had a short haircut, which resembled something that Halle Berry had once had; with incredibly long legs and the build of a video vixen that any rapper would love to have working on his team.

Her body oozed sex, and she had a command over men that Alexis; however pretty she thought she was, had never been able to master or quite understand the workings of. Vanessa was always able to make men, from all backgrounds and all ethnicities get caught up in her essence as if there was no other woman in the room. The thing about Vanessa was that she knew that she had this power and she always used it to her advantage. Although she and Alexis came from a family full of opportunities, Vanessa never wanted to go the route that would require her to build anything on her own. She decided long ago that she would rather rely on her own sexual prowess to get her to where she wanted to go. So far, it had worked.

"Well, what are you here for? I'm getting ready to go out," Alexis said as she turned away from Vanessa, and made her way back over to her vanity to grab some lotion. As she headed over to her window seat, she took a quick glance at Vanessa and noticed the odd look on her face. Vanessa seemed to be struggling to say something, and this was not her usual way. Vanessa had always been very direct and unafraid to say even the most inappropriate things, so the fact that she was hesitant to speak made Alexis stop in her tracks, and wait for her sister to answer.

"I need to move in with you for a little while. I've been having some...issues and I just need a place to stay," Vanessa said as her confidence returned. She straightened her back and looked Alexis square in the eyes as she waited for what she expected to be an immediate answer.

"Vanessa," Alexis sighed as she walked over to the window seat and sat down. "What is the matter? I thought you were staying with Sasha...didn't she move into the condo with you that daddy bought? Why can't you stay there?"

"Lexi, Sasha and I are not getting along right now. She moved out, and I really don't want to stay alone right now. I can explain later. Can I please move in with you?" Alexis paused as she thought about the possible issues that could arise by Vanessa staying with her. There were things regarding her relationship with Marc that she didn't want anyone to know about. However, Alexis' mothering instincts kicked in, and she felt the need to protect her sister although she had a feeling that it would lead to much regret later on.

"Sure, Vanessa. I will clean out the guesthouse, and you can stay there. When do you need to move in?" Alexis looked down and began applying lotion on her legs. She tried to hide the tense look on her face, and shoo away all of the warning signs going off in her head. *She's my sister, and she needs me. I just have to hope that she has grown up.*

"Today...like right now, actually. I have all of my things in the car outside. I can leave everything else in the condo for now," Vanessa said as she got up from the bed, and started for the door. Alexis looked up, and her mouth dropped open.

"Right now? So, you pretty much knew that I would allow you to move in, huh? Well, since that is the case, *you* can clean out the guest-house. Don't make a mess in there, and no men are allowed in there, Vanessa!" Alexis yelled to Vanessa's back as she walked out of the bedroom door. The last thing she saw before Vanessa turned the corner was her hand waving off her comments.

"Damn it!" Alexis huffed.

She got me again!

KAYLEN

"*D*amn, K. You always late!" Kaylen looked at Alexis and placed her hand on her hip and then waved Alexis off as she walked over to hug Jazmyn. She looked back to Alexis, watched as she crossed her arms in front of her, and scrunched up her face into a frown.

"That's the way we greet each other now? I had a late start. Had to take care of some business." Kaylen said as she glanced around the club. *Compound* was definitely the place to be tonight. Kaylen took a quick look at the crowd, and immediately noticed some labels that told her she was in the right place. She felt the heat of Alexis' stare and looked back at her friend.

You left me with her! Alexis mouthed, and now Kaylen knew just why she was so upset. Apparently Jazmyn had been doing her usual thing, and Alexis was upset about playing babysitter alone.

"Jaz, how are you doing? I heard the news. You holding up ok?" Kaylen asked as she turned her attention to Jazmyn, who looked flawless as usual. Her eyes looked slightly puffy, but you wouldn't be able to tell unless you were looking for it. Her makeup was perfect, and she had her eyes done in a way that accented their almond shape and sat well against her mahogany skin-tone. Jazmyn blew her breath out sharply causing her bang to ruffle as she rolled her eyes, and drummed her nails on the tabletop on front of her.

"No, Kay. I can't believe that nigga would do that to me! How could he kick me out of the place that we shared after all this time? I've done nothing but be good to him! I've been holding him down for a whole year!" Jazmyn started to continue, but thought twice, and quickly downed the rest of her drink. Kaylen raised her brow and looked over at Alexis. Alexis had a look on her face that said a clear "I told you so" then she turned her back to them to survey the crowd. Kaylen couldn't tell what Jazmyn was drinking, but thought she caught the scent of Hennessey. Jazmyn was a lady, but when she was angry, she let the hood in her shine through. There was no telling how much she had already drunk of the strong liquor, but from the way that she was wavering back and forth in her seat, Kaylen knew that this had definitely not been her first...or second...drink.

"That's ok! It's a lot of men in here who will help me forget about that motherfucker!" Jazmyn said as she waved her hands in the air to point around at the crowd. She then motioned for the bartender to pour her another drink. Kaylen looked at Alexis and sighed. This was about to be a long night.

"Jaz, why don't you just have a little fun? That's what we came here for. C'mon, dance with me." Right on cue, Kendrick Lamar's *Bitch, don't kill my vibe* came on. Kaylen smirked as she thought to herself; *that's exactly what I need to hear.* She grabbed Jazmyn's hand and led her to the dance floor. Before Jazmyn gave in to Kaylen's pull, she took a long swig of her freshly poured liquor, and then slammed the glass back down and followed Kaylen to the dance floor. When Kaylen turned her back, she saw Alexis hand the glass back to the bartender and whisper something in his ear. Kaylen knew that Alexis was letting him know not to pour Jazmyn anymore drinks for the night unless they were severely watered down.

When Kaylen arrived on the dance floor, she decided that she deserved a little fun as a reward for the tough day that she had. She made sure that Jazmyn was enjoying herself before she closed her eyes and zoned into the lyrics of the song. "*I am a sinner, who's probably gonna sin again. Lord forgive me. Please forgive me...*" Kaylen began moving her body on the dance floor slowly to catch the beat. She felt the high slit in her dress open up exposing her thigh, and she continued to twerk her body to the beat as she lowered herself to the floor, and then picked herself back up slowly.

She felt a man try to position himself behind her, and she stopped dancing immediately to turn towards him and shake her head "no." Tonight was all for her. She was not worried about dancing with anyone or worrying about how many numbers she could get tonight. She needed to relax and relax was what she intended to do.

Kaylen started back moving her hips slowly to the beat when she began to feel like someone was looking at her. She looked up and glanced quickly around the dark club in an attempt to figure out the reason behind her feeling. She quickly brushed off the feeling and decided that she was probably right. Someone *was* probably looking. Shit, *everyone* should have been looking at her.

She was having a good time and dancing like someone was throwing money at her feet. Kaylen noticed that the dance floor had filled up pretty quickly, and people were crowding in on her, but that didn't stop her from dancing. Her hip softly bumped another female in the club as she danced. The woman turned sharply and eyed Kaylen angrily.

"Bitch, you know this is a club, and it's thick in here. If you worried about getting touched, get your ass off the dance floor!" Kaylen checked her quickly, and then turned her back to her to look for Jazmyn just as the girl looked as if she wanted to respond.

I ain't even trying to hear that shit.

Kaylen weaved her way through a few people dancing by and found Jazmyn on the opposite side of the dance floor booting up her ass on the same guy that had tried to grab onto her earlier. She laughed to herself, and then put her hands in the air as the next song came on. It was a joint by Erykah Badu, and it was just what she needed to hear at that moment to calm her mood. This was exactly what she had wanted to get into tonight.

Two songs later, Jazmyn and Kaylen decided to head back to the table. Alexis was busy talking to a fine brother dressed in what looked like a tailored suit. It fit snuggly against his athletic build, and the material must have felt nice too from the way that Alexis was running her fingers up and down his lower arm as she leaned in close to him to whisper in his ear. The brother smiled widely and licked his lips slowly as he reached over and squeezed Alexis' ass firmly. Kaylen shook her head and sighed.

Poor thing don't even know he is wasting his time. Alexis loved attention, but she would never cheat on Marc. However, she got a high off of pushing her limits. And she really did push her limits. Kaylen had warned her on quite a few occasions that it was dangerous to take these men all the way to the edge and leave them the way that she did. Most good brothers don't have a problem spending time with a woman that they know they will never have sex with, but when you lead them to believe the whole night that you are going to put it on them, they become a different person when you don't.

Kaylen had barely got settled into her seat when she noticed that she had that feeling again. Someone was watching her, and she felt the hairs on her arms begin to rise. She flipped her bang out of her eyes and began to look around the club. It was hard to see anything in the dark building, and the black lights and strobe lights mixed with the thick smoke in the air, made it even harder.

She shuddered as she tried to ignore the feeling and turned her attention to Jazmyn, who looked as if she was trying to flag down the bartender again. Kaylen started to intervene when her eyes caught the stare of a man towards the back of the club. He was bald, with evenly toned, caramel skin, athletic build, and was dressed in crisp white, linen pants and a simple blue shirt. He was leaning on the wall, and stared at her so intently that she had to take in a quick breath and look away. She ran her hands through the front of her hair and started to bite on her fingernails before looking back up to see if he was still watching.

She saw that he was still looking at her as if he was studying her. It was something about the gaze that interested her and made her feel nervous all at once. This was not a feeling that she was used to, and she was unsure of how she should react. Something about him looked so familiar, but Kaylen couldn't pinpoint where she had seen him before. She watched as he nodded his head in a way that seemed to respond to her unasked question and also acknowledge the fact that he felt her stare, as well. Kaylen reluctantly turned away from him when she noticed a short young woman dressed in the tiniest sequined, black shorts possible standing in front of her with her hand outstretched holding a drink on a platter.

"Someone bought you a drink," the cute young woman said to Kaylen with a smile. She dipped her head and winked at Kaylen in a way that seemed to signal that she approved of the buyer. Kaylen immediately looked to her admirer on the wall and smiled, assuming the drink was from him.

"Who bought it?" Kaylen asked.

"That fine specimen headed this way," the woman said as she nodded her head pointedly to her right. Kaylen followed her line of sight and saw a fine chocolate brother with long dreadlocks headed her way. He had a small smirk on his face, and his hands were placed in his pockets giving him a boyish, but sexy, look.. He was wearing a long-sleeved, collared white shirt with a gold design on it, and black jeans. His long dreadlocks were pulled in a style that made them fall to his side and cascade down his back with a few falling forward and lying on the edge of his chest. She glanced quickly at the familiar face standing on the wall and noticed that he looked slightly irritated.

Oh, well...snooze you lose; Kaylen thought watching her new suitor as he headed her way.

"Hello, miss, my name is Salem," he said as he licked his lips and sat down next to her, extending his hand. Kaylen looked at Jazmyn and almost laughed out loud. Jazmyn was looking at Salem in a way that let her know that if she could have her way; Salem would have been laid out on the table, butt-naked with her straddling him, and bouncing away like dick was going out of style.

"I'm Kaylen. It's nice to meet you." Kaylen said as she placed her hands in his to shake it. But Salem had other plans and brought her hand to his mouth for a gentle kiss.

"And I'm Jazmyn!" She announced from across the table and reached out for Salem's hand. Salem chuckled as he brought her hand to his lips as well and kissed it. "But you can call me Jaz." Jazmyn smiled sexily and took her time sliding her hand out of Salem's. Kaylen looked at her smile and rolled her eyes.

Hoes always be winning; she thought looking at her friend and shook her head.

"Jaz," Salem said as he looked at her smitten face. "I have a homeboy who I know would love to meet you. He's the quiet type, but don't let that shake you. You look like a lady who likes nice things and would love to be treated right. He's the type." Salem looked at Jazmyn and winked.

Kaylen appreciated the fact that Salem didn't dismiss Jazmyn although he had come over initially to speak to her. The last thing she needed was Jazmyn to feel the rejection of a man, on top of everything else that had happened to her that day. That would definitely ruin the mood.

"Ok," Jazmyn stated looking curious but doubtful that whoever his friend was would be able to rival what was already in front of her. "He better be good though. Where is he?" She said as she smoothed down her hair.

"Oh, you sit right there. He will come to you," with that, Salem nodded to someone across the room. Kaylen looked in the direction of his nod and saw her admirer on the wall headed their way. As he came closer, she noticed he began to look finer and finer. He still had a look of irritation on his face as he walked towards the table, and he seemed to be struggling to fix his expression. When he came close, Kaylen immediately remembered where she had seen him.

That's the dude that tried to holla at me earlier today! Kaylen frowned to herself. This man right here couldn't be the one that she saw at the bus stop. Not the one with the white t-shirt and basketball shorts on who tried to get her number while he waited at the Marta station. She looked at his Armani shades tucked in the collar of his shirt and the Presidential Rolex on his arm. He obviously could afford a car and a few other things if he were able to rock a Roley. Kaylen felt instantly embarrassed as she smoothed the wrinkles out of her electric blue dress.

"Hey, I have someone that I think you should meet," Salem said as he stood up and put his arm around the man standing at the table. "This here is Ms. Jazmyn. She told me that I could call her Jaz, but I won't assume you have that privilege yet." Salem chuckled as he looked over at Jazmyn whose face showed obvious approval.

Kaylen lifted her face to look at this new man as he stared at her for what felt like an hour, ignoring his friend who was pointing in Jazmyn's direction. Finally, he pulled his attention away from Kaylen and turned towards Jazmyn, who was grinning up at him and nearly foaming at the mouth. He held out his hand to extend a friendly greeting.

"Hello, Jazmyn. My name is Lorenzo. But you can just call me Zo."

"And you may call me Jaz. Nice to meet you, Zo, " Jazmyn sat up straight to make sure that she gave Zo a full glimpse of the top of her breasts. " It's so very nice to meet you."

"You know...I actually like the name Jazmyn. It has a nice ring to it." Zo said as he pulled a chair up to sit next to Jazmyn.

"And I like the way you say it," Jazmyn smiled and leaned in closely.

Damn, Kaylen thought. *Hoes always be winning.*

KAYLEN DRUMMED HER NAILS ACROSS HER LEG AS SHE AND ALEXIS listened to Jazmyn speak on and on about how her night ended. Apparently, Zo had been the "perfect gentleman."

"Jazmyn, you really have to stop having sex with these guys on the first night," Kaylen said to her friend, hoping that she was actually listening. She worried about her when she got in these types of moods. Actually she worried about her all the time. Her hope was that Jazmyn would find someone that she could really settle down with instead of these random guys that she hooked up with just because they had money.

"Oh, I didn't have sex with him. I just let him bring me home after we left the club. Thank God I kept this apartment after I moved in with Raymond." Jazmyn had begun calling Ray by his government name now that she decided she was aspiring to be Zo's main girl. *Out with the old and in with the new.* "I wanted to have sex with him, but he just shrugged it off whenever I tried to do something sexual. He's playing hard to get is all. It's been a long time since I've been with such a gentleman, but I like the challenge."

"Well, did you get his number?" Kaylen asked as she relaxed and fell back into the recliner that she occupied. She pulled her legs up and rested the base of her chin on her knees. Her curiosity was more for her own benefit than for Jazmyn's. She wanted to see if the guy that seemed so interested in her would go for her friend instead.

"No, but I gave him mine. He will call, though. I'm sure of it."

"How are you so sure?" Alexis asked, folding her legs up under her on the plush, red sofa. Jazmyn paused from painting her toenails to look up and answer the question.

"I left my purse in his car. So he should be calling any time now to return it." She smiled, obviously basking in her shrewdness.

"You don't think that is a little obvious? How you leave your purse but not your phone?" Kaylen asked. Jazmyn shrugged and went back to painting her toenails.

I really shouldn't be jealous; Kaylen thought to herself. She'd had a good night with Salem. He had danced with her most of the night and even took her out to grab a bite to eat after the club. He followed her home in his pearl white Escalade truck since she'd had a few drinks at the club, and made sure that she got in safely. They had exchanged numbers, and he had already texted her this morning. A simple "Good morning, Beautiful" was all.

She was feeling him and looking forward to spending more time with him. He was definitely a nice change from Caleb, who had not bothered to call her at all since she hung up on him the last time they spoke. Salem seemed to be doing all the right things. However, something about Zo had piqued her curiosity. She couldn't shake the feeling.

"HA...I told you!" Jazmyn said as she looked at her phone. "Kaylen, answer the door while I fix my hair. He texted saying he is outside with my purse." Jazmyn stood up and ran up the stairs to her master bathroom.

Kaylen looked over to Alexis, thinking about asking her to answer the door instead. When she saw Alexis frowning down at her cell phone, Kaylen sighed loudly and pulled herself off of the sofa. She smoothed down her hair and began to walk to the door. She was not dressed to impress. Sure, she looked decent in her Juicy Couture tracksuit, but she did not put it on planning to see anyone but her girls this morning.

Kaylen opened the door and squinted out into the front of Jazmyn's apartment. She put her hand up to shield her eyes from the glare of the sun and saw an all-black 2-door Porsche pull up and park right in front of her.

Now that's more like it; she thought as she leaned back against the door. Zo stepped out of his car wearing black basketball shorts and a crisp, pure white t-shirt, with black Jordan sneakers. He looked very similar to the way that she had first seen him. He placed Jazmyn's purse under his arm loosely and headed in her direction with his head down. He was obviously very uncomfortable holding it. When he looked up and saw her, Kaylen could have sworn she saw a twinkle in his eye and a small smile teasing at the corner of his lips, but she couldn't be sure.

"Hi, Ms. Kaylen. How are you doing this..." he checked his watch. "...afternoon?"

"I'm doing ok. You?"

"All is well," Zo said. Kaylen noticed that his eyes never left hers. Although her jacket was open, and her shirt had a dipping neckline, Zo remained focused on her face. Kaylen looked back over her shoulder at Alexis. She was still pecking away at her phone, texting. Kaylen took the opportunity to close the door behind her in order to speak to Zo more privately.

"So that was you, yesterday. Downtown...right?" Kaylen shifted and placed her hand on her left hip. Zo's eyes darted quickly to her hip. They had lingered there for a moment before he lifted his eyes back to her face.

Bingo, Kaylen smirked. *All man after all.*

"Yeah...noticed you didn't want to give a nigga no attention. I get it. Couldn't blame you though."

"I thought you were tryna ask me for a ride or something. Since you were at the bus stop," Kaylen lied. She knew he didn't believe it, but she was trying not to seem too shallow. She also wanted to know why someone who drove a Porsche would opt to take the bus. "Obviously, you didn't need it." She tilted her head towards his ride. Zo turned toward it and scoffed.

"That car ain't nothing. Nothing wrong with the bus. Sometimes I just have to take it back to what I know." Kaylen paused to think about what he said. So he was like her - came from the bottom up. Nice. She could appreciate a man that worked for what he had, especially if he had a lot.

"So, is Salem a good guy?" Kaylen asked, admiring Zo's bold stance. He stood like a boss. She could tell that there was something more to him than what you could see. A part of her wanted to know more about that side to him, but she decided it might be disrespectful to him to flirt when he was friends with Salem.

"Yeah. You just be careful around him, ok?" Zo said lowly, dropping his voice barely above a whisper. Kaylen wasn't even sure she was supposed to hear the warning, but she'd had enough experience dealing with Levi's whispering that her hearing could pick up the lowest murmur. Before Kaylen could ask what he meant, the door swung open, and Jazmyn appeared looking unbelievably perfect for so early in the day.

"Hey baby, thanks for bringing my purse. Would you like to come in?" She said in her normal chipper tone. Zo shifted his weight as he looked at both women staring at him.

"Naw, I'm heading to the gym. Check you later," he said quickly. With that, he handed Jazmyn her purse, and turned around to walk back to his car. Jazmyn pouted a little, and then immediately perked back up.

"Ok, see you!" she said. She shot an accusatory look over at Kaylen and walked back into the house. Kaylen walked behind her and glanced over at Alexis. She had finally put her phone down but had a strange look on her face. Kaylen couldn't quite place the look, but she made a mental note to ask her about it later.

"Dang, Kaylen, what...do you want both of them for yourself?" Jazmyn pouted. Kaylen gave her a confused look and sat back down on the recliner.

"What? What do you mean?" Kaylen had to admit she was curious about Zo, and there was no denying that he was sexy, but she didn't think she had made it that obvious.

"I saw how he was looking at you at *Compound*. I just didn't think that it mattered all that much. But I can see where his real interest lies. So now you have him and Salem to choose from," Jaz narrowed her eyes at Kaylen.

Two seconds later, she immediately perked up. "It's ok because Ray texted me while I was in the bathroom! I'm about to meet up with him in about an hour. Maybe you can do both, Kaylen. It's always more fun that way. Or have them engage in a little competition. You gotta learn how to use that power you have between them thighs, girl!" Jazmyn said as she winked at Kaylen and headed to her bedroom. Alexis and Kaylen shared a glance and sighed.

Back to the old bump and grind.

"ALRIGHT...WHERE WE HEADED?" KAYLEN ASKED LEVI AS HE SAT ON THE porch of their shabby meeting spot. She really didn't like doing too many jobs this close in time. She preferred to space it out to about every few months or so, but Levi seemed to have picked up more business for them, so here she was - filling another order not even a full day later.

"Someplace close. We out?" Levi rose up from his chair and took a quick glance at the top of Kaylen's mocha colored breasts. He let his eyes linger for a second longer than he probably should have, before turning to walk towards his truck.

"Let's get it," Kaylen stated as she quickly turned and walked towards Levi's vehicle.

This nigga just got caught slipping, she thought as she lightly touched her back to make sure that her Desert Eagle was tucked just right. Kaylen stayed strapped. One thing her father had always taught her was that men always saw women as weak. While many women thought of this as something to be upset about, Kaylen's father had taught her how to make this an advantage. If a man thought you were weak, he would keep his guard down, and that's the perfect time to attack. She wasn't worried about Levi trying her; it wasn't like he'd never had it. But every now and then a nigga tried to get pussy whipped and may need a good pistol-whipping to correct the damage done to his mind.

After driving for about an hour, Levi pulled up to an abandoned building and turned off the car. Kaylen looked at the building before jumping out and then let out a sharp breath of annoyance. It looked like a small warehouse, tucked and forgotten in the middle of the woods. From the looks of it, the place should have been condemned and torn down a long time ago.

The front area of the building leaned in slightly making it seem as if it was due to come crashing down any minute. She started forward and hesitated slightly before placing her shoe into the moist soil. Luxury never coincided with her place of business. It was part of the occupation, and it was something that she had come to accept. The luxury came after business was done. *Gotta pay to play.*

Kaylen watched Levi grab all the materials that were needed and waited while he headed to the entrance of the building. After he opened the door and went in, she quickly took one last glance at her surroundings before following his lead.

Showtime, she thought. It was time to get to business and cook up somebody's meal. Kaylen was a chef. But food was never on the menu. She cooked meth.

ALEXIS

*A*lexis could tell that Kaylen knew something was up. So she had dodged as many of her questions as she could, put on a face that said she was perfectly happy, and headed out the door to her car. Kaylen was too good at knowing when something was bothering Alexis and it was becoming harder and harder for her to hide the truth from her. Throughout the years, Alexis had become a professional at pretending and hiding the truth.

Hell, I deserve an Oscar; she thought to herself as she stopped at the traffic light. She picked up her phone and quickly read the message for the hundredth time since she had received it hours earlier while at Jazmyn's house. Alexis ran her fingers through her long, auburn hair and sighed.

Marc is home. That thought had been circling through her mind since before she left Jazmyn's apartment. Marc had texted her stating that he was going to be home early. Although she was happy to see her man, she was mentally unprepared for what she knew would come when she arrived home. For that reason, she had been driving around on faux-errands, taking her time getting back to the home that she shared with her husband. Marc had arrived back early, before she had time to prepare and before she had time to get her mind together. She had always tried to be a good wife to him…a *great* wife to him. But it still didn't make her plight any easier.

As she turned onto their beautiful property and paused at the gates to enter the code, she began to slow her breathing in order to calm herself down.

It only works if you get into it. You have to stay calm, she told herself. Alexis pulled up to the house and parked in the front. She looked over to grab her purse from the passenger seat. When she looked up Marc was already standing at the door with a huge smile on his face. *It only works if you get into it. It only works if you get into it.*

"Hey baby. I missed you!" he said as he came over to open the car door for her.

"I missed you too, Marc," Alexis looked up at him and smiled. Marc was exactly the type of man that she had ever wanted, and she loved everything about him. He was tall and very handsome. Alexis usually preferred them dark too, but Marc's ancestry originated from Italy, so he had a Mediterranean glow, but was pretty much as light as she was willing to go.

Two out of three ain't bad, she thought as she licked her lips and looked at her husband. She had waited what seemed like an eternity for this man. She knew from a very young age that she wanted to be married early on in her life. Although she had her own dreams and aspirations, one very real goal of hers was to find love and enjoy her life as a wife. Alexis was very traditional in the way that she believed in not having sex until she met the one and he became her husband.

While Jazmyn and Kaylen were out enjoying life and enjoying sex with whoever they deemed worthy, Alexis had decided that she was going to hold on to her virtue and pray that God hurried up and brought the right man to her. When she married Marc, she wasn't sure what she would get, but she was sure that he would be happy knowing that he was the first one to get what she had to give. Little did she know she got more than she had ever expected, and more than she had really wanted.

Marc helped Alexis out of the car and closed the door behind her.

Alexis looked up at her husband as he wrapped his arms around her waist.

"Is Vanessa here? You know she moved...." Alexis started.

"I know. No, she's not here. She said she was going over to your parents for the night." He planted a kiss first on her forehead and moved down to her cheek, then neck, before placing a soft, sweet kiss on her kips. He pulled back and looked at his wife longingly and Alexis could feel the passion radiating between them. Marc grabbed her sides and pulled her into a tight hug that made her knees buckle. He then scooped her into his arms and began walking towards the front door that was still ajar.

Marc carried her over the threshold as he did every time he came back home from a long business trip, and then kicked the door closed behind them. Alexis looked up into his eyes and saw pure love as he carried her through the house and up the stairs to their bedroom. He had lit candles and was playing soft music. The scene was perfect and very calming...much different from what she had expected.

Alexis looked into his eyes with trepidation as he laid her gently onto the bed. For a second, she thought that this might be the moment. This might be the moment that she was waiting for when everything would change for the better. Marc leaned over her and planted another soft kiss on her lips and gently nudged his tongue in between her lips at the same time. He was so perfect.

ALEXIS LAY ON HER BED IN A FETAL POSITION AS HER HUSBAND NAPPED, obviously exhausted from their lovemaking. They had been going non-stop for the past two hours and she was more than sore. Since Marc had been away longer than usual for his business trip this time, he took it extra hard on her and showed her exactly how much he had missed her.

Alexis twisted around and peeked under the covers to look at the skin on her back. It was already beginning to bruise and ugly whelps were forming on her light skin. She lightly touched one and winced at the pain that she felt. She opened the top drawer of the nightstand beside her bed and pulled out the ointment that she kept in there for days like this. Unfortunately, this had not been the moment that she wished for. She was hoping that Marc would finally get it...finally understand what she needed from him. But after five years of marriage, she was close to letting go of that small shred of hope that she had left.

When Alexis had finally been able to look around the room after Marc placed her on the bed, the first thing she noticed, after the candles, was that there was a new contraption set up in the bedroom. She wasn't sure what it was, but it looked like a swing set that had two chained handcuffs hanging from the top, near the ceiling, and two chained cuffs at the bottom. She then turned back to look at Marc with an expression that said nothing but pure fear.

She opened her mouth to question him about the gadget on the far side of the room, but was stopped short when Marc ripped off the front her clothing as she lie on the bed, destroying a nearly $1000 outfit. The fear that she had only seemed to excite him as he roughly grabbed the material from beneath her and pulled it to the side, dropping it over the edge of the bed. Alexis felt parts of her skin start to burn from where the remaining pieces of her dress had rubbed against her. Before she could even reach back to rub the area in an effort to soothe the stinging, Marc grabbed her by her neck and flipped her on her stomach in one quick motion. Squeezing her neck so tightly that Alexis could barely breathe, he leaned down and whispered in her ear.

"I missed you so much, baby. I've wanted to be with you for so long." Then he licked her starting from the base of her neck and slowly going upwards. His tongue swirled around the inner folds of her ear and Alexis almost moaned with pleasure. With that, he reached back and smacked her ass so hard that Alexis was sure that she would have a big, purple handprint on it for the next couple weeks.

He let go of her neck enough for Alexis to gasp for air and began her attempt at crawling away from his area on the bed. Marc grabbed her by one of her legs and pulled her back towards him. He then spread her butt cheeks wide, whistled happily at the sight, and then licked his lips.

He slid back on his knees to rest on the bottom of his feet, then kneeled down and licked Alexis' ass slowly from front to back a few times in a row. Alexis relaxed slightly, but not completely because she had an idea about what was to come and she was not ready. She never was, and this time was no different. Alexis braced herself for what was about to come. Marc sat back up on his knees, and then he spread her butt cheeks even wider than she thought they were ever supposed to go.

Suddenly, Marc pulled back quickly and slammed forward, diving his dick right in Alexis' ass. Alexis yelped and then grinded her teeth together as she took in the excruciating pain. She continued to grit her teeth while trying to make noises that sounded like she was experiencing nothing other than pure pleasure, and it only made Marc dig in harder.

"Take it, baby. Oh, I love the way you take it," Alexis squeezed the bed as hard as she could making her fingertips burn as she began to rip through the sheets. She tried to fight the urge to tense up. She knew tension would only make things worse.

After what seemed like hours' of shoving into a place where things should only come out, Marc pulled all the way out and pulled Alexis up by the nape of her neck. Alexis scrambled trying to make her feet catch her weight to stop the pressure of the pinching on her neck as he pulled her off of the bed. Marc tugged her over to the contraption and dropped her on the floor. Alexis moaned in pain.

How can he be so rough during sex and so gentle every other time? It's like Dr. Jekyll and Mr. Hyde! She thought as she massaged the spot on her elbow that hurt the most from the impact of her fall.

Marc reached down and grabbed one of her ankles, bending in a way to allow for him to place it more easily into the bottom cuffs. He walked on the other side and did the same with her other ankle. After he was done, he roughly grabbed her left arm and stretched her up off the floor, so that he could secure her wrist in one of the handcuffs hanging from the top.

Alexis' eyes opened wide in horror as she began to understand what this was. She looked at him with eyes pleading him to stop while he locked her other wrist into the last remaining cuff. She tried to mutter words to tell him to stop, but nothing would come out. Instead, her lips began to tremble and she shook her head hoping that Marc would stop on his own.

Looking at her husband, she saw that he was truly excited by his new toy. He took a moment to stare at Alexis as she was held captive by the machine and she saw that his eyes were filled with so much desire. He reached down towards her and Alexis' heart fluttered with hope as she began to think that maybe he had a change of heart and decided to release her. Her hopes were dashed as she realized that he was leaning down towards a small lever on the side of the metal contraption.

When Marc pulled the lever, it jerked the chains in opposite directions so that Alexis' legs and arms were spread apart from each other. She was overcome with so much fear that she was trembling although she was anything but cold. She turned her head to the side to look behind her as much as she could and saw Marc as he took out a whip and then looked hungrily at her.

"Have you been bad while I was gone?" He said to her, while he walked over and kissed her lightly on the shoulder. He stuck his tongue out and ran it along her shoulder and bent down to continue all the way down her spine.

"Mmmm, yes, baby. I've been bad!" Alexis said as she played along. She knew pain was coming, but the quicker he could get off, the faster they would be done. Her mama had taught her that it was a woman's place to please her husband. And that's what she planned to do. Marc was a good man. Never cheated on her, gave her everything that she wanted and he always catered to her every need. So what if he liked it a little rough from time to time? She was a big girl and she could take it. Or maybe not.

"AAAGGGHHHH!" Alexis yelled and her legs buckled underneath

her as she felt the whip smack her right in the middle of her back. As soon as she fell down, Marc pulled the lever, dragging her feet apart and making her attempt to scramble back to her feet to no avail.

"Oh, you been bad, huh? I'm going to teach you a lesson!" With that, Marc began to whip her with a vengeance that almost made her think to herself: *Well, what the hell did I do?*

Alexis moaned and yelled out for more as much as she could; hoping that the punishment would end soon. She grew weaker and weaker and Marc continued pulling the lever until she was no longer assisting in holding herself up at all. Instead her instrument of torture was supporting her totally and she gave in to her body's desire to let go altogether. She hung her head as she began to zone out to the thumps of the whip on her back.

Well this is what love is. And I love my man.

JAZMYN

ust a few more minutes and he will be done; Jazmyn thought to herself as she lackadaisically rolled Raymond's dick around in her mouth. Needless to say, Raymond had taken her back. *They always do;* Jazmyn rolled her eyes. She didn't even have to plead and beg, but she wouldn't have done that anyways. What she felt for Raymond was nothing close to love and a little more than like.

He was her sponsor...nothing more, nothing less. Of course, she had to cheat on him! Did this man, who was 15 years her senior, really think that she would be satisfied with him? This man who couldn't get it up to save his life? Jazmyn quickly moved her mouth off of Raymond's dick right before he let loose what he had been holding back for...all of about five minutes.

"Daaaamn Jaz, why you moved?" Raymond looked at her, and then fell back on the bed. His breathing was so quick and labored that Jazmyn almost felt a little concerned that he may have a heart attack.

His old ass; she thought as she rolled her eyes and moved to the edge of the bed. It was not always this way. When Jazmyn first met Raymond, it was not love at first sight, but she was definitely interested.

He was sweet, attentive and loaded with money. He gave her everything that she wanted, and he treated her like a queen. But he bored her quickly, and the money was beginning to not even be a comfort to her.

Jazmyn didn't even need his money; she had her own rainy day stash, though pretty small since she had to support her own major spending habits. But she still enjoyed being taken care of, and she enjoyed the company of a man. However, her time with Raymond was about to come to an end. She was bored and ready to move on to something new. Sadly, her plans for Zo had fell through, and she ended up coming back to Raymond's open arms. But she knew it wouldn't be long before she found a replacement.

Jazmyn rolled completely off the bed and headed to the large adjoining master bath and turned the water on to start the shower. She sat on the edge of the Jacuzzi tub and placed her head in her hands as she waited for the water to heat up to the right temperature. She was bored with her life and didn't like herself when she was this way. She didn't like her constant need to jump from man to man, but for some reason she had been unable to stop herself from doing so. Even now, she couldn't completely remember a time in her life when she had been completely without man.

Am I that bad of a person to be with that I can't even stand to be with myself? Jazmyn brought her head up and leaned over to place her hand under the showerhead to test the temperature of the water. Satisfied with the temperature, she reluctantly pulled herself up from the ledge of the tub and started to place her foot into the shower when she felt a presence behind her.

"Where are you going, baby? We aren't through," Jazmyn turned and saw Raymond standing at the door holding his male essence in his hands and bouncing his hips from side to side as if he thought that would turn her on. Jazmyn stifled a laugh and turned back towards the shower.

"I'm getting ready for work, Raymond. I have to meet with a few clients today, and I also have a lot cases that I need to do a little research on." She stepped into the shower and closed the glass door behind her hoping that would signal to Raymond that this was the end of their conversation.

"Will Kingston be there?" Raymond said with an obvious change in tone.

Jazmyn glanced at him through the glass shower pane, and even through the obscurity of the glass, she could see the obvious disdain that he held for Kingston showing through in his face.

"Yes, he will. He does work there, too; you know," Jazmyn stated. Her lips curled into an automatic smile as she thought of Kingston.

Kingston was her co-worker as well as her competition. Both were aiming to become the next partner at the law firm in which they worked. And it was a combination of this rivalry and his sexiness that made Jazmyn get hot whenever she saw him walking around the office. Jazmyn was somewhat young to be aiming for a slot as ambitious as the next partner at her law firm, but she brought in a lot of money thanks to the connections she was able to make with the help of lil' mama between her legs, as well as some friends from the past.

Kingston was not quite as young as Jazmyn, but he was only a few years older and in his early 30s, so he was just as ambitious as her. Somewhere down the line during their early morning coffee runs and late nights working on cases, they had begun sleeping together. And the sex had been amazing. Jazmyn was a sexual creature anyways and loved sex. If a man could work it right, she had no qualms about lying in bed for days at a time doing the deed. But it wasn't just that with her and Kingston.

Sex with Kingston had awakened a feeling that she had never felt with anyone else that she had ever opened herself up to. When he touched her, it felt electric; she was pulled towards him in a magnetic way. Sometimes before even seeing him around the office, she felt as if she could feel him enter her into her consciousness. He awakened a feeling in her that was just that strong and she craved it most times, but she had to keep herself from feeling that way.

Jazmyn would have left Raymond in a heartbeat to permanently warm Kingston's bed if it had not been for one thing. Kingston was very, very married. Jazmyn didn't have many rules when it came to love and war, but one that she consistently abided by was not to mess with a married man.

Kingston refused to leave his pregnant wife, and Jazmyn wouldn't have let him either way. But the fact was that he was not able to give her the attention that she needed and that meant that she couldn't deal with him. Jazmyn needed a man that was able to be with her every day and every night. She wanted a man to call her own. Kingston could never be that. So instead of dealing with the constant frustration of dealing with a man that she knew could never be hers, she decided to let Kingston make love to her one last time before sending him on his way. Unfortunately, that had ended in drama.

Jazmyn glanced over at Raymond, who was now standing with a frown on his face and his arms crossed, and she sighed. Raymond had heard very graphic details of her most recent session with Kingston last week, thus the reason he kicked her out of the apartment. Apparently, she had accidentally butt-dialed Raymond before Kingston pulled off her pants. He had of course been concerned when he heard her moaning, thinking that she may have been in trouble. So instead of hanging up, he stayed on the line and heard every last sexual detail all the way up to Jazmyn screaming out Kingston's name like she was trying to proclaim it to the world.

Jazmyn still wasn't sure if Raymond was more upset that she had sex with Kingston or that he had never made her scream like that. He had held on to the knowledge of all of this until a few days later when he finally had decided that he couldn't take it anymore, and kicked her out.

"Don't worry, Ray. It's all business between us. You have nothing to worry about baby." She was deliberately vague with her actual meaning regarding *whom* she was referring to. With that, she lifted her arm and waved over the top of the glass door for Raymond to leave, hoping that this time he got the message. He stayed a little longer, looking through the glass at her as she showered before he turned away and closed the door behind him. Jazmyn groaned with relief and continued on.

᪻

JAZMYN WALKED OFF THE ELEVATOR AND RESUMED HER STRUT TO HER office. No matter how many times she'd walked through this building in all the years that she's worked here, most things remained the same. The men still couldn't control their eyes and the women still couldn't control their envy. Jazmyn couldn't help it that while she was making sure she stayed on top of shit and kept herself right and tight, other women had gotten a tad too comfy with their men and decided to let themselves go.

Get like me, bitches, she thought as she unlocked her office door and walked in. She closed the door behind her, and then walked over to place her Prada bag in the bottom drawer of her large dark cherry-wood desk.

Sighing heavily, she smoothed out the wrinkles in her short, tan skirt and looked up to sign in to her computer. Work and more work, the amount of it was almost never-ending, but the good thing was that it would keep her mind off Kingston. She opened a few emails from clients and decided that since she had a few hours before her morning meeting, she would reply back to a few to reduce the amount of emails she would have to send later on.

She grabbed the Starbucks coffee cup that, undoubtedly, her assistant had placed there for her earlier and took a long sip as she leaned back in her chair to read the first email. Jazmyn groaned out loud as she read an email stating that a case was going to be transferred to her due to another attorney's conflict of interest. This was really not a good time in her life to bring on extra work. She had enough to deal with as it was.

"Damn it!" Jazmyn yelled and quickly backed away from her desk as she mistakenly spilled a few drops of coffee nearly onto her skirt. Immediately upon looking up from her computer to place the cup back on her desk, she noticed that she was looking directly into Kingston's green eyes.

Hard to hide from someone with these damn glass walls! Jazmyn thought with a sigh, as her eyes remained locked on Kingston's. She watched as he walked to her office door and let himself in.

"Knock much?" Jazmyn stated and turned her attention back to her skirt to ensure there had been no damage.

"Why haven't you been returning my calls?" Kingston asked walking towards her desk and taking a seat reserved for her many high-end clients. "I have been texting you since you told me that motherfucker threw you out!" Kingston lowered his voice to a stern whisper and tried to relax his posture as to not sound off any alarms from their passing co-workers.

"You know why, Kingston! You are married, and you told me that she is pregnant! I can't continue to play this game with you. It was one thing when you told me you were in an "unhappy" marriage. Apparently, it's not as unhappy as you thought!" Jazmyn took a second to look up at Kingston before turning her attention back to her computer. That quick glance almost took her breath away.

Kingston was the furthest thing from unattractive as one could get. He had a chestnut-colored complexion and the most piercing green eyes that Jazmyn had ever seen. He wasn't the tallest man alive, but he was taller than Jazmyn with her signature 5-inch heels, and he wore his height well. He kept his hair cut very low, just like she liked it, so that it showed off the perfect angles in his jaw-line. Right now, he was sitting before her looking slightly boyish with his arms crossed and mouth formed in a straight line. The pouting did not subtract from his sexiness...not in the least.

Kingston was looking at Jazmyn with pleading eyes that said that he wanted to fix it, but in her opinion, there was no way to do that. Jazmyn already had issues with dealing with a married man, for falling for him the way that she did, but a married man with a pregnant wife was out of the question. She had done many things in her past that she wasn't proud of, but messing up a happy home had never been one of them.

She never wanted to get involved with Kingston in the first place, but somehow it had happened. Continuing on with him while his pregnant wife sat at home waiting for her husband to arrive, was out of the question.

"Jazmyn, I'm telling you, it was only that one time since you and I have been together! There is no way that she is pregnant...not by me! We have been together for three years, and she never got pregnant. Why now?" Kingston said throwing his hands up, looking genuinely confused.

"Kingston, I am not your sex education teacher. You stuck your dick in her, right?" Kingston just stared at Jazmyn with a guilty face. "You didn't wear a condom, right? Did she make you come?" Jazmyn stood up suddenly and looked down on Kingston.

He shifted uncomfortably in his chair and glanced over towards the glass wall where he noticed some of the young paralegals glancing over with interested eyes. This was sure to make its way around the office before lunchtime.

"Yes, Jaz. I get it, damn...look, just meet me somewhere later so we can talk. I miss you," Kingston said, standing up to catch her glare. "I need to speak with you. We can work this out...however you want to. We have to. We can find a way."

"No, we can't," Jazmyn said, sliding back down into her chair. "The fact of the matter is that I never asked you to leave you wife...never even wanted you to, but you never did. Now she is pregnant...and even if you do leave her now, I can't deal with a man that would do that to a woman that he once said he loved and to his child. Goodbye, Kingston." Jazmyn swirled in her seat to face the computer monitor.

"But, Jaz...," Kingston began.

"GOODBYE, Kingston. I have work to do. And you do too," Jazmyn said as she motioned with her head to a group of individuals standing outside of her office. Kingston turned and saw that a few of his clients were waiting for him. He turned back to Jazmyn, started to say something, but changed his mind. With his head down, Kingston ran his hand from over his low-cut fade and down over his face. He then shrugged and stuck both hands in his pocket and headed towards the door. Jazmyn didn't even bother to look up as he made his exit.

Jazmyn lifted her eyes from her computer in time to see Kingston greet his clients and lead them down the hall to his office. Once she was sure that he had made it to his own office, Jazmyn swiveled in her seat to make sure her back was towards the glass. She finally felt it was safe to let her face reveal what she had been feeling during the entire time speaking to Kingston. She felt torn and had no idea what to do. Jazmyn would never admit it, but she loved Kingston. She knew that, for her, he was "the one" that every woman hoped for. But, like everything in her life, he came with complications.

Just my luck, she thought. *Of all the men that I've been with, I would fall for the unavailable.*

KAYLEN

$\mathcal{K}$aylen rolled over, grabbed onto Salem's muscular back, and swung her leg over his thigh. They had been in bed all morning having the time of their lives. Well…Kaylen had and judging from the way Salem was next to her sleeping soundly and peacefully, she guessed he had also. Kaylen sighed happily, rolled over, and reluctantly pulled herself out of the bed. She would like to be nestled next to Salem all day, but her growling stomach decided otherwise. Apparently, it didn't agree with her dick diet.

As she walked into the kitchen, Kaylen heard something that sounded like a phone vibrating against her kitchen counter. Slightly confused, she began to look around until her eyes rested on Salem's vibrating phone. He must have left it on the counter that morning. Kaylen took a second to reminisce about how Salem had scooped her naked body up in his muscular and tattooed arms and sat her on the counter, pressing lightly on her inner thighs to spread her legs. That man could do things with his tongue that should have been illegal. There was nothing better.

Kaylen jarred herself from her daydream and glanced at Salem's phone. She didn't mean to pry, but something about the name that glowed on the screen made her halt. Zo was calling Salem. She still wasn't sure what it was about that man that tugged at her, and she didn't really want to find out. Salem was perfect. He seemed like the one. He *was* the one actually. He was the one who decided to buy her a drink. Who decided to come over to her. Who decided to dance with her all night...in spite of the envious glances from the surrounding women.

Whatever she thought about Zo didn't matter. Although she had only been with Salem for about three months, it had been the best three months that she had ever spent in a relationship. Her father had always told her to find a man that would treat her as well as he did... that is, how he treated her before he became addicted to heroin.

Kaylen's father had always been the most important man in her life. He taught her how to survive. He told her that if anything was to happen to her and she could not afford to complete school or pay her bills, she could always rely on her cooking skills. Her father cooked meth himself, for a long time before he was able to get others to do it for him, and he taught her everything he knew.

His skills helped him to become one of the richest men that lived in Atlanta. He treated Kaylen and her mother to everything that they wanted and anything that they thought they needed. Kaylen thought about all of the parties and fancy dresses; the beautiful jewelry and nice cars. All of that went away when her mother became addicted to cocaine. Her father resisted for a while. But instead of his deep love for her mother urging him to get her the help she needed, he fell captive to her addiction, as well.

Eventually, one of their "friends" introduced them to heroin, and it was curtains after that. Kaylen had to raise herself as best as she could. At thirteen years old, she was writing checks and paying bills. She was able to lie to her teachers and hide her parent's lifestyle for as long as she could, but not long enough. She would never forget the day she came home and found her father's lifeless body laid out on the kitchen floor. His eyes were closed, and his arm was outstretched, as it had been when the needle was still in it.

Her mother was sitting crouched down in the corner staring into oblivion. The needle that she had grabbed out of her husband's dead body was protruding out of her own arm. Her head was tilted back at an awkward angle, and a piece of drool was sliding down her chin in a long line that connected to the marble floor. Kaylen had screamed until one of the neighbors called 911, and the cops arrived. She was still screaming when the police busted down the doors and ran into the tragic scene.

That had been the worse day of Kaylen's life. Although she knew that her parents had become addicts, she had been able to pretend otherwise for a short while. She had to lie so much to cover for them that she began to believe some of the lies. But that day was the beginning of the point in her life when she had to leave her denial behind.

Kaylen shivered from the memories of her parents and headed towards the fridge. As she opened it, she smiled graciously. Salem had made sure that her refrigerator stayed stocked with all the necessary items. Kaylen was always too busy studying to make sure that she stayed on top of eating right. Matter of fact, she needed to get to the books now. Salem had been taking up a lot of her time, and her exams were coming up in two weeks. Kaylen sighed as she thought of all that she had to do that day, and pulled out the carton of orange juice and then scooped up a handful of grapes. She popped a grape in her mouth and followed up with orange juice that she drank straight out of the carton.

"That's my baby...undercover hood, huh?" Kaylen opened her eyes and saw Salem slowly entering the kitchen wearing a huge smile and a glitter in his eye. He stood in the entrance as naked as the day that God brought him to this earth, with only his long dreadlocks to cover him.

"Every now and then I have to take it back to my roots," Kaylen joked.

"Your roots?" Salem laughed. "You act like you struggled or something. Get the hell out of here."

Kaylen looked down quickly before turning around to place the carton back in the refrigerator. If only Salem knew how much she did struggle to get herself to where she was. After her father overdosed, her mother was sent to a mental health facility, and Kaylen was sent to stay with her aunt. Kaylen's aunt did not care about anything except for the monthly check that she received from Kaylen's father's estate to take care of Kaylen.

Most of that check went to assisting her aunt with her gambling addiction. What did not go to that went to her aunt's food addiction. Kaylen's Aunt Jessie was easily the largest woman that Kaylen had ever seen. She had to weigh over 500 pounds, and it was a wonder that she was even able to take care of herself. Although in the eyes of the state, Kaylen had a guardian, Kaylen's aunt was anything but.

"My bitch sister thought she was better than me. Laid up with that stupid nigga buying her all that shit. But look, bitch! Who better now? HA!" Kaylen's aunt used to say like clockwork every month when she collected her beloved check. Kaylen used to pray every day that her mother would get better so that she could save her from Aunt Jessie, but, unfortunately, this never happened.

"Baby, I was thinking that today you should go over to your place. I have a lot of studying to do, and I need to make sure that I can do it without your...distractions." Kaylen said as she looked at Salem's bare chest.

"That's cool, baby. I need to holla at my boy, Zo, anyways. It's been a while since I've hooked up with that nigga."

"Ok, baby. Want me to cook you breakfast before you leave? I have time," Kaylen asked. She was secretly hoping he would say no; she had a few other things that she had to do before she was able to study and would rather not have Salem in the way.

"Naw, that's ok. I will catch something on the way out," Salem said as he walked over to Kaylen and gave her a kiss on the cheek. "Let me get in the shower real quick and I will be out."

"Alright baby. Love you," Kaylen slipped and stopped suddenly in the middle of the kitchen with her eyes wide as she realized the gravity of what she had just said. She did not mean to say that to Salem. Sure, she had thought it, but she still wasn't quite sure of her feelings.

I guess unconsciously I know how I really feel. And damn...now Salem does also! Kaylen lifted her hand to her face and attempted to hide

49

herself from the onset of embarrassment that she was beginning to feel. If she were a few shades lighter, she was positive that her cheeks would be a nice rosy red by now.

"True that...I love you too, Kay," Salem said quickly with a wink. He then turned on his heels and walked out of the kitchen and back towards the bedroom. Kaylen stood stunned in the same spot that he had left her for what felt like hours.

He loves me back; she thought.

KAYLEN CALLED LEVI FOR THE THIRD TIME IN A ROW. THIS WAS NOT LIKE her to continuously call him, but she wanted to make sure that she got this done when she had time. Kaylen made up in her mind that this would be her last time working with Levi. Her father had told her that her cooking up meth was only to be used in dire situations. When she was no longer in a position that she needed to cook for a living, she should stop. Kaylen was finally at that point. She had enough money saved to live on for a long time and in addition to that, she was thinking of asking Salem to move in. Knowing Salem, he wouldn't let her pay for a thing even if she tried.

"Yeah?" Levi said roughly as he answered the phone.

"Did you not hear any of my other calls? Let's get a move on."

"Alright, Kay. Give me a couple hours and meet me at the spot." Levi said hesitantly.

"Everything ok?" Kaylen asked. Her radar was sounding off in her mind, but it always was, so she decided to ignore it.

"Yeah, see you in three." Levi said and hung up. Kaylen brought the phone away from her ear and stared at it.

No, this nigga didn't hang up on me; Kaylen thought. She would just have to tell him about that when she saw him. Something was up with Levi, and she was glad that she wouldn't be dealing with him much longer after today. They would always be friends, but it was time to put an end to this business.

KAYLEN OPENED HER EYES WHEN SHE FELT THE CAR SLOW DOWN. SHE had finally arrived at the spot that Levi was driving to. Kaylen felt slightly annoyed with herself for falling asleep. Her father had always told her to never get caught slipping. Falling asleep in the car with Levi's suspicious ass as he drove her to some unknown spot in the middle of nowhere would definitely be something her father would disapprove of. Kaylen looked up at another shady spot, courtesy of Levi, and sighed. She would be glad to be able to get out of this business.

"You got everything?" Kaylen asked, looking at Levi. She noticed that he was taking extra time surveying the area.

That's something you should have done before you brought me here! Kaylen thought. On cue, Kaylen checked her back to make sure that her Desert Eagle was in place. *Might need to use you today on this shifty motherfucker!* She watched as Levi pulled everything out of the car and headed to the door of the broken-down and nearly condemned building.

Walking into the building, Kaylen immediately began to look around. The place was disgusting, but it would suffice for now. Looking around Kaylen noticed something odd with the floor in one room. She looked over to Levi, who looked preoccupied with setting everything up, before she went to investigate. Kaylen walked into the room and looked around slowly trying to find anything that seemed out of place.

The room was small and uninteresting for the most part. There was no furniture or anything to indicate what this room would even be used for. Kaylen was about to leave out when she noticed a part of the floor that seemed to be protruding slightly. She walked over to the area and pressed down on the swollen floorboard with her foot. When she pressed down hard on one spot, another part of the floorboard popped up. She kneeled down and pulled at the opening, and noticed that it was a door leading to a small space under the house.

A secret hideout? Where the hell has Levi brought me?

"Kay, you coming?"

"Yeah, I'm on my way." Kaylen closed the door back down and stood up. She was thinking about telling Levi to hang it all up and take her back to her car. There were too many signs around indicating that this was not the place for her to be.

Stop being paranoid...you've known Levi for over 10 years! She thought trying to brush the paranoia out of her mind. Levi was the one who had saved her from dealing with the measly leftovers that her aunt gave her in order to make sure that she was able to at least survive...if nothing else.

In all the time that she lived with her aunt, Jessie never bought Kaylen anything new. Kaylen's clothes were the same ones that she had brought in with her. When they began to get too small or too tight, Kaylen would have to take it upon herself to go to find clothes wherever she could. She started out by stealing clothes from various small-time stores in the neighborhood. After she had gathered enough courage, she began stealing clothes from the mall.

It was there that she met Levi. Kaylen was leaving a store that she had just hit up for two pairs of jeans, and three shirts. When she walked out of the store, she hit the corner and sped up her pace towards the mall's exit. As she neared the door, she felt a hand on her shoulder. Scared that she had been caught, she readied herself to run when she noticed that it was not a security guard, it was a teenage boy no more than a few years older than she was. He was dressed neatly but not flashy, in jeans and a red polo. He had on a hat, pulled very low to cover most of his face, and a small Cuban link chain. Kaylen wasn't sure why he was touching her, but she knew that she wasn't interested in finding out. With a sneer, she pulled back out of his reach and turned back towards the door.

"You need to leave with me. I have a car," he stated. Kaylen started to respond harshly when she noted that he was pointing behind her. She turned around and saw one of the clerks from the store speaking to the mall security guard and pointing in her direction. Kaylen looked back to Levi trying to assess whether or not she could trust him. She looked back behind her and noticed that the security guard was jogging in her direction. With that, she decided that she would take her chances with trying to escape.

She touched her back pocket to make sure that she still had her knife tucked in the back of her jeans and followed his lead towards the door. That was her first encounter with Levi and it led to a lasting relationship of survival. Kaylen showed Levi the skills that her father had taught her in order to be able to make it during the low points in her life. Levi then made sure that she was always able to have access to anything she needed in order to get started. Then he would pay her up front and leave with the product. She never knew what happened to it after then. She was always one to mind her own business, and she never asked questions. Fortunately, neither did Levi.

Four hours after arriving at the shack, Kaylen was nearly done with what she had to do and Levi started packing up. This was a larger order than usual, and Kaylen had spent much more time than she had initially wanted to. She was sure that Salem had called multiple times, and she also still needed to study.

"Here is your cut. You got everything?" Levi asked, handing her a large, thick manila envelope full of cash.

"How much is in it?" Kaylen asked. If she had to guess, she would say about $50,000 from the look and feel of the envelope, but she often asked questions she knew the answer to so that she knew whom to trust. It was a habit, and she found it advantageous in her line of work.

"$65,000. Big order this time. I'm dealing with some new guys. Big timers, I guess."

"What do you mean, you guess? Shouldn't you know who you are dealing with?" Kaylen asked loudly. At that moment, she began to hear a car pull up to the building.

"Expecting someone, Levi?" Kaylen asked pulling her gun out of her back holster and ducking behind one of the ragged and mildewed couches in what she assumed was a living room at one time.

"Not at all," Levi replied as he took out a Glock that he had stashed somewhere on his body. Kaylen watched as he walked to the door and opened it slowly with his gun tucked at his side.

The next few seconds happened so fast that Kaylen barely had enough time to react. From her crouched position, she could see through the screen door as Levi walked out with his gun and hid behind one of the huge columns on the front porch of the house. He peeked out from the column ready to blast whoever decided to exit out of the SUV that sat in the front yard. At that point, about a dozen more vehicles pulled up, and Kaylen knew that she and Levi were surrounded. She could hear the faint thumping of an approaching helicopter and her heart sank. They were caught, and she knew it.

I've got to get to that room! Kaylen thought. *But how do I get there fast enough without being spotted?* Kaylen took another look out the door and noticed men jumping out of the cars and SUVs with their guns trained on the area where Levi hid. Each person that jumped out wore a vest with various acronyms, FBI, ATF, and DEA. *The alphabet boys got us!* Kaylen thought, breathing heavily as sweat began to form. Levi was pinned where he was, and there was no way out.

"Put down your weapon!" One of the agents yelled to Levi. Kaylen looked and saw Levi staring back at her with a look that could not be explained as anything other than pure fear as he continued to hide behind the column. Kaylen was surprised for a moment at what she saw. One thing that Levi had always told her was that in the business, you can't afford to be scared. If you do the crime, you pay the time, and it's that simple. It's the risk that you have to be willing to take.

Kaylen understood that as soon as he said it. That's why she always knew this was something that she could not rely on forever. She had to line up her life in a way that she could make money in other ways. Kaylen looked back to Levi, and she noticed that he was looking directly into her eyes. In a split second, the look of fear disappeared totally from his face. He winked at her then flipped out from behind the column with his gun raised and began to fire his gun at any and everything in front of him.

Kaylen had to suppress a scream as she saw the agents return fire and fill Levi's body up with multiple holes. His body popped back multiple times as if it was full of fireworks, and it crashed back against the front of the house with a loud thud.

Oh, my God! I need to get OUT of here! Kaylen thought. This was the perfect time to try to get to the other room, and it may be the only time that she had. She stayed crouched down and tried to run as fast as she could into the room with the trap door. *Oh shit! Which floorboard opens it?* She screamed to herself as she began stepping on all of the floorboards in the room.

Outside, she could hear the shooting stop and about a dozen footsteps on the porch of the house. She heard someone swing the screen door open so fast that it slammed back into the wall behind it as agents began to enter the house. Finally, after what seemed like a lifetime of stumping, she was able to locate the right one. She stuck her hands under the opening and propped up the floorboards. As she swooped her legs over into the opening, she noticed a small baggy of meth lying next to her.

SHIT! How did that get there? Kaylen thought. She quickly grabbed the bag, placed it in her pocket, and dropped herself down into the small compartment. She was able to close the lid quietly right before the agents began to file into the room.

JAZMYN

*S*hit! How the FUCK did I get here again? Jazmyn thought as she watched Raymond ranting and raving. It was to the point now that she saw his arms flailing in the air and his mouth moving but she was so zoned out that she didn't even hear a word. Normally, she would feel upset or even a little guilty about what she had done, but not this time. This time, she was too busy feeling exceptionally satisfied to even think about what Raymond was upset about this time.

"Raymond, I will send the movers to pick up my things, ok? I really don't have the time to speak about this. I'm sorry that this happened. But it's your fault, really," Jazmyn said nonchalantly as she pushed away the pictures sitting on the desk in Raymond's office. The pictures contained photos of her and Kingston as they each walked separately into *Twelve*, a high-end hotel in downtown Atlanta. Although they were on the tenth floor, the skilled photographer was able to catch photos of her and Kingston in various stages of undress as they enjoyed what ended up being a very eventful, long, and pleasurable night.

The photos were taken through the window and on the balcony. Kingston had wanted to close the window, but Jazmyn objected. She had always had a knack for doing the nasty in public areas. She felt it was her duty to appease the ones with voyeuristic tendencies. Jazmyn took one final look at the pictures and smiled. She was furious that Raymond had been having her followed, but she contemplated keeping the photos as a keepsake. They were memorabilia of what was an incredible night and the shots displayed her showing passion that she would love to relive at all times. She looked back up at Raymond and noticed his mouth gaping wide open as if he were trying to catch flies.

"MY fault? What do you mean it's MY fault, Jazmyn?"

"Obviously, *Raymond*," Raymond winced as she said his name like it were a disease. "If you hadn't been tracking me like a dog, you wouldn't have seen anything you weren't supposed to see." Jazmyn grabbed her purse and picked up her keys that were also on the desk. She glanced up at Raymond, who was still staring at her like he couldn't understand what had gotten into her.

"I want you out, Jazmyn. Right now. Get your shit, and don't come back!" Raymond roared. Jazmyn closed her eyes and placed her free hand over her ear.

"Didn't you hear what I said, Raymond? I will send the movers to pick up my things."

"No, I want you out NOW. Whatever is not gone will be tossed, I swear, Jazmyn. Don't play with me," Raymond threatened. He leaned back in his stance and displayed a face that showed his belief that he now had one up on her.

"Listen. Whatever you want to do with the small amount of things I have left here, you may do. I have no more patience to deal with your attitude, your demands, and your questions regarding every aspect of my day-to-day dealings. Have a great life," Jazmyn turned and began to sashay smoothly out the door.

"Actually, on second thought," she stopped and started walking back towards Raymond. His face relaxed with a look of satisfaction as he began to think that maybe she had seen the error of her ways and was ready to beg for forgiveness. Instead, Jazmyn walked over to the desk and scooped up all of the photographs of her and Kingston that lay on the table. "I think I want to keep these. You know, for my own personal reasons." With that, she walked out of the door and out of Raymond's life forever.

The sad truth was that although she didn't want to have anything to do with Kingston, that is not what ended up occurring. That day after Kingston confronted her at work, he began calling her relentlessly, leaving messages professing his love, and begging to see her. Although Jazmyn was moved by the voicemails and the text messages that said a little more than what she had already heard him say, it wasn't until he began to send images of his 11-inch dick that she was really moved to listen to what he had to say. About a week after sending over pictures of one of Jazmyn's most favorite parts of his body, she finally decided to answer his call.

"Hey, baby...how are you doing?" Kingston had answered the phone with pure confidence. He knew that once he started sending those pictures to her personal and work cellphone as well as email he would eventually get a response.

Jazmyn had a cold heart and a stubborn mind. She was able to ignore a lot when it came to hers or anyone else's feelings. That's what made her such a good attorney. But he knew that she was not able to ignore the tugging of her kitty when she was aroused. She loved sex just as much as he did, and he knew it.

"Kingston, what do you want from me?" Jazmyn asked as she sat in her home office in her condo. On her computer screen was Kingston's most recent email featuring his member standing erect in all its glory. The photo alone took up all of the space on Jazmyn's 27-inch computer screen. She had meant to take it down when she answered the call, but was unable to.

"I just want to see you, baby. Alone. We don't have to do anything. I just need to be near you," Kingston pleaded. Jazmyn hesitated as she thought about his request. Without exiting out of the image on her screen, she turned off her monitor and rotated in her seat. She was trying to think logically, and the photo was making that incredibly hard.

"What about your wife, Kingston? What would she think about this? She is pregnant with your child!"

"Jaz, that baby is not mine! I swear by it, baby. The timing doesn't match up, and I've been careful. Don't you think it's odd that she "all of a sudden got pregnant" after I hadn't touched her in months? She was supposed to be on the pill but..."

"But obviously she wasn't!" Jazmyn finished.

"Look Jaz, I don't want to talk to you over the phone. Can you just meet me somewhere? It can be somewhere public. You pick."

"Kingston...." Jazmyn tapped her fingers on the arm of her chair as she mustered up her last shred of self-respect in order to object. It was the last ounce that she had left, and she hoped that it would work.

"Jazmyn! Stop it....I'm not taking no for an answer anymore. Now, tell me where you want to meet. I'm listening."

"*Room at Twelve* in Centennial Park," Jazmyn said as she ran her fingers through her long, black hair. Her heart began to beat with excitement although her face was flushed with the shame of what she began to feel as she thought about Kingston.

"I will call now to make a reservation for 7 o'clock," Kingston replied, and Jazmyn could hear the smile in his voice.

"Fine. I will see you then," Jazmyn sighed and turned back to her monitor. She reached over to press the button to turn it on and smirked as Kingston's beautiful member once again decorated her screen.

"Great. I can't wait to see you," Kingston said.

"Oh,...and Kingston?" Jazmyn asked.

"Yes?"

"Make sure you get private seating."

JAZMYN SAT INSIDE OF HER RED AUDI RS 5 CABRIOLET AND contemplated what she was about to do. Although her intentions were only to sit and listen to Kingston rattle on about what should be a closed case, while enjoying a free dinner, her body was singing an entirely different song, and she knew herself enough to feel guilty already. She flipped down her mirror to make sure that her make-up game was on point. As she looked at her reflection, she could not help but feel slightly embarrassed, and betrayed by her feelings.

Jazmyn knew first hand that what she was doing was wrong. She was the child of a man who had left her and her mother after he decided that he no longer wanted to be with them. He had never offered her an explanation of why he had decided to leave, and Jazmyn wasn't sure that he cared. As she grew older and began to understand relationships, she knew that things happened, and people split apart, but she was never able to forgive Remi for leaving *her* and allowing her to grow up without a father. Everything she had learned about him, she'd had to find out on her own. Remi Baptiste was now a well-respected corporate attorney in Chicago, IL, and had another family to erase away the old one that he had forgotten.

His present wife was apparently the woman that he had decided was the better choice for his new lifestyle of riches and prestige. He had opted to leave her mother behind after he had arrived into his new lifestyle with a new yearning to shed his past self. This woman who was all of a sudden too low-class for him had also been the one that had been around when he was nothing but a little black boy in the ghetto with a half-combed afro, two pennies, and a dream. Now his wife of ambiguous ethnicity was the one that decorated his arm while he frequented the most exclusive parties with the new crowd of the haves who looked down on the have-nots.

Jazmyn had spent most of her adult life carrying a deep disdain for her father, however; she also had an inner conflict when it came to him because she felt the need to prove herself to him in some way. Her choice of career stemmed from a desire she had to prove to him that she was the one child he had that carried his talent and love for the law; regardless to the fact that he had never acknowledged her otherwise. She hoped that one day he would see her somewhere or hear about her and feel something - maybe a little close to guilt and regret, although less than love and absolute admiration.

Jazmyn flipped up the mirror and glanced over at the clock on her dash. 7:11. Kingston knew better than to expect her on time, but it was about time for her to make her entrance and get this whole thing over with. She checked her lipstick one last time and then drove up the rest of the way to the valet area. As the valet grabbed hold of her door and assisted her out of the car, Jazmyn looked towards the hotel.

My restaurant of choice WOULD happen to be inside of a hotel! Jazmyn thought to herself as she entered and walked in the direction of the restaurant.

"Not sure if I picked this place to satisfy my physical hunger or sexual hunger," Jazmyn said aloud.

"Excuse me, ma'am?" the hostess of *Rooms at Twelve* was a petite blond with a short cut that framed her cute face. Her large blue eyes looked at Jazmyn as she asked the question while clutching what appeared to be menus in both of her hands.

"Oh, nothing...sorry, I was thinking out loud. I believe the other person in my party should be here already. The reservation should be under Kingston Grant."

"Yes, ma'am. He is here. Right this way," Something about the way that the young woman looked at Jazmyn clued her in on the fact that Kingston had left a lasting impression on her and that she was all too happy to have the opportunity to interact with him once again. Jazmyn chuckled to herself as she watched the blond put an extra pep in her step as they neared Kingston's table. As requested, Kingston was able to get private seating, separated from the rest of the restaurant by a bamboo partition.

"Here you are!" the hostess motioned towards Jazmyn although her eyes remained fixed on Kingston. Jazmyn swept pass her outstretched arm and sat in the seat opposite him. "And if you need anything at all, be sure to ask me. My name is Desiree." She said as she leaned down and looked deeply into Kingston's eyes before turning around on her heels and strutting off towards the front of the restaurant. The whole ordeal helped to calm Jazmyn, and she was able to release the tension in her body enough to let out an actual laugh.

"So the hostess shows guests to their table now? I thought she was supposed to hand you off to our waitress." Kingston said joining in on her laughter.

"I guess that's what happens when one of the members of the party is Kingston Grant. I didn't know you had it like that," Jazmyn said taking a minute to give Kingston a full look over.

He was wearing a tan suede blazer with a white collared shirt. The top button was opened just enough for Jazmyn to get a glimpse of his chest and allow her mind to fill in the rest. He looked amazing, but he always did. His sense of style and proclivity for putting the most daring but visually appeasing ensembles together were two of the reasons why Jazmyn had felt so drawn to him in the beginning. Once she got to know him, he piqued her curiosity to know more. Once she had sex with him, it was all over...she was hooked.

"I don't believe I have it like that. But thanks," Kingston said smiling. "I'm sure you already know what you would like to have, am I right?"

Jazmyn nodded. This restaurant was one of her favorites since the first time Kingston had brought her here months ago. She was a creature of habit and always ordered the same thing although he reassured her every time that all items on the menu were perfection on a plate.

Somewhere between Jazmyn's steak entrée and Kingston paying the tab, while making sure to leave a hefty tip, Jazmyn had decided to ignore her inner caution and succumb to the desire to have Kingston alone. She was sure that if she could get him alone she would still be able to refuse to have sex with him, but she definitely wanted to try out everything else.

During the entire time dinner, Kingston had not even brought up their current issue pertaining to his domestic life. It was almost as if he knew that Jazmyn was his for the taking and that he had no responsibility to explain, refute, or speak on the issue of him proclaiming his feelings for her while being married and in the process of expanding his family.

Sadly, Kingston had been right. And now, here she was plowing out of Raymond's driveway after enduring him yell and carry on about something that she didn't even feel sorry about.

How could I feel sorry after a night like that? Jazmyn thought to herself as she pulled out of Raymond's neighborhood for the final time and turned the corner to head to the I-75.

Kingston had definitely performed at his best that night. And that was saying a lot. Jazmyn had experienced bad sex before. She had experienced good sex, as well as great sex. But what she had with Kingston was deeper than that. She connected with him on a level sexually that was different from anything ever before. He knew what she wanted before she knew, and he didn't stop until he put her to sleep, exhausting her from sheer pleasure.

By the time that Jazmyn and Kingston had entered the hotel room, she was already clutching at his jeans while he fingered the buttons on her blouse. The passion was evident by the way that Kingston kissed her: first tamely, inserting only a little of the tip of his tongue and then later more savagely as he grabbed her neck and explored all areas of his mouth.

Jazmyn felt Kingston tug once more at her blouse, making it drop off of her, freeing her *La Perla* decorated breasts as he placed his arms underneath her, lifting her feet off of the ground. Jazmyn wrapped her legs around him and allowed herself to be carried over to the bed, where Kingston dropped her gently and finally broke their kiss.

Kingston lifted up and looked into Jazmyn's eyes as he pulled her skirt down over her hips. Jazmyn saw the desire in his face and was absolutely confident that his matched her own as she laid back and allowed him to continue undressing her. Jazmyn watched with hunger as Kingston finally began pulling off his own clothes, first his shirt and then his jeans.

As he looked down to remove his boxers, Jazmyn decided to show him a preview of what was his. She let her legs fall loosely apart, with her knees touching opposite sides of the bed exposing herself to him. Once Kingston looked up, his eyes darted quickly from her face to his prize right at the spot where her thighs met. Jazmyn watched as he licked his lips slowly and she gushed. Kingston lowered himself down to his knees and gently pulled at her right foot, and then placed her manicured toes into his mouth.

Jazmyn felt her clit getting tighter as she relaxed back on the bed and enjoyed the feeling of Kingston nibbling on her toes. He then began kissing up her calves. Once he got close to her knee; he dipped his head and began to reach the area behind her knee, licking softly in circles. Jazmyn started to moan. Kingston knew that was her spot, and he never missed on the opportunity to show her how much he knew about her body.

"Kingston.....don't stop," Jazmyn moaned as he began to suck on her thighs. She loved the soft sucking noises he made as he teased her inner thigh. Right as she was exhaling a breath that she barely noticed she had been holding, Kingston slid two fingers deep inside her. Jazmyn arched her back, allowing herself to take in more of him until his knuckles were teasing her clit as he wiggled his fingers deep in her crevice.

"Ummmm, Kingston, baby...it feels so good." Jazmyn began twisting her torso around in circles so that she was rubbing her clit over the top of Kingston's knuckles. The soft friction was bringing her close to orgasm, and her body began to shudder.

"No, you don't," Kingston said between kisses. "Not yet." With that, he pulled his fingers out and the next sensation that Jazmyn felt was the warmness of his mouth. He slipped his tongue inside of her and Jazmyn continued to roll her body against his face.

"You taste so damn good, Jaz," Kingston mumbled before he became to suck more feverishly on her swollen clit. He reached up and grabbed onto her nipple and squeezed. Jazmyn took in a sharp breath and arched her back, driving his tongue deeper inside of her, and pushing her swollenness onto his nose. Kingston nestled his nose into her as he sucked, and it made Jazmyn lose control.

"Kingston...uhhhhnnnnn, I can't take it no more, baby. Please, give it to me. I need it, baby. NOW!"

Kingston loved to hear her beg for the dick. But even more than that, he loved to give her the dick. So with that, he rose up and brought his long, slender body up until he was parallel to her. He looked deeply into her eyes and lowered himself down and pushed forward. Like magic, he was able to enter her with no hands. That's how perfect their bodies were for each other. There was a magnetic energy, nothing that Jazmyn had ever witnessed before. It was amazing.

Kingston began moving back and forth slowly, but he made sure that he did not place the fullness of himself in her. He liked to ease himself in slowly and watch Jazmyn react. Jazmyn could hear the squishing of her wetness as Kingston slid in and out of her. She wrapped her legs around him and pulled him in closer to her. Kingston kissed up her neck and began pushing himself deeper inside of her.

"Yesssss, Kingston. Oh, my...damn, baby. I love this," Jazmyn whispered into him. She began gyrating her hips in a motion that made the curve of Kingston's dick tease her g-spot, and she could feel the orgasm building back up inside of her. Kingston knew it too, and responded by dipping his head and pulling one of her hard nipples into his mouth.

"Oh, shit, Kingston! This feels too damn good, baby!" Jazmyn began digging her nails into his back, and he began to suck even harder. Jazmyn dug deep and threw her pussy onto Kingston's dick, forcing him to shove the fullness of his length into her, and she sucked in a breath. Jazmyn could feel the orgasm rising up through her toes, and she gripped Kingston tighter with her legs as he pushed in and out of her at a faster pace.

"Cum with me baby, pleeeeaaaase," Jazmyn yelled out as she felt a wave of pleasure flow over her. She began jerking even harder against Kingston's dick, and she felt the contractions that signified the fact that he had reached his pleasure peak, as well.

"Daamnnn, Jazmyn. Shit, baby!" Kingston said as he released everything into her that he had been holding back since he had last been able to feel her. He squeezed tightly onto her, and she watched as he kept his eyes tightly shut until his breathing began to slow.

"Damn, Kingston. That was too damn good." Jazmyn said as Kingston fell onto the other side of the bed and reclined onto his back. Jazmyn threw her leg over him, and he began to rub on her thigh.

"You wanna rest a little here? We can stay here all night if you want to," Kingston said, turning to look at her.

"Hell, no, I don't wanna rest," Jazmyn replied looking over at Kingston. Jazmyn noticed the twinkle of amusement in his eyes because he knew exactly what she wanted.

"Want some more?" Kingston asked.

"Yeah...but this time on the balcony," Jazmyn said as she rose up out of the bed and walked sexily over to the glass doors that separated her from the large balcony that surrounded a third of the suite. Without hesitation, Kingston got up and followed behind her; eager to please.

ALEXIS

*A*lexis picked up the huge bottle of Jose Cuervo, put it up to her lips, and swallowed the last drop before tossing the glass onto the floor. The heavy bottle made a loud cracking noise, but the glass did not shatter. Not like Alexis cared. She was not in the mood to care about anything right now. Marc was gone on another business trip, and she was doing the only thing that she cared to do at the moment...draining the largest bottle of liquor she could find in their upstairs bar.

Alexis had called her mother that morning to vent about her marriage. She had thought that maybe Duchess, as she preferred her children to call her, would be able to sympathize with her...or at least give her some motherly advice on what to do. As usual, when it came to her mother, Alexis was wrong.

"Alexis, I really don't understand what your issue is. You have a man who gives you everything you want. He pampers you and he is barely home long enough to get on your nerves! Why can't you be a good wife like I taught you," Duchess stated. "So what if you have to have *sex* with him every now and then. We all have to suffer when our men get a little frisky and want to stick those things in us. Even your father is trying to get the little pills now to help out his situation..."

Alexis began to tune her mother out. She couldn't believe this! Duchess always had a way of making every conversation about her, but Alexis thought that in this case, Duchess would be able to put that aside and focus on the needs of her daughter.

Alexis was unhappy. Although she loved her husband dearly, she could not help but think that there had to be something more to it that she was missing. She wanted the level of intimacy that her friends had with their men during sex. Even Jazmyn was able to describe most of her encounters with men as romantic, fulfilling, and fun.

She had endured countless phone calls from Kaylen where she continued to go on and on about how attentive Salem was, how he treated her like she was so fragile, made her feel so feminine and precious during sex. Why couldn't Marc give her that? Why did he prefer to cause her pain? It was like pain excited him...each time he came home; he had a new idea of something that they could do that would cause her to yell even louder, cause even more bruises. Alexis was tired of pretending she *liked* that shit. She *hated* it, and she wanted more from someone who said that he loved her more than anything.

"Duchess...I am not happy. I'm tired of pretending. Isn't it supposed to be fun and romantic? Aren't I supposed to *like* it?" Alexis asked. She had her Bluetooth on, and she was pacing back and forth in her room wearing sweatpants and a tank top with her hair pulled back in a long ponytail.

"Absolutely not!" Duchess' declaration made Alexis stop mid-pace. "Alexis, stop watching all of those romantic comedies. Real life is not like that, and if anyone tells you anything different; they are telling you a lie. Sex is *work*, my dear. Always has been, and it always will be. But sex is power! If we, women, do it just right, we can get a man to give us anything we want. Stop complaining, Alexis, and put on your grown woman panties. This is what marriage is about! You act like I didn't raise you, child!" Duchess huffed at her daughter.

"Look, Alexis. I have to go. I am in the middle of preparing for a dinner party, and I am absolutely tired from having to direct the staff on how to do every single thing. I will talk to you later." With that,

Duchess hung up without even saying "bye" and Alexis began to pour her first glass of tequila.

Now that Alexis had finished the bottle, she peered over her bed, onto the floor and looked at the emptiness of the bottle with a slightly confused look on her face.

"How am I supposed to refill it?" she muttered to herself, slurring her words together. Belching loudly, she flipped herself over on the bed so that she was facing upwards towards the ceiling and her head was dangling off the side of the bed. "That's not lady-like! Duchess would not like!" she giggled to herself and picked up her cellphone.

She contemplated calling Marc herself and telling him how she felt, but she decided against it. Getting on the phone with Marc in her current state would only worry him, causing him to return home and give her some more good "loving." Alexis slumped back down on the bed. Just thinking about Marc made her depressed. She used to love to think about him. Back in the days before the sex, he excited her in every way. Not only did he look good, but he dressed good, was smart, charismatic, and was the perfect man...seemingly.

People felt magnetized by his presence. His personality seemed to make women and men alike want to befriend him, be near him, and take everything he said as gold. No one would ever understand her if she left him because he was the man of her dreams and every woman's dreams! It was just that one small thing that she could not get over.

Why couldn't he just leave his dirty clothes in the bathroom or fuck around like most men? Alexis thought. But no, she had the man who was organized to a fault and cleaner than anyone she ever knew. Alexis should have known when they first began dating that he was too good to be true.

She had met Marc at a party that she had been invited to by a co-worker while she was in college. Alexis had worked as an intern for LaChic, a clothing boutique that belonged to Ranell Stu, a famous designer in Atlanta. He had an office in Atlanta as well as an office in New York. Alexis was working for the Atlanta office while in college with hopes to transfer to the New York office after college in order to work permanently alongside Ranell himself.

Alexis and her co-worker, Dexter, were friends outside of work, but inside of work, they were fierce enemies and competitors. Alexis and Dexter were both competing for the most coveted position of head intern. The first day that Alexis saw Dexter, she liked him. He was impeccably dressed in a tailored suit and his Gucci shoes peeked out from the bottom of his crisp pin-striped pants. His cologne hung to the air around him and Alexis noticed it at the same minute that she looked into his face and admired his smooth caramel-colored skin. The corners of his mouth turned up as he caught her stare and Alexis began to feel heated. Although Alexis was caught up in Dexter's good looks, she wasn't dumb.

Damn...it's a shame that he is not playing for my team. Alexis was not too naïve to think that a man that had been able to receive one of the most coveting fashion internships in the nation would actually be interested in her - or any woman for that matter. Especially not one that dressed the way Dexter dressed. His style was absolutely flawless, and he knew it. He had an air of confidence that made everyone in the room aware of him and although he looked friendly, Alexis did feel slightly intimidated by him. That feeling quickly went away because Dexter became her friend quite quickly, and they often took lunch together and spoke outside of work.

One day Dexter suggested that she went to a party with him, and that's where she met Marc. Marc had actually come to the party with a date - he and Alexis often joked about what may have happened to her. All Alexis knows is that she was the one that Marc drove home that night.

Alexis entered the party, slightly frustrated at the fact that she was not able to fit into the skirt that she originally had wanted to wear. She had been trying for quite some time to lose weight and had been very successful...however, she still was not able to fit into the size twelve skirt that she had bought for this party.

All that working out five times a week for nothing! Alexis tried not to get discouraged, but her weight had become a soft spot for her ever since she had met up with some of her high school friends two months prior, and they commented on her twenty pound weight gain.

Alexis knew she still had a great shape and could pull any man that she wanted, but she did things for herself and based on how she felt. She felt like she wanted to be lighter and healthier, so that was her goal. Alexis ran her hands down the front of her skirt to smooth out the material before grabbing Dexter's outstretched hand and letting him pull her into the room.

Actually, the word "room" was an understatement. The party, although it took place inside of a home, it looked nothing like anything that Alexis had ever lived in. Alexis was used to nice things being that she came from a family with money. Her father had always worked hard, and it paid off nicely. He had acquired multiple businesses over his lifetime, and his family lived well because of it.

Even though Alexis had older siblings that had been around before the family had gotten to the state of wealth that they currently enjoyed, Alexis had never witnessed that. She was born into her life of privilege and enjoyed every second of it. Even then her father always made sure that the things he bought were bought out of necessity and that his purchases were practical. Therefore, she had never lived in anything as outrageously luxurious as the home that she now stood in.

"Dex, who did you say was throwing this party again?" Alexis said as she walked into what she could only call a grand ballroom. She looked up at the mural that was painted on the ceiling and framed in gold. As she walked past one of the many columns stationed in the room, she ran her beautifully manicured fingers down the side and looked down to admire the mosaic tile beneath her feet. A server passed by Dexter with rose-colored champagne and mini appetizers. Dexter grabbed two champagne glasses and handed one to Alexis.

"This party is being thrown by the parents of a person that I met outside of *LaChic* last month. I met him on my way to work, and he seemed to be having a serious wardrobe malfunction - in other words his pants had split straight down the back and he was a little exposed, if you know what I mean," Dexter winked. "So, I had him come in, I fixed his pants and he invited me to this party. He said his parents know a lot of important people here in Atlanta, and it would be a great networking opportunity."

"Hmmm....well that was nice. I guess I better get to networking then," Alexis started and looked over to Dexter, who had already walked away towards a group of people standing in a circle. As usual, as soon as Dexter approached them each person immediately seemed to accept him into the circle. Alexis huffed, and blew out a sharp breath that made her feathered bang fly off to the side. She would love to have that effect on people. Instead, most women hated Alexis when they first met her, and most men felt slightly intimidated by the fact that her father took such great care of her. She even had a boyfriend break up with her because he stated that he couldn't compete with her father.

Well, duh...no man can compete with my daddy, Alexis had thought to herself. *But at least your ass could try.*

"Hi, can I get one of those?" Alexis asked as another waiter passed. The man smiled at her and held out a tray filled with small quiche-looking delights that were filled with various sweet toppings. Alexis eyed the one that looked like it had a pecan-custard filling. "Actually, never mind." She had come to realize that she was an emotional eater, and she wanted to make sure that she wasn't just eating to cover for the fact that she felt out of place and alone. She looked over to Dexter and noticed that in that short of time, he seemed to have become the center of attention. He was speaking, and everyone around him seemed to be enjoying what he had to say.

After the group suddenly erupted in laughter, Alexis decided to head back towards him. She stopped short when she felt a light touch on her arm. Alexis turned sharply towards the touch, and was immediately caught up by the oddest looking eyes that she had ever seen. They were blue with gray and brown flecks, but that's not what made them look odd. It was the streaks of auburn that spread throughout that made her pause.

"Good evening...I'm sorry for stopping you. I saw you about to walk away, and I wanted to make sure that I introduced myself to you." Alexis eyed the man that spoke to her with genuine curiosity. He had boldness about him that she had not seen in many men outside of her father. He had soft eyes and olive colored complexion with short, dirty blond hair. His chiseled jaw line accented his dramatic, but gentle eyes and his pouty lips made Alexis have to clench her thighs to calm her womanly nature. Alexis had always preferred to keep a brother tucked in her pocket because the thought had never even occurred to her to date any other type of man. But there was no denying the sexiness that stood in front of her.

She allowed her eyes to quickly drop down and admire the effortless sexy in front her of her. He was wearing a soft grey pant suit, European cut, just like she liked them. He had on a pale blue shirt with the top button undone to show a small sliver of his smooth and tan chest. Alexis looked down and finally noticed the outstretched hand; she quickly placed her hand into his and smiled sheepishly. She noticed the small smirk and minor tilt of his head which let her know that she had been caught while admiring this stranger, but apparently he didn't mind.

"I'm Marc. I wanted to make sure that I introduced myself to you because I don't believe we have met." Alexis noticed that although the handshake was over, Marc had not yet let go of her. Instead, as she relaxed her arm; he relaxed his, as well, but continued to gently hold her hand.

"No, we haven't met. I actually don't know anyone here. I came with my friend Dexter." Alexis said as she gently pulled her hand away. Although she was physically attracted to Marc, the realness of the situation is that she didn't know who he was and didn't appreciate the way he had begun running his thumb across the inside of her palm. Alexis looked over at Dexter, and noticed that he was staring straight at her. Dexter had an odd look on his face and it made Alexis stop for a second to try to read his facial expression as he began to walk in her direction. She couldn't exactly place the look, so she decided not to dwell on it.

"I didn't catch your name," Marc stated adjusting the sleeve on his tailored suit.

"Alexis," she replied as soon as Dexter approached them.

"Hey there, Marc. I see that you have met Alexis," Dexter stated wrapping his arm around Alexis' waist. The gesture stunned her, and she turned to look Dexter in the face, but could not read his expression. He was smiling and looking directly at Marc; one hand was extended to offer Marc a handshake while the other remained tightly snuggled against Alexis' hip. She shifted uncomfortably but didn't move. She looked at Marc, who hesitated for a minute before answering Dexter's question and observed her body language. The smirk returned.

"Yes, I have. I was just wondering who this beautiful woman was that decided to come to my parents' party all alone. I thought they were trying to set me up again. Apparently not this time. Shame, too, because I would have loved this pick." Alexis felt her face getting hot, and she bowed her head to conceal the smile that crept up on the edges of her lips.

"I see. Alexis, this is the person I was speaking to you about...with the wardrobe malfunction," Dexter winked. It was now Marc's time to be embarrassed, but he didn't seem to be bothered at all. He tilted his head back and laughed in a way that made Alexis have to squeeze her legs closed again. His laugh had a rough sound to it, but it was also deep and commanding - with each chuckle; Alexis could feel her female essence begin to thump. She could feel the heat rising up to her cheeks again, and she began to examine her French manicure as they continued speaking.

That night had ended with Alexis hopping into Marc's car and touring around the city in his Mercedes Benz convertible. Although, she had lived in Atlanta most of her life, she had never seen it the way that she saw it that night.

Fast forward ten years and here she was, lying on her bed in a drunken stupor trying to escape the realities of her marriage. She had married someone that she loved. Hell, she married someone that *everybody* loved! But they were missing something that she needed. She needed the level of intimacy with her husband that her friends bragged about with men that they barely knew but found themselves ruffling the sheets with.

"It just doesn't seem faaaaiiirrrr!" Alexis whined to herself as she wrapped herself up in her covers and pulled the top over her head.

"What doesn't?" a condescending voice said from above her head. Alexis recognized it instantly, and groaned as she heard the click of the light switching on in the room.

"Duchess? What are you doing here?" Alexis shouted a little louder than she had intended and tried to adjust her eyes to the light as she tugged the covers from off of her head. She sat up quickly - a little too quickly - and tried to focus her eyes on her mothers' brown glaring eyes that looked back at her in a way that perfectly displayed her displeasure.

Duchess stood in front of Alexis in a black, Prada suit with a hat pulled on over her long dark brown curls. She had her excellently manicured hands crossed in front of her as they held onto her small, black clutch with her fingers clasped together. "I thought you were prepping for your dinner party?"

"Countess Alexis! How long have you been sitting in this bed? Do you know what time it is?"

Alexis winced at her mother's use of her first name. Countess... definitely something only the Duchess could have come up with. Alexis stared blankly at her mother and blinked a few times. She looked over at the beautiful Breitling wall clock across from her bed.

11:30 at night?! It was JUST 6:00 o'clock! How have I lost track of that much time? Alexis looked back at her mother trying to hide the surprise on her face. She knew from the way that Duchess pulled her lips into a tight, thin line that she had not been successful in fooling her mother...she never was.

"Duchess, do you need something?" Alexis stated crossing her arms in front of her. She was attempting to steady herself by crossing her arms and also appear lucid in hopes that Duchess would find that her impromptu visitation was no longer needed.

I need to remember to collect her spare key.

"First of all, Countess, you will *fix* your tone when you talk to me, "Duchess said between clenched teeth. " Secondly, you will get your *ass* out of this bed and listen to what I have to say. I will meet you in the sitting room in five minutes and you *better not* make me have to come back in here!"

Duchess had not been born into wealth, but she had adjusted with much ease; however, every now and then she was able to shed the "Duchess" and step into "Mama" when she deemed it totally necessary.

Alexis groaned loudly and headed over to the master bath. She knew that Duchess expected her to get herself together and look "presentable" for their little chat.

Or lecture, Alexis thought.

She walked into the bathroom and looked at her reflection. She looked absolutely horrible even with her blurred vision. She pressed her hair down on the sides to try to smooth it as much as possible, then she thought back to the look of disapproval that she had received from Duchess, and decided it was best to at least run a comb through her it. After checking her breath, she decided that she should brush her teeth as well. Maybe even use a little Listerine.

Alexis walked into the living room with a bright smile and as much of a positive attitude as she could muster up. There was nothing odd to her about how she had spent the day. This was her ritual. She always drank her troubles away the day after Marc left for work. It was the only way that she knew how to cope with her life as it was.

"Alexis, sit down, darling. Right here beside me," Duchess patted the space next to her on the small designer loveseat in Alexis' living room. Alexis looked around the room before sitting down. It wasn't often that she was able to enjoy this area. During the last few months, Alexis had grown accustomed to spending most of her time in her bedroom thinking about her marriage and feeling sorry for herself. Pathetic, yes, but that's the reality of how she had been spending her life. The high points were the few days that she was able to spend time with her girls. Unfortunately, with Kaylen and Jaz booed up, she'd had to live life alone when Marc wasn't around.

"So, I wasn't going to come down here, but your father suggested I make the trip based on our conversation earlier and the fact that we haven't seen you in a while," Duchess said as she wiped the top of the coffee table in front of her with her finger. She looked down at her finger and frowned at the dust before she continued. "Judging by how I found you, wrapped up in your sheets with empty liquor bottles tucked under your bed, I am thinking that there is something amiss. What is the problem, Alexis? And I do hope that it isn't that silliness regarding you not wanting to have sex with your own husband."

Alexis sighed and sat back in the sofa, tucking her legs beneath her. "No, Duchess. That is not it. I'm just depressed that Marc is gone all the time for work. That's all," Alexis lied. There was nothing that her mother worshipped more than her own husband, so Alexis knew that this was an issue that even the Duchess wouldn't be able to understand.

"Oh, darling, I can definitely identify with that. Your father certainly works a lot as well, so I know the feeling. We must have focus on the fact that they *are* coming back...." Alexis steadied her gaze on her mother as much as she could, but her mind began to drift off to another place as Duchess continued her lecture on how it was the wife's duty to wait for and *please* her husband. "If he can make the sacrifice to work hard and provide all of these things for you, the least you can do is wait for him to return home and please him. You don't want him to go out and have a fling with some random woman, do you?"

YES! "No, Duchess. I don't. But I understand. I think I just need to rest; that's all. I know it will all be fine," Alexis said standing up. She hoped that Duchess saw this as a hint that it was time to leave. Fortunately for her, Duchess sighed deeply and began collecting her things. Duchess stood up slowly and then began searching around the room. Alexis continued walking towards the front door and then stopped when she noticed that Duchess was not following her.

"Where is Vanessa?" Duchess asked, her eyes still surveying the area as if Vanessa would jump out any second.

"I have no idea. Maybe she is with Sasha," Alexis responded drily. The last thing she wanted to speak about at this time was her sister. Who knows what she was up to. Alexis was just glad that she wasn't there.

"No, I doubt that," Duchess said slowly.

Alexis hesitated as she continued to watch her mother. Duchess' shoulders slumped over, and the expression on her face was one of worry and sadness. Alexis had never seen her mother this way and it began to concern her. Even in her drunken state, she could feel the alarm rising in her body as she watched her mother.

"Alexis, watch out for her, please?" Duchess asked, picking up her head to look Alexis in the eyes. Although her parents had told her many times to watch out for Vanessa, something was different about this request. Alexis began to walk over closer to Duchess.

"Duchess...is something wrong with Vanessa?" There was a long silence as Alexis waited for her to respond. Slowly, Duchess raised her head all the way to its normal position that situated her nose directly in the air, and she straightened her back.

"Just do as I asked, Countess. I'm glad you are doing fine now. I will let your father know the news." With that, Duchess let herself out, and Alexis stood in the foyer pondering her mother's request regarding her sister.

KAYLEN

The first thing that Kaylen noticed once she dropped into the small compartment was the smell. There was a distinct smell of musk and spoiled milk. She had to hold her hand over her mouth and nose in order to keep herself from coughing at the combination of the smell and the dust that she was inhaling with each breath. Kaylen could hear the thumping above her. It seemed like they were right above her head. With each step that the agents took, dust and other debris fell from atop and landed in her hair, face, and in her eyes. She ducked down low and tried to cover her head with her arms to prevent any more debris landing in her face and going up her nose.

The LAST thing I need to do right now is sneeze. Kaylen thought as she crouched low to the floor.

"This room is clear," she heard the muffled voice of one agent and then heard a stampede of footsteps scampering out of the room. Kaylen let out the breath that she had been holding, and took the opportunity to take a quick look at her surroundings.

She noticed that there was something that looked like a door in front of her. She started to push at it, and decided not to at the last minute. Kaylen sat still for a minute and listened to see if she could hear any more steps to indicate that someone will still in the room above her. Sure enough, she heard the slow steps of what must have been an agent who stayed behind to make sure the room was, in fact, clear.

Your spidey senses are correct! Now get the hell out! Kaylen thought trying to will the agent out of the room. As soon as she finished that thought, the steps picked up speed, and she could hear the person retreat to one of the other places in the house.

Kaylen decided to give the door a try this time, hoping that she could go deeper into the underground compartment and find a way into a space that would help her hide until all of the agents searched the place and left. The door gave out a small creak as she opened it, and Kaylen snatched her hand away to listen for any approaching footsteps. After a while with no noise, she became confident that she wasn't heard and proceeded to open the rest of the door. From the sound of it, all of the agents were gathered in the main room and probing through all of the evidence that lay on the table right where she had left it.

When Kaylen entered the space, she noticed it was very large and covered the entire bottom of the house like a basement. However, the smell still lingered in the air. Kaylen turned up her nose at the filth that covered the ground including what appeared to be small animal droppings. Suddenly something brushed against her foot; Kaylen jumped backwards, and then covered her mouth with her hand to hold in the scream that had nearly escaped her mouth. She looked behind her and saw a small mouse racing into a hole near the corner of the house.

Disgusting! She thought curling up her lips in repulsion. Kaylen walked to the opposite corner of where she saw the mouse escape, careful not to step on any of the rat droppings scattered throughout, and sat down with her knees up and her arms wrapped around her legs. She decided the best thing to do was to stay in that spot and listen for when the agents left the home.

KAYLEN OPENED HER EYES AND NOTICED A SMALL SET OF EYES LOOKING back at her. She jumped up faster than her legs were probably ready for and kicked her foot at the gray mouse that had been inches away from her face. Lifting her arm, she looked at her watch and noticed that it was three a.m. the next day. She walked through the basement slowly, making sure to place her foot down in spaces not currently occupied with rodent feces, and listened intently to figure out if she was alone in the house. After feeling confident that she couldn't hear any activity above her, she counted to 100 quietly in her head and then pulled out her cellphone. She turned on Google maps and tried to map the distance from her current location to her home.

Thank God for technology. Wait...2 hours?! Kaylen squinted at the screen in disbelief. It hadn't even seemed like she had been asleep that long in Levi's car.

Kaylen walked over to the wall and pushed the door that allowed her entrance into the small compartment that she had first been in. Kaylen hesitated a moment before pushing the small door up and moving it to the side. She felt a cool breeze of air...still stale, but slightly less stuffy, as it hit her face. She grabbed the sides of the floor above her and lifted herself up as much as she could. Suddenly, she felt her grip loosen and she fell back down, smacking her head on the side of the wall in the process.

The rug that she had been holding on to in order to hoist herself up came flopping down the opening and landed on top of her. Along with it came a thick covering of a combination of dust and dirt that must have been accumulating on the rug for years. Kaylen groaned loudly as she picked herself up from beneath the rug and tried to shake off some of the filth that covered her. She tried once again, this time successfully, to pull herself from the basement and rolled onto the floor in an attempt to regain her breath.

Didn't know I was THIS out of shape; she thought as she huffed loudly while massaging the spot on her head that still throbbed from her tumble. Kaylen reached into her side pocket and quickly dialed a number.

"Kaylen?" Salem said after the first ring. Although he sounded tired, he didn't seem to have been asleep. His voice was filled with concern and Kaylen immediately regretted calling him. She thought about hanging up and dialing Alexis or Jaz, but then decided against it.

"Salem....I need your help. I don't know where I am...but I need you to come get me." Kaylen said as she actively tried to control her breathing so not to worry Salem.

"Kaylen! What happened? Are you ok? I've been trying to call you for hours! What do you mean you don't know where you are?" Kaylen could hear through the phone that Salem was moving quickly. She could hear him as he closed what must have been the front door. She knew he was in his car when she heard the beeping reminding him to put on his seatbelt.

"Calm down, Salem. I will explain when you get here. I will text you the address....just be careful, ok?" Kaylen sighed. This was not a story that she even wanted to tell, but she knew that Salem would want some answers. There was no other way to explain what she was doing here.

"Ok, baby. Send me the address...I'm already in the car and ready. See you soon."

Kaylen dropped her phone, not even bothering to hit the "end" button. She was grateful that Salem hadn't wanted to keep her on the phone while he drove. She needed to figure out a way to explain what happened while revealing as little about her past as possible.

"KAYLEN...WAKE UP! KAYLEN! WHAT THE FUCK HAPPENED HERE?" Kaylen was jerked out of sleep by Salem, who was standing over her, leaning down in her face. His long dreadlocks were draped over the sides of his face and drifting back and forth across Kaylen's face as he moved. Kaylen blinked a few times as her eyes attempted to adjust to the blaring light in her eyes coming from Salem's cellphone.

"Salem, let's get out of here. I will explain on the way home," Kaylen mumbled as she picked herself off of the dirty floor. Apparently, instead of brainstorming how to explain her current situation to Salem, she'd ended up falling asleep. Salem grabbed onto her in order to keep her steady as she began to walk, and he led the way with his flashlight.

After walking out the door, Kaylen gasped when she made it to the porch. Salem's light shined on what she knew to be Levi's dried blood splattered all over the front steps of the house. Until that moment, Kaylen hadn't fully thought about what had occurred with Levi. Her knees began to buckle, and Salem grabbed her tightly to keep her from falling to her knees. Kaylen let out a loud moan as the tears came and fell down her face.

Her mind replayed the last of what she had seen of Levi as the bullets filled his body. She let out all of the emotion and all of the fear that she had felt within the past 24 hours as Salem picked her up and cradled her in his arms, carrying her to his car. Kaylen allowed him to place her in the passenger's seat of the car, and she fell against the window after he closed the door behind him.

Salem moved quickly to jump into the driver's seat of the car. With what seemed to be one swift motion, he started the car and pulled out of the lot. It wasn't until they had made it onto the highway that Salem glanced Kaylen's way. Kaylen had shifted in her seat so that she could see him out of the corner of her eyes, but she was trying hard not to make direct eye contact. Although she could not fully make out his face, she knew that he was looking at her with concern. She prayed that he would think she was sleeping and drop the subject altogether.

"Kay...I need to know what happened there. I need you to speak to me," Salem pleaded. The car slowed as he turned multiple times between looking at the road to observing the side of her face. Kaylen looked towards Salem with fresh tears in her eyes.

It's either now or never. Kaylen cleared her throat and began to speak. She hadn't wanted Salem to know, but somehow her story started at the beginning. She began by telling Salem about her father and how he had raised her, the skills he taught her and how much she loved him. She told Salem about what happened when she went to stay with her aunt and how she'd met Levi. She told him how she had been supporting herself all these years and how she had been able to afford her apartment, clothes, and car.

Lastly, she told him about the horrific day that she'd had, how she had seen Levi die and how she had hid in the rat infested basement for hours until she was able to call him. As Kaylen spoke, she made sure not to look over at Salem. He was so quiet that she was able to pretend that she was all alone and speaking to herself. She was able to be honest, and tell it all without feeling ashamed and afraid of what he might think.

As Kaylen finished her story, she exhaled loudly and fell back in her seat. It wasn't until then that she noticed that they had arrived in front of her apartment and were sitting in front of the garage. She glanced over at Salem and tried to assess his face. When she looked over to him, she noticed that he looked confused, angry, but mostly something else that Kaylen wasn't sure of. He actually seemed slightly embarrassed, but Kaylen couldn't find a reason why he would be embarrassed from her story, so she ignored it.

Salem's expression shifted to one of concern and he leaned over to kiss her lightly on her lips. His kiss quickly became something else as she felt him part her lips with his tongue and roam throughout. He grabbed onto her tightly and began to kiss her with so much passion that Kaylen could feel nothing but utter relief. Her eyes began to fill back up with tears, and they fell down her face, mixing in with their lips.

Salem pulled away and looked Kaylen in her eyes with so much love. He then pressed his lips on her cheek following the trail of tears down her face. Salem pulled back once again, turned off the car and then opened his door. He walked slowly over to Kaylen's side, opened her door, and lifted her effortlessly out of the car and carried her into the house.

Salem's face showed no expression as he carried her up the stairs and to the bed. He laid Kaylen on it and began to peel off her clothing slowly as he inspected every inch of her body. Kaylen watched as Salem fingered a small bruise on her lower left leg that must have been a result of her fall. He leaned down and kissed it softly and when he rose Kaylen could see that he had tears in his eyes. Kaylen lifted herself up slightly while looking at him with a worried expression on her face.

"Sorry, I couldn't protect you," Salem said as he continued to look at her. He blinked the tears away before turning to walk towards the master bathroom. "I will run you some bath water so you can relax." Kaylen fell back on the bed and looked to the ceiling, but her mind followed Salem as she thought about how incredible a man he was.

KAYLEN SWUNG HER FEET AROUND THE SIDE OF THE BED AND PLACED them on the floor. She let her head hang as she massaged the side of her neck with her right hand. Her body was sore as a result from sitting in a crouched position in the corner of that basement for so long and also from the fall that she took.

The baths that Salem had been running for her each day made her feel a little better, but there was still some discomfort that reminded her that what happened a few days back had not been a dream. Since "the incident," as Salem called it, Kaylen had been having trouble sleeping. Each night she felt like the agents would break down her door and rush into her home looking for her. She had always been safe to wear gloves when she worked with Levi, but she wasn't completely sure that she hadn't left any of her DNA at the house. She had probably been the last person that Levi had called also...what if they checked his phone records?

Kaylen would wake up in the middle of the night at any sound that she heard or *thought* she'd heard. The night before, she'd heard the sound of ice dropping into the bin for the ice maker, and she nearly jumped out of bed and into the closet. Salem had been sleeping over and taking care of her the whole time since the incident. He had not mentioned what happened at all, and when Kaylen was watching the news and the story showed up about the huge drug bust, Salem turned off the television quickly and suggested that Kaylen take a walk with him.

Another thing that had not been brought up was the issue of him finally moving in. Kaylen had thought about it a few times, but she wanted Salem to bring it up. Although Salem stayed with her the past few days, he still had to leave to go back home and get clean clothes. Kaylen was still a little unsure how comfortable she would feel when he decided to go back home.

"Still sore?" Salem asked placing a glass of orange juice in Kaylen's hand.

"Just a little...nothing big," Kaylen said as brought the glass to her lips. Looking over the rim of her glass, she was able to see her school books. She had been neglecting her studies, and the emails that she'd received from her professors assured her that she had a lot to catch up on. If that were even possible...missing a week in medical school was equivalent to missing a semester's worth of information within an undergraduate program.

"Going to class today?" Salem asked following her gaze. Kaylen shook her head.

"No, I've already missed most of today's lectures. I'm just going to take some time out to look over the material that I've missed."

"Well, I will do anything that I can to help," Salem said flipping a few of his long dreadlocks out of his eyes. "Why don't you get up and put on some clothes? I was thinking about going over to my place today to grab a few things. I would love if you would ride over with me." Kaylen thought for a minute before getting up to walk over to her closet to find something to wear. Salem walked behind her and leaned on the side of her closet door.

"Hey, I wanted to ask you about something, Kay. I was thinking about the possibility of us moving in together." Salem paused and looked at Kaylen in an attempt to gauge her reaction. Kaylen slowly looked towards Salem with a smile on her face. It was the first smile she had seen since the incident had occurred.

"I think that would be a great idea. I mean....might as well, right?" Kaylen smiled. Salem returned her smile, showing his deep dimples that gave him more of a boyish look which contrasted his serious grown man swag that she was used to seeing.

"Ok,....well why don't we work out the details over dinner?" he said walking close to her. He wrapped his arms around her waist and planted a kiss on her cheek. Kaylen's clit began to throb as he slowly moved the kisses down to her neck. They had not been intimate since before everything had happened. Kaylen had been too stressed to even think about it. But at that moment, she wanted Salem. She needed him. And from the way that his manhood was pushing against the back of her ass, he needed her just as badly.

Kaylen turned around to place her arms around Salem and began rotating her hips over his throbbing member as she pulled him into a deep kiss. She let his tongue enter her mouth, and he kissed her even deeper making sure to grab tightly around her waist, and pull her even closer to him. He reached down under her short, hot pink dress and pushed it up exposing her backside as well as her nicely trimmed hot spot.

Kaylen didn't believe in sleeping with panties on for the most part, and Salem enjoyed this about her. Salem pulled back just enough to slip a finger deep into her wetness. Kaylen caught her breath as he entered her, and she began gyrating against his finger as he opened her wider by sticking another finger in...and then another. Kaylen moaned and hugged him even tighter, lifting one leg up to wrap around him.

Suddenly Salem began to kiss her even more forcefully. So hard that it made Kaylen gasp out loud with pleasure as he began pushing his fingers further into her more roughly than he had before. He lifted Kaylen up by placing his other hand up under her and dropped her onto the bed. Kaylen moaned slightly when he pulled his fingers out of her throbbing pussy. She barely had any time to react before he pushed her to the side making her land on her hands and knees, with her ass tooted straight up in the air.

Kaylen bit her lip and looked back at Salem. He was her man, and he knew exactly how she liked it. Salem quickly unbuttoned and dropped his white linen pants to the floor, wasting no time before he long-stroked directly into Kaylen's tight walls. The smooth force of the first thrust made Kaylen groan with pleasure.

Salem groaned as well as he felt her pussy grab tightly around his dick.

He reached out and grabbed Kaylen's hair firmly, wrapping it around his fist. He pulled back hard which made her back arch even more so than before. Kaylen exhaled deeply with pleasure as she felt Salem began sliding in and out of her slowly. She grabbed the sheets tightly and pressed back as hard as she could, opening herself up for him to ram further up into her.

"Yessssss, baby! Mmmhmmmm, that's so....fucking good, Salem!" Kaylen yelled loudly. Her breast bounced happily in the air as her nipples became hard as a rock with pleasure.

"You like that? Huh? You liked that, don't you?" Salem said through gritted teeth as he continued thrusting forward. The wet smacking sound began to turn Kaylen on even more and she further arched her back to allow Salem to go deeper inside her.

"Oh, shit...this pussy is too good!" Salem said. He paused for a minute and pulled out quickly. In one quick motion, he flipped Kaylen onto her back and pushed her legs apart by the knees. He pushed her them up towards her head and then pushed three fingers deep inside her, rotating them in a forward motion to tickle her g-spot.

"Mmmmhmmm..." He moaned after he pulled out his fingers and slid them into his mouth to suck off all of her gooey juice. Before Kaylen had any time to react, Salem slammed his dick deep inside of her and continued hammering away. Her thick, cream began oozing out of her and onto his long, plump dick. Then Kaylen looked up into Salem's eyes and felt true and absolute happiness. He leaned down to kiss her, and she moaned into his mouth as he continued pounding away into her.

I could do this forever.

JAZMYN

"*W*ell, ain't this some bullshit?!" Jazmyn said to herself as she smacked her steering wheel so hard the palm of her hand began to sting. She was sitting inside of her mother's car across the street from Kingston's house. She had been sitting there for hours waiting for something to happen…anything that would provide her some clarity about the situation that she was in.

Kingston had been visiting her more frequently at her condo, but while he repeatedly stayed late, he never spent the night. They had been going at it nearly every day since that night at the hotel two months ago. He always jumped up around the same time every night, took a shower in her bathroom, and then threw on the clothes that he had arrived in. Jazmyn began to grow increasingly suspicious of him as the time wore on, and she began to feel more like a mistress than someone whom he loved. That line of thinking led her to borrow her mother's car for the day to drive over to his house and camp out for a few hours. Her mother had been happy to assist and nearly threw her keys in Jazmyn's direction as she ran to get dressed and show off her new car for the day. Jazmyn had been just as anxious to get a move on and figure out if Kingston's home was as unhappy as he claimed.

Unfortunately, after nearly two hours of waiting, she was

rewarded with watching Kingston exit out of his home with his very pregnant wife and while assisting her as she entered into his white Porsche Cayenne.

This nigga even opened the door and everything! Jazmyn waited until they had backed out of the drive-way and stopped at the stop sign at the end of the street before she continued her pursuit behind them with horrible intentions.

Jazmyn picked up her phone and began dialing Kingston's cell-phone number. She already knew what would happen, but for some reason decided to set herself up for failure anyway. She needed the rage to continue fueling her anger. She waited for the line to begin ringing, but was alarmed when it cut short after one ring and went directly to the voicemail.

"That's how we do Kingston? We ignore calls? You could have at least let it ring out to the voicemail instead of diverting me yourself!" Jazmyn spat into the phone after it began recording her message.

She pressed her foot down on the pedal to follow a little closer behind Kingston's SUV in order to escape being stopped at an approaching traffic light that was currently yellow and about to turn red. At that exact moment, Kingston pressed the brakes and began to slow his car to a stop at the light. Jazmyn hit the brakes and tried to slow down in time to not run her vehicle smack in the back of Kingston's SUV, but she was going much too fast to stop so soon.

"Oh, shit!" Jazmyn yelled as she pulled on the steering wheel and swerved to the right in order to avoid colliding with Kingston's which had finally come to a full stop. Jazmyn squeezed her eyes shut as she entered the lane to the right and waited for the crash that was sure to come from any vehicle that may have been on the side of her. But it never came.

"Thank you, God!" Jazmyn yelled when she looked up and noticed that she was still in one piece, and had been fortunate enough to swerve into an empty lane. She ran her hand through her hair and took a deep breath as she looked in her rear view mirror to glance behind her, checking the scene to ensure she had not caused a wreck. Finally, she placed her hands back on the steering wheel and glanced up at the traffic light. It was green, but she had an odd feeling because the car to her right was not moving.

Oh, my God! I forgot about Kingston! Jazmyn thought and looked to her left. Kingston and his wife were staring directly in her face with very different expressions. Kingston wore a look of absolute shock mixed with a little bit of embarrassment and also a side of...anger? Jazmyn started to slant her neck a little to the side to try to decipher if Kingston really did seem to be mad at her, but she could not ignore the heat on her face from the glare coming from the passenger seat.

Mrs. Grant was almost seething as she looked at Jazmyn. Her thin lips were pulled into an even thinner line, and her eyes were so narrow that they almost looked like slits. Although she may have been a beautiful woman at any normal period of time, the way that she was looking at Jazmyn distorted her features in a way that seemed almost demonic.

BEEEEEEEEP, BEEEEP! Jazmyn was jarred back into reality as cars pulled in behind them and honked with understandable impatience at being stopped at a green light. Jazmyn turned forward and placed her foot on the gas to accelerate, but instead of continuing forward, she took a sharp right towards the interstate in the direction of her mother's home. She needed a little bit of an escape from her normal reality in order to better her mood.

"I can't believe I did that! What was I thinking? How could I do that?" Jazmyn was certain that following Kingston, sitting outside of his home, the home he shared with his *wife,* was the dumbest thing that she had ever done in her life. "Well, one of the dumbest things. Getting involved with Kingston from the beginning is number one!"

Jazmyn felt tears rise up in her eyes as she thought about her life at that exact moment. The last two months had been spent with her falling behind on her cases, some that included very high paying clients. Her work performance was at an all-time low since she was spending every night with Kingston rather than studying and preparing to defend her clients. Her boss had been making an increasing number of "casual visits" to her office to check on the status of things, and Jazmyn knew this was more so him checking on her more than anything else.

That's it! Jazmyn thought to herself as she pulled off of I-285 towards the exit for East Point, and directly towards one of the roughest neighborhoods in Metro Atlanta. *Kingston must think I'm stupid. He's been using me!* It all became so clear to Jazmyn at that very moment.

When she and Kingston were not involved, she spent most of her time competing with him for the top spot. Both of them had always wanted to become partner at *Duncan & Associates,* and Jazmyn Elizabeth Thomas, Esq. was his primary competitor. Besides Kingston, no one else who was not a partner brought in more money than her, or more high-end clients. Since becoming involved with Kingston, Jazmyn spent her after work hours romping around with him in her condo. Her nights were spent clutching her pillows, alone in her bed, as she replayed their love in her mind and wished that he would return to spend the night with her. She spent her nights alone hoping and wishing while he probably went home, cuddled with his wife, and reviewed case law.

"I'm so stupid! Oh, my God, I am so, so stupid!" Jazmyn lay back in her seat and smacked her palm against the top of her forehead before running her hand back over the top of her head. She had finally arrived at her mother's small, wooden home in the heart of East Point, Georgia. Her car was not in the carport, so she knew her mother had not arrived back home yet from the "showing off" spree that she was most likely doing around town.

Jazmyn looked at her watch and decided that it would only be a matter of time before she returned. Denise liked to flash off her daughter's nice things, so she would be back at the house shortly in order to park it in front of the house just long enough to give the neighbors their gossip for the day.

Jazmyn didn't like coming on this side of town at all. Although she saw her mother weekly, they would often meet up at her condo or a restaurant for lunch or dinner. Jazmyn did not come on this side of town unless she absolutely had to. It wasn't that she had a problem with being in areas like these or around people who were not as blessed as she was. She definitely wasn't afraid to be on this side of town either. Granted she was a little more refined at this point in her life, but she wasn't against placing her razor back under her tongue or throwing on some sweatpants and duking it out in the streets, if it ever came to it.

Her issue with this area stemmed back to a long time ago, and it was something that she did not like being reminded of that had happened right in the very house that she was now parked in front of. It was a thought that was hard to think about, but it was just the reminder that Jazmyn needed at that moment. She needed to think about the last time that she had ever seen her father in person. The time that he had walked out of this door and told her the one lie that she would remember forever: "I will be back, baby girl." Though he had known that he had no intentions of returning, the seven year old Jazmyn had been eager to believe anything that her father told her. So, she sat on top of her mother's car all day and waited for her father to return home so that she could show him the document that she had written up herself.

It was her version of a legal notice stating that he was being sued for unfair wages. She had been giving her parents free labor, in the form of household chores, and was demanding payment. Unfortunately, she had never gotten a chance to serve him with the papers and her heart was broken when she realized that her daddy wouldn't be returning as promised.

Jazmyn jumped in her seat as her quiet thoughts were invaded by the smooth voice of Tweet as she began to sing the sultry lyrics of her song *My Place*, one of Jazmyn's most favorite songs and also her ringtone for Kingston. She picked up her cellphone from the middle console and almost pressed her finger on "ignore" before quickly changing her mind and answering the call. She didn't say anything, mainly because she felt ashamed and angry, but also very unsure of what she should say. Therefore, Jazmyn thought the safe route would be to listen first. She answered the call and heard Kingston breathing on the other line, but he did not say a word. Jazmyn reluctantly opened her mouth to speak.

"Yes?" she let out, barely above a whisper. *Wait, a minute. Why do you feel guilty? He is using you!* Jazmyn cleared her throat and tried again. "Yes, Kingston. What do you want?" she said as she slowly regained her confidence. Her trip down memory lane, along with her current surroundings, had made her think of her father and the hurt little girl she had been. That was still her at other times and other places, however, at this moment she was a grown woman, and she was very pissed off.

"Jaz...what is going on? Why were you behind me and my w...."

"You and your *wife?* Why was I behind the two of you?" Jazmyn finished for him.

"Yes...." Kingston said slowly and easily as if he knew that he was messing with a ticking time-bomb.

"Listen, Kingston. Don't worry about it," Jazmyn sighed heavily and released as much of her anger as she could. There was no reason for her to be upset. All's fair in love and war. She had been played, but she couldn't even be mad at him. "I have already figured everything out. I know all about what you're doing, and it's whatever, really. I'm not mad at you. I hope you get the promotion. I truly do, Kingston. I hope you become partner. I'm done. Don't bother me anymore, I mean it."

"Jaz, what the hell are you talking about? Wait a minute; I need to know what happened this morning. I don't care about work!" Kingston sounded genuinely confused, and Jazmyn almost wanted to laugh out loud. If he weren't so good an attorney, he would make an excellent actor.

Well, I guess those two professions could actually go hand in hand. Jazmyn thought looking to her right. Denise had pulled into the driveway and was observing her daughter with concerned eyes.

"Kingston, it's always been about work. I will be changing my number. Do not try to contact me, I mean it. Goodbye."

"Wait, baby, I just wanted to tell you..." Jazmyn cut off her phone and threw it into her *Hermes* bag. She was sure that he would be calling back frequently until she got the number changed, and she didn't want to be bothered with his lies. Somehow Kingston had gotten to her in a way that she hadn't ever really let other men do in the past, and now she sincerely regretted it because it really was too late. Regardless to what she had said over the phone, it wasn't over. Her feelings were very real, and it would take a while for her to get over them.

Jazmyn looked up and noticed Denise standing at her door, looking down at her through the window. Jazmyn opened the door and gathered all of her things out of the car before getting out and closing the door behind her.

"What's new, baby girl? You alright?" Shortly after he had left, Denise began calling her by the same pet name that Remi had once used for her.

"I'm ok, mama. Just needed a little change," Jazmyn said as she looked around the neighborhood. It had not changed at all. People were still nosy, and the dope boys still owned the corners. Jazmyn glanced over to the corner right on the edge of the neighbor's house and saw a pair of eyes looking back at her.

Dom. She thought his name so loudly that she even moved her lips as if she were speaking it while staring back at the man that stood on the corner. She winked at him, and he smiled, showing his mouth full of gold teeth. Dom was Jazmyn's first. She never had any real feelings for him that went deeper than friendship, but he had taught her a few things that she was still using in the bedroom. Dom nodded his head to acknowledge her and then turned back to face his companions on the corner. *Times must be hard for him if he's out here with the dope boys.*

"Well, that's not the type of change you need, baby girl," Denise warned as she watched the quick interaction between Dom and Jazmyn. "Let's go on in the house."

Jazmyn chuckled to herself and followed her mother into the house. A part of her missed the noise on this side of town. She stopped for a moment and looked in the other direction of the street corner before going into the house. She could hear the sound of a neighbor yelling at her children to come in the house, the sounds of said children's laughter, and the thumping from the bass of a drop-top Cadillac. She walked into the small house and closed the door behind her. The familiar smell of home was the first thing that greeted her. She headed over to a cookie jar that was always on the kitchen counter and reached in, knowing that she was sure to find fresh baked cookies. Jazmyn pulled her hand back out and looked into the jar.

"Oh...I stopped eating that mess. You need to be healthier. I eat carrots instead now," Denise said dismissively and sat down on one end of her chocolate colored sectional. She patted on the side near her for Jazmyn to sit down.

"Well, I might as well since you have ruined my need for a sugar rush to pick me up," Jazmyn said as she walked over to the spot next to Denise and plopped down on the soft cushions. She leaned all the way back into the plushness of the pillows and lifted her feet to place them on the ottoman in front of her.

"Now, tell me what's going on, because I know it's something, and I better not hear no lies," Denise warned as she turned to look Jazmyn directly in her face.

"I'm in love, Mama," Jazmyn sighed loudly then turned to look at Denise. "I'm in love with a co-worker of mine." Denise's facial expressions changed suddenly from worry to relief and then to joy.

"Well, that's nothing to sulk about, Jaz. I've never heard you say a thing about love before. It makes me happy to hear that I haven't passed my own bitterness down to you and made you incapable of love. Maybe I can get some grandbabies outta you." Denise wrapped her arm around her daughter and pulled her close. She then bent down enough to kiss her on her forehead gently.

"That's the problem, mama," Jazmyn said pulling out of her mother's embrace. "It's not that simple and I'm not sure that you are the one that I should be telling about this. How about we just leave it at that and not speak on it?" Jazmyn looked down at her hands in order to avoid the probing of her mother's eyes. After a while of silence, she looked up and noticed that Denise was still staring at her, however, her eyes were now filled with tears.

My God. She knows he's married. Jazmyn felt her face flush with the heat of embarrassment and guilt. She lay back in her seat again and stared upwards to the ceiling.

"I understand baby girl. I understand." Denise said as she rose up out of her seat. She walked into the kitchen and began clanking around with dishes left in the sink. Jazmyn knew Denise's ways, and she knew what this meant. She decided it was time to go and leave her mother with her thoughts. She knew that Denise would call her soon to offer advice or guidance, but at the moment she was trying to find a way to cope with the fact that her daughter was sleeping with, and in love with, a married man. Jazmyn knew that this realization had brought forth pain that Denise had tried to bury on the daily.

"Mama, I need to get to work to do some research on a few things for my upcoming cases. I just wanted to stop by to switch up the cars," Jazmyn lied and Denise knew it was a lie, but didn't mention it. Instead, she walked over to her purse and grabbed the keys.

"Here you go baby. I love you and I will pray that you are given some guidance on this in order to find your way," Denise said as she pulled Jazmyn into a tight hug. She walked back into the kitchen, and Jazmyn let herself out.

KAYLEN

here the fuck is it! Damn it, Kaylen! Kaylen threw the tenth pair of jeans onto the floor of her closet before dropping to the floor and placing her head in her hands. All of her "work" jeans were scattered around her on the floor with the pockets pulled inside out. It had taken her a while to pull herself together, and work on getting her life back on track. The Feds had not come knocking at her door, so she said her blessings to God for sparing her life, prayed for Levi's soul and decided to keep it moving, leaving her past life in the past where it belonged.

However, there was one thing that she needed to handle. She needed to find that baggie of Meth that she had thrown in her jeans and get rid of it. Salem had undressed her that night, but she wasn't sure which jeans she had been wearing or what had happened to them.

"God, I hope Salem threw it away!" Kaylen yelled out as she fell back onto her floor. Tiny came over and nudged her head with his nose. He seemed concerned about her frantic state and began to whimper softly.

"Threw away what, Kay?" Kaylen looked up as Salem rounded the corner and came in to stand over her head. Kaylen pulled herself up from the floor and allowed him to help her up. She looked at his face and focused in on its scruffiness. Salem had always been on top of his appearance when they met, however; it seemed like since everything had went down some time ago, he'd adopted a new look.

Kaylen let her eyes fall and take in the balance of his appearance. He had on a wrinkled blue t-shirt and dingy blue jeans. Kaylen couldn't tell if the jeans were supposed to look worn and discolored or if that was the result of missing a few washes.

"My jeans from that night. I had something in the pocket...I just wanted to make sure that it wasn't still in the house."

She looked up at Salem and noticed a strange look on his face again. The same look that she had seen when she spoke about what had happened with her and Levi; what she did for a living and about her father. He looked surprised, then a little embarrassed.

"Oh yeah...I know what you mean. I, um....I threw it out. It's all good, Kay," Salem looked at her and smiled nervously. Kaylen tried to return his smile, but something felt a little off. She looked at his smile and noticed that it looked like he hadn't brushed in a while. His teeth were stained with a deep yellowish color, and it looked like leftover meals where still gunked up in-between.

I know he likes to drink coffee, but gotdamn! That don't explain all that!

"Where were you last night, Salem? Is everything ok?" Kaylen asked as she pulled her eyes away from the disgusting state of his teeth, trying hard not to show the repulsion she was feeling.

"Yeah, I'm good," Salem said raising his arm in the air to scratch his underarm. Kaylen ducked under his raised arm to walk out of the closet and caught a whiff of the tart and sour smell of musk.

Damn, this nigga ain't take no shower either? What the hell? Kaylen thought as she sat down on the edge of her bed and looked back at him. "I was over at Zo's....shiiiiit....we wasn't doing nothing. Just coolin'. Naw mean?"

No, not really. Actually, I DON'T 'naw' what you mean', Kaylen thought as she watched Salem walk out of the bedroom. Salem had officially moved in shortly after they had agreed that he should. Initially, he played a key role with helping Kaylen to overcome the trauma of everything that had occurred with Levi. She was even able to sit for her exams, and although she had not done as well as she should have, she passed, and being that she had missed about a week and a half of lectures, this was quite an achievement in her opinion.

Kaylen began to walk in the direction of the kitchen. Tiny stood up from his resting place at her feet and followed closely behind. Kaylen heard the clanking of dishes in and figured that Salem was in there putting them up. She decided that this was the perfect time to talk about his new disheveled look that he had been rocking for the past few weeks.

"Hey baby," Kaylen walked into the kitchen and sat on one of the barstools. She leaned her elbows on the edge of the bar countertop and dropped her face into her hands. Salem was placing the clean dishes from the dishwasher into the cabinets.

"I'm glad you came out here. There is something I need to ask you anyways," Salem said without looking up. Kaylen noticed his movements were rushed, which was odd because Salem had always done his movements slowly and surely. He never rushed to do much of anything and this was something that took some time for her to get used to, but it also was one of the reasons that she loved him. He did everything with ease and great precision. It was something that he often said she had to work on. Kaylen was a quick thinker and a quick mover and Salem had to remind her often to slow down and breathe a little before she reacted to things. From the look of Salem's hastiness in the kitchen, Kaylen thought that maybe it was time for her to remind him of his own advice.

"What is it that you need to ask me? And...Salem, why don't you slow down a little? I can barely make my eyes keep up with you!" Salem stopped after placing a plate into one of the top cabinets. He grabbed his dreadlocks off his back and tied them up with a rubber band that he kept wrapped around his wrist before turning to face her from the opposite side of the counter. They looked a little dry and Kaylen made a mental note to ask him if he wanted her to oil them later.

"Zo is having a party...a birthday party. My man is turning thirty, and we got a pretty big thing in the works for him. Anyways, I just wanted to know if you wanted to come with me. You can invite your home girls too, if you want."

"Yeah, I will be there, of course." Kaylen instantly felt nervous, but she wasn't sure why that name still had that effect on her. The palms of her hands felt hot in their position on the top of her legs, and she clasped them together, and then quickly changed her mind as she felt them start to get clammy. She had not seen Zo since he showed up outside of Jazmyn's condo months ago. Every now and then, Salem would mention him and every time he did, it piqued her curiosity.

Is it possible to have a crush on someone that you don't know...that you never see? She was unsure, but she wasn't really sure why whenever Salem mentioned Zo, it made her stir a little inside. There had always been a part of her that wanted to know Zo better since she met him, but she had ignored it when she decided to get serious with Salem. But now, with the subtle differences occurring in her relationship with Salem, her interest in Zo had become more of a constant nagging than a passing thought. Salem was still someone that she felt strongly about, but something in her felt that it wasn't quite love. Although she had told him that she loved him, she felt guilty about the fact that she might have spoken too soon. Her and Salem matched in that they seemed like a couple that ideally *should* work, but after the initial excitement of the relationship subsided, there was no real passion.

Salem had changed, and there was a roughness about him that made Kaylen feel uneasy at times. Even now he had a wild look in his eyes that had not been there when she first met him. The eyes, combined with his unkempt appearance and his new found love for southern slang was such a sharp contrast from the person that she had met, and there had been no explanation for the change.

"When is it?" Kaylen asked Salem. He looked deep in thought, and his eyes were incredibly glossy and wide open as he stared off into the distance. He was so still that if she had not heard the softness of his breathing, Kaylen would have been convinced that he was dead, frozen while leaning on the counter in her kitchen. "Salem?"

"When is what? Oh...the party? Tonight." Salem said as he stood up and went back to putting up the dishes from the dishwasher.

"Tonight?! Why are you just telling me?" Kaylen thought touching her hair and attempting to smooth it down a little. "My hair appointment isn't until next week!"

Salem paused for a minute to glance up at the top of Kaylen's head.

"You hair looks fine, Kaylen. This party ain't about you no way," Salem said scratching fiercely at his arms and then his back.

Maybe your ass should have bathed and then you wouldn't be scratching! Kaylen fumed.

"Whatever, Salem. If you wanted me to go, you should have told me earlier. I will call to see if I can get in to get my hair done this morning." Kaylen got up from the bar stool and headed back to her bedroom to grab her cellphone.

"A'ight. I'm pulling outta here round 10 tonight for the party," Salem said still scratching. "And I'm 'bout to leave right now anyways, so I will see you after your appointment."

"Where you going?" Kaylen asked. She usually didn't check up on Salem this much, but the last couple weeks made things a little different. Salem was gone more than he was home, and lately he had been pulling a lot of "late nights with the boys." Last night, she had waited up for him until nearly three in the morning only to fall asleep and not see him until he showed up earlier inside her closet.

Though not as obvious with his shit as Caleb had always been, Salem's moves were beginning to look suspicious. One thing that she could always appreciate about Caleb was that he was always upfront with what he did. She never had to guess about whether or not she was the only one because she knew she wasn't. If Salem thought that she was going to play the fool with him then he had another thing coming.

"Nowhere, really. Probably just going to go out and hang with the boys for a lil' bit," Salem answered. He seemed a little annoyed to have to explain himself, but Kaylen did not care.

"Really? Well, why don't you wait 'til I get dressed so you can drop me off at the salon?" Kaylen watched him closely to track his reaction.

Salem's shoulders slumped a little, and his face twisted up into a frown that showcased his utter irritation at her request. Kaylen crossed her arms in front of her and threw her weight to one hip in a way that dared Salem to object to her request.

"I thought you said that you had to see if she had any openings for today. I can't wait that long, Kay. I'm about to go now," Salem said raising his voice a touch.

"First of all, you just got here. You were gone all night 'with the boys' according to what you told me. They can wait a minute before seeing you again. Secondly, I'm sure that Nesha can squeeze me in, so I'm going to get dressed, and you can take me to the shop." With that, Kaylen turned on her heels and continued in the direction to her room. *He must think I'm stupid. I got something for that ass!*

SALEM PULLED INTO THE PARKING LOT OF *NATURAL BEAUTIES* AND parked the car with a scowl. Kaylen matched his expression with a scowl of her own and reached over to open her door.

"I got it," Salem said jumping out of the driver's side to walk over and open her door.

Oh, now he can be a gentleman! Kaylen thought to herself. Salem drove her to the salon as she asked, complete with much attitude, although she had hurried to get ready. He fidgeted the whole way and seemed like he couldn't sit still. Something had him nervous and anxious, and Kaylen was determined to get to the bottom of it. Upon arriving at the salon, he had pulled up to the front door and pushed the button to unlock the doors while he kept the car running. Kaylen looked at him like he had lost all his marbles and then some.

"What...you expect me to hop out of the car? You can't park and walk me in, like you normally do? What's SO important, Salem, that you are in such a rush?"

Salem grunted his displeasure, but had smartly decided to acquiesce to her request.

"Well, thank you for opening my door, baby," Kaylen said, planting a kiss on Salem's cheek. The fighting was tiring and frankly; she just wanted it to be over with. Especially since Salem had done everything that she asked and was going to pay for her to get her hair done.

"You're welcome, Kay," Salem responded. He wasn't looking at her when he said it. Instead, he was surveying the parking lot as if he didn't know where he was. He still seemed rather fidgety also, and Kaylen began to think twice about letting him walk her into the salon. He still had not changed or washed, and he didn't look as presentable as he normally did when he brought her to her hair appointments.

"Let's just go on in, Salem," Kaylen said grabbing onto his hand and walking in the direction of the salon. *Natural Beauties* was the best salon in the worst side of town. The salon was in an area of Atlanta known as The Bluff. Though there had been some effort by local government to help the area by increased police presence and new development projects, it hadn't changed a thing.

The increased police presence had just led to an increase of police corruption in the area and a more structured drug ring. Kaylen had started going to this salon at the recommendation of Levi. Nesha was the hairdresser that did his braids during his teen years before he cut his hair. She also had done his sister's hair before she moved to California. The salon had been convenient for Kaylen at the time since her aunt's house was also located in The Bluff and only a short walk away.

"Heeeey, girl! I haven't seen you in a while, what's been happening?" Nesha stopped re-twisting a customer's dreadlocks and walked over to give Kaylen a hug.

"I know. It has been a while, and I'm sure you can tell," Kaylen said pulling at her messy half ponytail.

"Uh huh," Nesha agreed. "Go ahead and put your stuff down. I will meet you at the shampoo bowl."

"Ok," Kaylen said, and then turned to Salem. Salem's face still wore a scowl, and he was fidgeting worse than he was earlier. Kaylen sighed heavily and then held out her hand to him. Salem responded by looking back at her angrily and shifting from foot to foot.

"What you want? Can I go now?" he said gruffly as he pushed away her outstretched hand. Kaylen felt the heat rise to her cheeks as she tried to mask her embarrassment. She was positive that every eye in the salon was watching the exchange between her and Salem.

"What do you mean 'what do I want'? I need money for my hair, Salem," Kaylen said quietly. She was hoping that no one in the salon could hear her, but that was a very high hope. The salon was so quiet that you could hear the faint blaring of an emergency vehicle in the distance.

"I ain't got nothing. You pay for it," Salem muttered then turned around and scurried out of the door. As the door fell back into place, the bells that hung at the top chimed loudly and seemed to echo around the quiet salon. Kaylen could have sworn she heard a few light chuckles and teeth sucking coming from behind her.

I know this nigga didn't! Kaylen thought. She was still facing the door; willing her mind to accept what had just occurred. She looked down and checked her purse to make sure she had her wallet.

"Kay, if you ain't got it right now, girl, it's ok. I know you good for it," Nesha said from the back of the salon. Instead of making her feel be that just made her cheeks even hotter as Nesha's statement solidified Kaylen's thinking that everyone in the salon had heard every detail of her interaction with Salem.

"No, girl. You know I'm good. I got you." Kaylen said as she turned and headed towards the back of their store where Nesha was waiting.

"What you want done to this hair?" Nesha said as she ran her fingers through Kaylen's rough mane. She had a look on her face that said she would have preferred that Kaylen came to see her months ago. Kaylen didn't say anything about it though, as she was grateful for the change of subject...even if the new focus was her split ends and dry hair.

"Just cut it off," Kaylen responded nonchalantly. She was tired of her hair as it was. Although it wasn't very long, she preferred something a little shorter and sexier. Her morning had caused her stress levels to rise, and change is what she needed. Salem had always gone on about how much he loved running his fingers in her hair.

"Cut it all off?" Nesha said looking at Kaylen with a touch of intrigue.

Nothing quite piques a beautician's interest like letting them chop off all your hair. Kaylen could understand Nesha's curiosity; however, she had been trying for the last five years to get her hair to grow to catch up with Alexis' and Jazmyn's. Now she was asking for it to be cut short when normally she didn't even like her ends to be clipped.

"Let's do a bob-style. Shorter in the back than in the front," Kaylen said as she sat down at the washing bowl and leaned back to get her hair washed.

"Ok, then. Whatever you would like!" Nesha said as she started the water.

KAYLEN RAN HER HAND THROUGH HER SHORT HAIR AS SHE LOOKED AT her reflection in the mirror. She could see Nesha smiling from behind, obviously happy with her work.

"Wow...it's going to take some getting used to, but I definitely like it," Kaylen said slowly. The new style framed Kaylen's face in a way that made her look at herself in a new way. Alexis and Jazmyn had always been the "pretty" ones of the crew, with their long hair; smooth skin and confidence that made men flock to lick their feet. Kaylen had never had an issue obtaining a man, but their first compliments to her had never included "You are so beautiful." However, with this new style, her features were being brought out in a way that made her appreciate herself in a new way. For once in her life, she felt naturally pretty and sexy. "Actually I love it. I'm going to a party tonight, and I think this is exactly what I needed. Thank you, Nesh." Kaylen said and pulled out enough money to pay Nesha for her work as well as a $50 tip.

"Thank you, as always, Kay," Nesha said. "Your man here yet?" She said as she looked through the glass door at the front of the shop. Kaylen grabbed her phone and thumbed to her text messages.

"Yeah, he says he's waiting outside the door."

"Ok, well....I just wanted to tell you that I've seen him round here." Nesha had a peculiar look on her face, and it made Kaylen drop her phone back into her purse and give Nesha all of her attention.

"What you mean? Like with another girl? He brought some hoe up here to your salon, Nesh?" Nesha's expression changed, and she seemed like she was struggling to say what she wanted to say. She twisted up her face in a way that let Kaylen know that whatever she needed to tell her was serious and wouldn't be taken too well.

"No, Kay. Nothing like that. I haven't seen him up here at the salon with anyone but you. I mean....I've seen him around here. Around The Bluff on a few occasions," Nesha said lowering her voice and ushering Kaylen over to the side of the salon and away from the nosy ears of the other stylists and customers.

"Well, what else would he be doing round here in The Bluff, Nesh?" Kaylen asked. She was genuinely confused. If Salem were up here, there had to be a reason. People who didn't need to live around here didn't just visit for no reason.

"Well......" Nesha started and then looked down and fumbled with her fingers. The bells on the door rung loudly announcing someone's entrance or departure and both women looked up and towards the door. Kaylen felt a mixture of emotions as she looked over at Salem, who looked a great deal cleaner and put together than he had earlier, though still quite different than what she was used to.

His dreadlocks were braided back into a long ponytail, and he was dressed in a red and white striped shirt with dark blue jeans. Though not ironed to a crease, his clothes were not quite as wrinkled, and he looked as if he had at least showered. Kaylen was relieved that he had pulled himself together enough to look presentable when he picked her up, but she was still irritated about what had occurred that morning.

"You ready, Kay?" Salem said looking at Kaylen. His eyes swooped over, and he looked at Nesha who was staring at him with an accusatory expression on her face. His mouth began to twist into a sneer, but he hastily replaced it with a pleasant visage when he realized that Kaylen was observing the exchange. "Ready?" he repeated firmly, holding out his hand for hers.

107

"Uh...yes," Kaylen said as she walked forward and accepted his hand. She was confused about what had just transpired, and still wanted to know what Nesha was about to say. She made a mental note to check with her later.

Kaylen walked out of the salon in silence and followed Salem as he led her to the car. Her mind was still on everything that had happened, from the argument that morning to the incident inside of *Natural Beauties* to the looks between Nesha and Salem when she was leaving.

Something ain't right, but I'm about to find out. Kaylen thought as she sat down in her seat on the passenger side of Salem's SUV. She watched Salem as he walked over to his side of the car. He seemed fine, but something was still a little off about him. Kaylen couldn't place it, but the feeling she was getting felt all too familiar. She felt a warning in her spirit about Salem like there was something that she should be watching out for.

Strange.

Just as Salem got in the car, buckled his seatbelt, and ignited the ignition, Kaylen was startled by a loud rapping at her window. She jumped and turned towards the noise to see where the sound had come from. What Kaylen saw standing at the window was enough to make her pee in her designer pants. In front of her, stood a small, frail woman with hair standing on end on top of her head; her face was pressed against the window and her eyes were wide open as she struggled to peer through the dark window tints.

Her mouth was open in what may have been a smile; showing teeth that appeared to be in some state of premature decay. Kaylen's mouth dropped open, and she let out a small whimper that probably was only heard by her own ears. Slowly, she reached down and pressed the button to lower the window.

ALEXIS

"*R*eally? Wow...that seemed like quite an amaaaaazing trip, Marc. And, how was the food there? Did you get to try any authentic Italian cuisine or only what was in the hotel?" Vanessa said as she leaned in close to Marc and smiled.

He grinned from ear to ear as he looked at his sister-in-law before shoving another handful of the red velvet cake she'd made into his mouth. Alexis looked up from her book and rolled her eyes. She had been watching Vanessa and Marc carry-on in the kitchen like love-birds for what seemed like over an hour, although it probably was only about thirty minutes or so. Alexis couldn't really blame Marc for being caught up; it was something that she had been used to seeing when it came to men and her sister. However, she could blame Vanessa for the fact that she was so close to Marc's face that she could probably taste a little bit of the red velvet cake that he was munching on.

"Yeah, it was a really nice trip. I didn't get to enjoy it as much as I would have liked to. A lot of my partners had their wives along, and I didn't want to drag along with the couples," Marc said it in a way that made Alexis' skin crawl because she knew that his comment was directed at her. *He ain't even been home two hours and already starting up about me going on his trips with him. DAMN!*

"Well, that's horrible! How about next time you go, you drag me along? I don't have much that I need to tend to here, and I would love to be able to see the world." Vanessa patted Marc on his thigh and tilted her head to the side.

I know this bitch didn't! Did somebody crack her over the head, and make her forget who she is talking to? Alexis had enough and smashed her book closed before throwing it onto the coffee table and walking over to the kitchen.

"I think that if any woman is going with Marc on a trip, be it business or personal; it will be me," Alexis said as she entered the kitchen. Marc turned to face her with humor showing through his eyes. He liked when Alexis showed jealousy, and he looked back and forth between the two sisters as if he were waiting for the main event.

"Well, from what I hear," Vanessa said as she leaned forward to place her chin in her hands. "You don't like going on trips, and would rather leave poor Marc all alone for another woman to just snatch him up." Vanessa looked over at Marc and poked out her bottom lip in a faux-pout. Alexis wanted to snatch her by that bottom lip and flip her across the bar. She gave Vanessa a look that said, "Don't get your ass kicked out" and watched as Vanessa turned back towards Marc to drop the subject.

"Anyways, Marc, we will have to continue this conversation later on. I am feeling a lot of tension in the room right now," she said darting her eyes quickly at Alexis before getting up from her barstool and strolling seductively out of the door.

Alexis was seething as she watched Vanessa make her signature exit, but when she looked at Marc, he began laughing and shook his head.

"Are you two always going to be at each other's throats, Lexi?" Marc said then shook his head as he continued to laugh.

"Yes, some things never change," Alexis said and sat down next to Marc at the bar. "Listen, Kaylen told me about this party that Salem is throwing for his best friend."

"Who is Salem?" Marc said pulling his phone out of his pocket. He began jabbing at the screen, and it annoyed Alexis to the max.

His ass can listen to Vanessa talk allllll day, but I have something to say and all of a sudden he can't focus?

"Marc, Salem is Kaylen's boyfriend. I told you about him a while ago when they first starting dating," Alexis said as she ducked her head a little trying to make a point of catching Marc's eye. Marc was able to catch the hint and placed his phone down on the table. He looked up at Alexis with wide eyes as if to show that she had his full attention.

"I remember you saying she had a new guy. I guess I just forgot the name, baby. So, what's going on?"

"Well, the party is tonight, and I was wondering if you wanted to go with me. It should be fun...we haven't been anywhere in a while, and it may be nice to get out," Alexis said as she observed the look on Marc's face. It seemed that he was genuinely thinking about it. Alexis needed to get out of the house tonight more than he knew. It was not about the fact that they had not been anywhere together in a while; she needed to get away before she was subjected to another "session of love."

When Marc arrived home, the first thing he had done was run upstairs to the bedroom where Alexis was lying down reading a book that had put her in an erotic mood. Marc walked in and found his wife lying on the bed with her nose nestled between the pages of the book and her hands down the front of her pink lace panties in an attempt to give herself the type of orgasm that he had never been able to provide.

She was reading hungrily about a woman whose husband was pleasing her in a way that she wished Marc did; with light nibbles on her nipples, gentle kisses around her navel, and tender sucking on her clitoris. Just as she was about to bring herself to the point where she was moaning lightly, Marc appeared peering down over the top of the pages with a sexy grin on his face and lust in his eyes.

Alexis was happy to see him, but mortified that he had caught her in the act of self-pleasure. She knew that she had only helped to ensure that he would be able to go extra-long and extra hard this time.

Alexis shuddered as she thought about how Marc had flipped her over and rammed his dick into her so hard and so long that all she could do was grit her teeth and cry silently as her husband dug his fingers deeply into the sides of her ass and forced himself to go as deep as he could. She had suffered silently because she hadn't wanted Vanessa to hear. But when she looked up and glanced towards the open bedroom door, she could have sworn that she saw a shadow and someone pull away from the door. Vanessa hadn't mentioned it later on, so Alexis thought that maybe it was the pain she felt that was making her see visions.

Or at least I hope it was a delusion. Alexis thought. *God, I would die if Vanessa knew this. She would love to know that I had a man who didn't love me. Or does he? Can you love someone and do this to them?* Alexis tried to shake her thoughts away and focus back on Marc. He still hadn't answered her and was back to clicking away on his cellphone.

"Marc?"

"Oh, baby, I'm sorry. Just following up on some emails. What was it again?" Marc said as he placed his phone back down on the counter and grabbed at a piece of Alexis' hair. He pulled her into an embrace and then kissed her forehead gently.

I wish it could be like this all the time; she thought allowing her husband to kiss her. "The party, right?" he said between kisses and Alexis melted.

"Yes, baby. The party," she said as she allowed Marc to pull her thin black dress down over her shoulders. She sucked in a sharp breath when she felt the warmth of his mouth cover her nipple and his tongue began to drift back and forth across the top. Her nipple responded by growing harder and her pussy answered by getting wetter. She clamped down hard on her tongue when she suddenly felt him bite down hard on her nipple. The pain was excruciating.

"Owwww, Marc! Dammit!" Alexis said and pushed Marc away from her breast. She reached down and pulled her dress up from around her waist, and glared at him. "That shit hurts, Marc! Don't you think it would be nice to be a little soft and gentle sometimes?"

Marc looked genuinely confused and a little embarrassed. He

scratched at the top of his head, and had a boyish look about him that would have made Alexis smile if she wasn't so angry. She had never seen Marc so unsure of himself, and it was almost a little comical. Alexis felt herself began to calm down, but then the throbbing of her nipple brought her anger back up to level 50 on a scale of 1-10.

"What the fuck is wrong with you, Marc? Do you think I like that shit? Do you think I like for you to jam your dick into me all the time? To scratch me? To bite me? You sick, sick, son-of-a-bitch!" Alexis jumped up off the bar stool and smacked her hand on the counter with frustration. "I am tired of this! Is it too much to ask to be pleased by my own husband? I know you have seen a sex scene in a movie or something? How about you watch a movie and get a clue!" She stood in front of Marc for about two seconds waiting for a response. She got none at all and just watched him stare at her with his mouth open. He looked hurt and ashamed.

That's how you should feel! Your ass has been shaming me and hurting me for years! Making me feel ashamed to be so weak that I took this!

"Marc, I'm done with this shit!" Alexis yelled out as loud as she could, then turned and ran up the stairs to her room. She slammed the door behind her and fell face-first onto her bed. She had barely hit the sheets when the tears came.

Alexis felt like all of her frustrations about her marriage had built up to a point that she could barely contain it. Part of her felt bad about the way that she had blew up at her husband, but most of her felt frustrated about the fact that she had let it get to this point. Marc had no idea why she was so upset, and she was to the point where she did not care. She resented him for taking from her the thing that she had saved for the right man. Her first sexual experience had been wasted, and there had been nothing but suffering, disappointment, and sexual frustration to follow.

Alexis picked up her head a little to look towards the room door. She had left the door ajar, and the entrance was as empty as it had been before she ran through it.

"Oh and this nigga ain't even gonna come back here and check on me?" Alexis fumed as she picked up the pillow she had been lying on and tossed it at the door. Fresh tears started in her eyes, and she was just about to succumb to her desire to let out a loud wail like a two year old child when her cellphone began to ring.

Wiping her tears away, she looked at the number displayed on the screen. Alexis didn't recognize it, but decided to answer anyways.

"Who is this?" she said, not yet rid of her attitude. She wasn't sure who it was on the line, but they were about to get more than what they bargained for by calling at the wrong time.

"Hey, there! I bet you don't know who this is!" the deep voice on the other end teased. Alexis' eyes widened in surprise, and her mouth fell open as she instantly recognized the voice on the other end. God worked in mysterious ways because this was exactly whom she needed at this moment. Someone to take her mind off of her current situation by reminding her of her happier days.

"Dex! Of course, I know who this is! What is going on with you? I haven't heard from you in forever," Alexis said as she tossed herself on the bed and looked up at the ceiling. Her mood had totally changed in less than a second with just a simple phone-call from her old friend. She had not heard from Dexter since shortly after she met Marc. She had begun spending more time with Marc than she had with Dexter and soon after, she dropped out of her internship program and traveled with Marc as he pursued his dreams. Dexter had tried to talk her out of it and seemed very jealous that he had lost a friend, but at the time, Alexis didn't care. She was in love, and to hell with anyone who didn't agree with it.

"Nothing really. I'm in town to do some work for Ray and thought I would contact you to see what you were up to."

"Ray?" Alexis asked, instantly thinking about Jazmyn's ex. *I didn't know Raymond was into the fashion industry.*

"Ranell Stu? Girl, college hasn't been that long ago! I know you aren't that out of touch to forget your fashion idol!" Dexter laughed, and it made Alexis smile. Dexter always had such a sexy voice and the only thing that could top it was his laugh. It was slow and sexy and the bass thumping in his voice always made Alexis want to rip her panties off until she thought about the fact that he definitely was not interested in her. Or any woman for that matter.

"Oh, no, I remember him. I just didn't know you two were on a pet name basis," Alexis teased. She knew that Dexter had idolized Ranell just as much as she had, and it seemed that he had won out on more than just an internship if he was coming to Atlanta to work with 'Ray'. "So, are y'all an item or something?"

"Excuse me?" Dexter asked quickly. His tone seemed as if he was offended by her question and Alexis struggled to backtrack on her statement. She had never mentioned Dexter's sexual orientation in the past, and now she was certain that it was something that he wanted to remain private about.

"Oh, nothing, Dex. Anyways, I'm glad you called. I want to ask you something," she said desperately trying to save face. Though she and Dexter had argued furiously in the past about many things, this was not the way that she wanted to start the reunion.

"Sure, Alexis. What is it?" Dexter said nicely, however, Alexis could tell that he still was a little annoyed by her question.

"Well, obviously, I would like to catch up with you while you are in town...so I would like for you to go to a party with me. It's tonight... one of my friends; Kaylen's boyfriend is throwing a party for his best friend."

"Oh, she still messing around with that loser? He finally decided to make her his official girlfriend, huh?" Dexter said with an extra pep in his voice. He had always been a sucker for gossip, and it automatically brought him out of any funk.

"Who? Oh, you must mean Caleb. No, she's left that asshole alone as far as I know. She's been dating this guy named Salem for a while now," Alexis said as she crossed her leg on top of the other one and relaxed. She felt like she had pressed rewind on her life and was back in her dorm room lying down and gossiping with Dexter. He had been her best friend in college. She had always had Jazmyn and Kaylen, but Dexter knew all of her secrets. Although he was always reluctant to share a lot about his life and his background, he was always eager to listen to Alexis when she needed to share.

"Salem? What kind of name is that? Well, anyways, I will be there. Should I pick you up or you want to meet me there? I don't want to start any problems with the hubby." Alexis looked towards the bedroom door again. Marc still had not even bothered to come up and speak to her or see how she was doing. He probably was still downstairs with his mouth open, catching flies.

"Fuck, Marc," Alexis spat. "You can pick me up at 9." Alexis said and rolled over on her bed to face the wall just as Marc backed away from the doorway and made his trek back down the stairs. Alexis could have never imagined the pain that her husband felt at hearing her words.

JAZMYN

*J*azmyn stared at the screen on her cell phone almost as if she were willing it to ring. Since she had changed her number, her phone had become eerily silent. Besides the occasional calls from her mother, Alexis, and Kaylen, her phone did not ring at all. Her business cell phone, on the other hand, was all the rage. Her dedication back into work meant that her supervisors were calling more often, either to continue checking in on her progress to ensure that there was no backsliding, or to add more cases to her growing case load.

Avoiding Kingston at the office had been pretty easy so far. He had been out for the week after their altercation in the streets, and she had also switched up her hours so that she came in earlier and left earlier. A lot of her work was done on the weekends, as well. Jazmyn looked around the office and saw that she was not the only one who preferred Saturdays at work. A few junior associates were also spending the day catching up on case research and racking up billable hours for the firm. The quiet was what Jazmyn needed this morning to get her day started in the right direction. She had to leave earlier than she wanted in order to get ready for a party that Kaylen invited her to, but there was still time to get work done without interruption.

When Jazmyn opened the door to her office, she noticed that there was something on the desk that was not there when she had left late last night. She walked over to it and directly towards the vase of flowers that sat right on the edge as if she had placed it there herself. It matched perfectly with the scenery around it and Jazmyn lost herself momentarily as she stuck her nose into the bushel of flowers, and took a deep breath. She loved the smell of Jasmine. They were her favorite flowers, and she could not resist. Jazmyn sat down and pulled her laptop out of her bag, before it hit her.

Wait...who bought me these flowers? Jazmyn thought as she turned back to face the vase. She looked through the stems and did not see a card. It made sense, since the flowers looked like they came from a garden rather than a flower shop. Someone had taken the time to pick them for her. It really could have been anyone. Kingston was not the only one who had not been a recipient of her new number. Jazmyn started to shrug off the mystery and return back to her work when she noticed a small Post-It note lying below the flowers on her desk.

We need to talk. At least give me that.

"At *least* give me *that*?!" Jazmyn fumed. "How dare he think I *owe* him anything?!" She had a mind to pick up the flowers and throw them in the trash, but stopped at the last minute. *No need to waste such beautiful flowers.* Jazmyn grabbed the vase and walked out of her office. Her assistant, Sitha, was at her desk with an annoyed expression on her face...most likely at being dragged in on another Saturday for work, at Jazmyn's request. Jazmyn dropped the flowers on Sitha's desk.

"These are for you, Sitha. Thank you for coming in again on a Saturday," Jazmyn said as she tried to squeeze out a small smile to show her sincere appreciation.

"Wow, you're welcome, Jazmyn. Anytime!" Sitha looked happily at the flowers and smiled back at Jazmyn before smelling them.

Satisfied, Jazmyn turned on her heels and headed down the hallway towards Kingston's office. She knew he was here, because she had seen his car in the parking garage and figured he was trying to catch up with her. Kingston had a nice corner office towards the back. Jazmyn had enjoyed making this walk in the past when she and Kingston used to "work" well into the late hours of the night...on his desk, in his expensive leather desk chair and sprawled out on the floor or against the wall.

Jazmyn tried to shake away her daydreams and clutch on to her anger as she stormed into Kingston's office. Her intentions were to yell at him for the flowers and the note, for the lying and pretending to love her when he was instead trying to squash the competition. For the most part, pretty much everything that he had ever done to upset her was lying on the tip of her tongue and ready to shoot out like daggers. But when Jazmyn walked in, and her eyes centered in on Kingston, she felt her heart let out a cry.

Kingston was sitting at his desk looking like he had not slept in days. His skin was pale and seemed slightly discolored. Kingston had always had a light brown complexion, but there was something about his skin that looked lifeless...almost like a corpse rather than a living, breathing person. When he turned to look at Jazmyn, his eyes were bloodshot red and drooped to the sides in utter despair. Jazmyn opened her mouth to start on her rant, but after fully assessing the sight in front of her, nothing came out, and her mouth remained just like that...partially open, as she struggled with what she should say. He looked back down at his desk.

"Kingston....the flowers," Jazmyn started to say. It wasn't coming out exactly how she had meant it because she wasn't quite sure if she should be angry or not anymore. "Thanks. They are pretty."

Kingston lifted his head and looked back at her with a confused stare. "I didn't..."

"It's ok! I'm not mad," Jazmyn interrupted and sat down in front of him. Kingston still looked confused, but seemed to dismiss it and looked back down at the paper on his desk. "What is going on with you, Kingston?"

Kingston didn't say anything at all and didn't even lift his head to acknowledge that he had heard what she'd said. Jazmyn crooked her neck to look at the sheet of paper that he was staring at. She couldn't read the top exactly, but she was able to make out the word "diagnostics" in the title.

It's the DNA test! Jazmyn thought, and her heart dropped to the pit of her stomach and died.

"It's yours, isn't it, Kingston?" that could be the only reason that he was sitting here looking like his life was gone. He knew that it was now truly over. There was definitely no getting back together now. "Isn't it, Kingston?" Jazmyn said, raising her voice and rising up out of her seat. She leaned over to get in his face.

"You know it's over now, don't you? I'm done, Kingston. I'm not standing by while you play hubby and daddy to someone else and her child!" Jazmyn barely had time to react before Kingston jumped out of his seat and lunged at her. He grabbed her by her upper arm and backed her against the wall of his office, lifting her up off of her feet.

"Don't you know when to fucking shut your mouth, Jaz? Everything is not about your ass! This is not about you!" Kingston said quietly, but with enough venom that tears came to Jazmyn's eyes. Kingston had never grabbed her in this way. And though he was holding her so tight that she couldn't move or struggle, she was feeling a mix of feelings that she could not explain. She felt afraid, angry, guilty, and turned on all at once.

Jazmyn looked at him through tear-filled eyes. She willed them not to fall. She gritted her teeth and held her breath in an effort to dispel the tears, but it was no help at all. One lone tear fell down her cheek, and she couldn't even struggle from Kingston's grasp in time to wipe it away before he saw it. His eyes focused on her tear and his demeanor changed. It seemed that he finally realized what he was doing and where he was. He released his grip on Jazmyn and lowered her to the floor. She struggled to catch her balance and leaned back against the wall. Kingston walked back over to his desk and sat down. He placed his head in his hands and exhaled loudly.

"The baby is not mine, Jaz. That bitch…my wife. She lied. The baby is not mine, and she's been cheating on me for, I don't know how long." Kingston looked as if he would cry, and Jazmyn could not understand why.

"Isn't this what you wanted? You told me it wasn't yours! You weren't lying, baby." Jazmyn said as she walked over and sat back down in front of Kingston's desk. She grabbed his hands and held them in hers. "It's going to be ok, baby."

"No, it's not, Jaz," Kingston said and pulled his hands away from hers. "I wanted the baby. I know I said it wasn't mine. But I had hoped it was mine." Kingston stood up and walked over to his window and looked outside at the crowds outside enjoying their weekend. "I wanted this baby. I can't believe she lied to me about this."

Jazmyn could not believe her ears. Her mouth flopped open again for the second time since she had graced his office, but for a very different reason.

Did this Negro really just say that he wished the baby was his? I KNEW he was playing me! This muther....

"Fucker! I knew you were playing me!" Jazmyn said out loud, not even fully aware of the fact that she had merged her thoughts and spoken language into one. Kingston turned to face her, and looked at her with what Jazmyn recognized as sympathy.

"No, Jaz. I love you...it's just crazy right now. I..." Kingston started walking over to her.

"Back up, Kingston!" Jazmyn yelled. She no longer cared that everyone who had decided to work on this particular Saturday was getting an earful of what was sure to be Monday's office gossip. "You probably still would have told me you loved me while you had your wife's legs wrapped around your neck!"

"Jaz! Really, I can't deal with this right now. Can't you see I'm hurting, baby? It's not about her; it's the baby!" Kingston pleaded. He looked pitiful. Normally, Jazmyn may have felt a flutter of compassion in her heart, but not any longer. He looked like he was ready to kneel down and beg, and Jazmyn almost wished that he would so that she could kick his ass square in the jaw.

"That's right. It's about the baby. *Your* baby that you wanted with *her!* All this time, you have been telling me that you were going to prove that it wasn't yours so you could leave her with nothing and be with me. Now that day has come, and your ass is acting like a lil' bitch because she cheated! Newsflash, Kingston! You've been sleeping with me for over a year now!" Jazmyn said only halfway aware of the crowd gathering outside of her door.

Kingston looked defeated, and Jazmyn knew that there was nothing else she needed to say. She didn't even care to go on because she felt defeated herself. This was not a battle that she had won. She'd had many wins in the courtroom, as well as had many losses. But this was by far the worst feeling of loss that she had ever experienced, and she had no more fight in her.

Jazmyn took one final look at Kingston before turning towards the office door. She walked past the associates outside of the door and continued into her office. She logged onto her computer and wrote a quick email to her boss announcing her resignation as well as a current address to forward her belongings, and then gathered her purse and laptop where she walked out of the building for the last time.

"HEY THERE, SHAWTY. I KNEW YOU WOULD CALL," DOM SAID WITH THE confidence that Jazmyn had always admired about him. Their relationship had always been a crazy one filled with reckless thinking and a preference for the dangerous side of life.

Throughout the years, Jazmyn could not count how many times she had to step in to provide quick legal defense to Dom for something that she knew he'd done before she had even bothered to read the details. She was the official attorney for him and his team, and he was a large part of how she was able to make so much money.

Dom was a product of his environment. His father, grandfather, and uncles had all been deep in the drug life. There was really nothing else that they taught him other than how to take over a business for them in the event of the two inevitable paths that lay before them: death or jail. Though Jazmyn's mother had always strived to keep her from experiencing that side of life, the side of life that most of the other kids in the neighborhood thought of as a guaranteed life-path for them, it did not matter in the end. Denise still was not able to keep Jazmyn away from Dom.

The first time Jazmyn had seen Dom was when she had snuck out of her house to go down to the basketball courts two blocks behind her home. Jazmyn had been tired of being the mystery girl in the neighborhood; the girl that went to private school and was never able to hang around the neighborhood. She was tired of hearing the snickering whenever she sat out on the front porch and the questions and comments from the other kids about how she felt she was 'too good for them'.

She had heard during a conversation between her mother and one of the neighbors that the older people in the neighborhood needed to get together to get rid of the basketball courts in order to stop children from congregating there at night and starting trouble. As soon as Jazmyn heard that, she decided the basketball courts would be the perfect place to make her debut. That night she pulled on the tightest and shortest pink jean shorts that she had in her closet and paired it with a white tube shirt that she borrowed from a classmate, tied up her white Nikes, and swooped up her long hair into a ponytail. She had an intention to prove that she was just as real as everyone else and could hang out whenever she wanted.

Dom was the first person that she noticed once she arrived at the basketball courts. He was standing with a group of guys outside of the gates that surrounded the court. He was dressed in all white, even down to his shoes and socks. He even had a white sweatband pulled around his head, which Jazmyn knew was more for style than catching sweat. When Jazmyn began walking in their direction, she noticed the group of guys around Dom immediately stop what they were discussing and look in her direction. Although Jazmyn was used to men staring at her, they were not staring at her with interest, they were staring at her with caution, and Jazmyn had the feeling that she'd better not make any sudden movements, so she stopped in her tracks.

"I'm just trying to get to the game," she said softly.

"What you want to go there for?" one of the guys said to her as he walked up closer. "No reason to go there when you could hang out with me tonight."

Jazmyn had recognized him as Dom immediately. She knew his name after hearing it multiple times from her mother and neighbors as the "trouble-maker" in the neighborhood. She knew more about him and his history than he knew, but it piqued her interest in a way that would not have happened otherwise.

Jazmyn spent that night with Dom and it led to a long teenage relationship that involved a dangerous life, many close calls, and many wrong decisions. Eventually she and Dom decided to end what turned into a tumultuous relationship, but it didn't stop them from linking up every now and then to reflect on old times. However, he kept her on call as his legal counsel.

"Hello Dom," Jazmyn said slowly. She was still unsure about why she had called him in the first place. The last time she messed with Dom; she almost ended up in a situation that would have led to a long prison sentence. But for some reason, the combination of seeing him the other day, and the hurt she was feeling because of Kingston made her want to reach out to him again on a personal level.

Though Dom led a life that meant she was susceptible to danger and crime, he had always been upfront with her about everything. Their relationship never quite made it the level of love, but Dom had always been a good friend when she needed one.

"I'm going to a party tonight. You want to come?" Jazmyn said with a little more confidence in her decision to call Dom. She needed some fun, and that's what Dom had always been. Life on the edge appealed to her.

"Where at?" Dom said gruffly. His voice had a sexy, raspy quality to it that added to his sex appeal.

"Don't worry about it. I will get you," Jazmyn answered.

"Naw, shawty. You know I gotta know where we headed before I pull up," Dom said in a way that let Jazmyn know he was smiling. Dom always smiled even when he was dead serious, as he was now.

Jazmyn had seen Dom give men their death sentences with a smile on his face. He had executioners on his team that would kill as soon as he mentioned the word. Many times his orders were given with a smile, nod, and wink. Something about that screamed power to Jazmyn, and it also made her aware of how close she was to the dark side. She would like to think that being so near to death and crime would be repulsive and cause her to run in the other direction, but it didn't. Kingston and Dom were exact opposites. Kingston had a moral compass that must have been given to him by God himself, and it was a marvel that he was able to be such a successful attorney. He encouraged her to be a better person than she had been in the past and that played a major part in why she loved him.

"Kaylen, you remember her, anyways, her boyfriend is throwing a party for his friend. The party will be near Midtown."

"And you want the Dom to hang with you and your uppity friends, huh?" Dom said with a light chuckle.

"I'm sure you will fit in just fine, Dom. I will see you round 10," Jazmyn said and ended the call.

KAYLEN

*K*aylen continued to stare at the woman that stood outside her window. She felt like she was in an alternate universe. After her mother was let out of the mental facility, she was placed into a rehabilitation center. Only two weeks after leaving the center, she left, and Kaylen had tried for a year to find her. She had finally seen her about five years ago, and she was greatly disappointed to see the dope fiend that she had become.

Kaylen tried a few times, with no success to get her into various rehab facilities and to give her money, but it never changed anything. So Kaylen forgot about her mother and decided to continue living her life. Every now and then, she would get a call from her aunt complaining that her mother had been outside of her house begging, but Kaylen had begun to ignore those calls; forgetting the two of them all together. Now here she was, looking at her through the window of Salem's car.

"Mama?" Kaylen repeated a little louder. This time the woman shifted her eyes quickly from Salem back to Kaylen. She blinked once, and a smile crept up on her face.

"That you, Kay? Damn, nigga, you dating my daughter?" the woman looked over to Salem.

"Uh...yeah, um...," Salem stammered. He looked incredibly embarrassed as he struggled to answer. Kaylen looked over at his face, and she began to feel her own shame creep up. She ducked her eyes and turned back towards the window.

"Kay, these the type of niggas you date now? Well, you and me ain't that much different, huh? Mudder fuggin junky ass niggas...We the same like that!" Kaylen looked at her mother as she smiled through the opening of the window. She showed nearly all the gaps and holes in her gummy mouth.

Did she really just call Salem a 'junkie'? What the hell? Kaylen thought to herself.

"What? What's going on? Mama, where have you been? Are you alright?" Kaylen started. She had so much to ask, but wasn't able to properly string her words together the way that she wanted to.

"Listen, Kay....you got $20 I can hold?" Kaylen watched as her mother started shifting her weight back and forth between her feet while she scratched at her hair. Kaylen looked down in her purse and scrambled around the inside to find whatever she could at the bottom of her purse.

"Mama...I don't have anything. I don't carry cash like that. You want me to take you to get something to eat?" Kaylen looked at the woman standing in front of her with sad eyes. She was not at all what she had remembered growing up. Before her mother had gotten hooked on heroin, she had a regal air about her. The woman that now stood before her was pitiful, dirty, and disgusting. Although Kaylen felt the need to take care of her in some way, she wasn't too comfortable with opening her home up to her.

"Hell no, I don't wanna go nowheres with you!" Kaylen watched as her mother twisted her face up into a sneer and lifted her nose to the sky. "You probably think you too good for me, now, huh? Sitting in here with this nigga! If you only knew, chile." The woman turned away from the car and started walking in the opposite direction, as she came up to the corner, she nearly ran directly into a handsome young man who looked like he was in his early twenties.

"I will suck your dick for $20! I know you got $20 on you, don't you?"

Kaylen shook her head as she stared in horror at the backside of her mother. Her clothes were torn apart from behind, and Kaylen could see straight through to her bare and filthy ass. She realized that there was nothing that she could do, and she didn't really want to try.

"Ready to go?" Salem said softly, and then cleared his throat. Kaylen looked in his direction and directly into his eyes. He was looking at her with compassion, and his eyes said an unspoken apology. Kaylen grabbed his hand and looked down in her lap as she nodded in response. She felt that the appropriate action would have been to cry, but she was not sad. In some strange way, she felt a freeness that she had been waiting for. Kaylen took a deep breath, and as she exhaled, she allowed herself to release.

"DAMN, KAYLEN! YOU READY YET?" SALEM GROWLED AS KAYLEN PUT the finishing touches on her make-up. Kaylen rolled her eyes and continued to dab at her cheeks as she applied her foundation.

"I'm almost ready. Give me a minute, Salem, please!" Kaylen said as she finished up and then placed her make-up back into her make-up case. Salem's caring mood hadn't last as long as she would have preferred, and now he was back in asshole mode.

At least he looks nice; Kaylen thought as she looked over at Salem. He was standing near the front door with his arms crossed in front of him and a deep frown on his face. Although he had lost a lot of weight and wasn't as muscular as he had been when they met, he was dressed so sharply, it was hard to not notice how attractive he looked. He had gotten his dreadlocks washed and re-twisted, had a clean shave and was dressed nicely in a sweater vest over a nice, plaid button-up shirt. His jeans were ironed with a crease and fell nicely over his black Madden dress shoes.

"Ready?" Salem asked dryly. His eyelashes flicked as he gave Kaylen a quick once over and began to move towards the door. Kaylen sighed to herself and forced her face to stay neutral as she walked out of the door.

Once in the car, Salem paused for a while and began texting on his phone.

Funny how you were in such a hurry, but now you got time; Kaylen thought as she watched him. Salem was concentrating pretty hard on the texts that he was sending and receiving, and Kaylen grew suspicious when she saw a smile curl up on the edge of his mouth.

"Who you texting got you smiling like that?" Kaylen asked with attitude.

I know this nigga ain't tripping. I am not about to be played!

"Nobody. Damn, Kaylen. What's your problem this time?" Salem asked looking over at Kaylen. He did not even try to pretend that he wasn't annoyed, but Kaylen didn't care.

"You better not be fucking around on me, Salem. I swear I don't play that shit!" Kaylen yelled. Salem burst out laughing, and it did nothing but piss Kaylen off even more.

"Bitch, please. Nobody fucking around on you. You a headache all by your damn self," Salem said with a chuckle. He reached down to place the car into gear, but before he could reach the gear shift, Kaylen slapped him straight across his face.

WHAAAAAACK!

"What the FUCK?!" Salem yelled.

"That's what your ass get for calling me a bitch, motherfucker!" Kaylen yelled and looked at Salem like she dared him to do something else. Suddenly Salem reached over and grabbed her by her neck and squeezed tightly. Kaylen gasped and tried as hard as she could to breathe.

"Don't put your fucking hands on me, ever again. Do you hear me?" Salem said through his teeth. His eyes seemed to be bulging out of his face, and white spittle was collecting on the corners of his mouth. "I said, do you hear me?!" Kaylen nodded her head quickly as she looked at him with wide eyes. She was shocked, and her state of panic was only making it harder for her to breathe.

Salem released her throat, and she gasped loudly in an attempt to take in as much air as she could. She placed her hand up to her neck and rubbed the spot where Salem had been squeezing.

"Let me out of this fucking car, Salem!" Kaylen said through her teeth. Salem didn't even listen and began backing the car out of the garage. "Salem, I mean it! Let me out now!"

"Listen, bitch. You are going to go to this party, and you are going to act like nothing happened, or I will really fuck you up," Salem said with such intensity that Kaylen was truly afraid. She lay back in the seat and looked out the window, willing the tears not to fall from her eyes.

THE FIRST PERSON THAT KAYLEN NOTICED WHEN SHE WALKED INTO THE party was Zo. He was dressed in a way that was simple, yet still drew attention. He was wearing black, as Kaylen had suspected he would, and he was looking directly at her when she entered the ballroom. Kaylen watched as he bowed his head slightly to acknowledge her presence and then turned his attention back to the older woman that was speaking to him.

Kaylen noticed that there was a younger woman holding tightly to his arm. She was very pretty, thin, and was dressed to kill. She had very fair skin and what appeared to be silky long black hair. She was looking on at the conversation that Zo was having with someone whom Kaylen assumed must have been his mother. The large smile that she donned showed that she was delighted to be Zo's plus one.

"Who is that with Zo?" Kaylen asked Salem as they walked over to where he was standing. She was trying her hardest to forget about what had happened back in the car. She reasoned with herself that she should not have hit him first. Her mother had always taught her that if you put your hands on a man, you can't be surprised when he slaps your ass back.

"That's some new lil' mama he been dealing with," Salem replied and Kaylen fought the urge to say "DUH!" right before they approached Zo and his date.

"Hey, moms," Salem said to the older woman that Zo had been speaking with. Salem leaned over and gave the woman a hug.

"How have you been doing, Salem?" Zo's mom said as she pulled back and looked Salem in the eyes. Kaylen noticed that she looked at him very intensely and with great concern. Salem had never mentioned this woman before, but she could tell by the way that she searched Salem's face that she thought of him as her own son. Kaylen tried to remain calm although she was starting to heat up about the fact that she was beginning to realize that Salem had never introduced her to anyone, with the exception of Zo. She glanced away from the exchange of expressions between Salem and the woman and her eyes locked instantly with Zo's.

Although he was not saying a word, Kaylen felt seduced by his stare. He was looking at her in such a serious way that Kaylen felt as if she was being assessed or examined. The way he looked at Kaylen made her have to catch her breath, and she dropped her eyes to inspect her manicure.

Damn it! She thought to herself. She hated the way that Zo made her feel nervous whenever he looked at her.

"And who is this?" the woman asked Salem. Kaylen turned in the direction of the woman that Salem was talking to when she noticed that her eyes, as well as Salem's, were fixated on her.

"This is my lady, Kaylen," Salem said as he grabbed her hand. Kaylen tried not to suck her teeth at Salem as he pulled her closer to him. "Kaylen, this is Mrs. Jackie. She is Zo's mom and she's like a mom to me." Salem smiled in a way that made him look like a little boy as he made the introductions. Kaylen extended her hand to Mrs. Jackie.

"Hi, Mrs. Jackie. It's nice to finally meet you," Kaylen said and cut her eyes at Salem.

"Oh, I don't shake hands, dear," the woman pulled Kaylen into a hug. "And you can call me Mrs. Jay." Kaylen squeezed the woman back as they hugged.

"Well, nice to meet you, Mrs. Jay." Kaylen opened her eyes and almost fainted as she focused on what she saw across the room. She quickly let go of Mrs. Jay and froze in position before bolting off in the direction of the front entrance of the ballroom.

"Jaz?!" Kaylen said as she walked over to where Jazmyn stood.

"Hey, Kay! Damn, it's thick in here! I ain't know all these people would be here," Jazmyn said as she held on to Dom's arm. Kaylen wrinkled up her nose at Dom and rolled her eyes as he looked her up and down, gave what he must have thought was a seductive smile, then sucked his teeth.

"What are you doing here, Dom?" Kaylen sneered.

"The same thang you doing here, lil' mama. Just trying to have a lil' fun. What? That's illegal now?" Dom smiled, showing all of his gold teeth from front to back.

"If it was, you wouldn't give a fuck," Kaylen responded.

"Yeah, you right, lil mama," Dom chuckled.

"My name is Kaylen," she said crossing her arms in front of her.

"Damn, right," Dom winked.

"Alright, you two, that's enough. Can't we all just get along?" Jazmyn sighed. "Where is Alexis?"

"I don't know. We just got here, and I haven't seen her," Kaylen said still eyeing Dom with disgust. She couldn't deny that he looked damn good, but she still couldn't stand him. There had been plenty of times that Kaylen had to answer midnight phone calls from Jazmyn about various shit that she got mixed up in thanks to Dom and his criminal activity. Kaylen did her own illegal activities, but she had never mixed up any of her friends in it and left them hanging. Levi had already been involved in that life, and Kaylen was always careful not to let Alexis or Jazmyn know what she was up to.

"I saw her car in the parking lot, so she must be somewhere in here," Jazmyn said looking around the room. "There she is! Wait...who is that?" Kaylen turned around sharply to follow Jazmyn's eyes and saw Alexis walking towards them holding the arm of a man who was definitely not Marc. Kaylen grabbed Jazmyn's arm, and they started off in her direction.

"Hey!" Alexis said with a big smile on her face when her friends approached her. "I want to introduce you both to Dexter. He's an old friend, not sure if you remember him." Dexter held out his hand to Kaylen and then turned to shake Jazmyn's hand, as well.

"Oh, we remember him!" Jazmyn said and smiled. "Well, I can say that we have heard a lot about you in the past, Dexter, so it is nice to meet you. How are you doing?"

"I'm doing well. Thanks," Dexter said and placed his arm around Alexis' waist. Alexis smiled widely as she watched Jazmyn and Kaylen exchange glances.

"Dexter, can we speak to Alexis really quickly? We promise to return her to you soon." Kaylen said and grabbed Alexis before waiting for Dexter to respond.

"Lexi, what are you doing?" Kaylen asked. "Why are you here with him?"

"Oh, please, Kaylen. Dex is gay. I'm just having some fun; that's all," Alexis said and rolled her eyes. She placed her hand on her hip and looked at Jazmyn for justification. Surprisingly, Jazmyn did not seem to condone Alexis' actions.

"Alexis, that man is *not* gay. I don't know why you are still hanging on to that notion, but it is not the case." Kaylen couldn't believe that Alexis was being this naïve. Marc was such a great husband. She understood that from time to time she needed attention, but bringing this man to a party when her husband was waiting at home was crossing the line.

"You don't think he's gay?" Alexis said slowly. She stopped for a minute and seemed to be thinking about what Kaylen had said. "Well that actually would explain a lot, I guess." Alexis glanced over at Dexter, who was still standing where she left him. He was looking directly at her while seductively taking a sip out of a champagne glass.

"He is *not* gay, Lexi. I don't think it; I know it," Kaylen repeated.

"I agree," Jazmyn said. "And you know that I know men," Jazmyn added.

"Well, in that case, let the fun begin," Alexis said and walked back over to Dexter. Once she reached him; she pulled him into a hug and made sure that there was not an inch of space left between them, and then she covered his mouth with hers and gave him a deep kiss.

Kaylen looked on with utter shock and disappointment at her friend's actions. Alexis finally pulled her lips away from Dexter's and looked over at Kaylen.

"You're right. He is *not* gay," she mouthed and then turned back to her date.

"Wow...on that note, I am going to head back over to Dom," Jazmyn said, grabbing a glass of champagne off of a tray that a server had pushed towards her.

"I can't believe this, Jaz. What should we do?" Kaylen asked.

"Nothing. She is grown. Let her do whatever the hell she wants to do," Jazmyn said and left Kaylen standing there with her mouth still hanging open.

ALEXIS

amn this nigga know he can kiss! Alexis thought to herself. Before Dexter picked her up, she had taken quite a few shots from her favorite bottle of Jose Cuervo, and she was loving the courage that it had given her. Alexis had never been so forward with any guy, but once her girls told her that they didn't think Dexter was gay, she thought the best thing to do would be to test it. After that first kiss, coupled with the way that he had grabbed her ass and slipped one finger under her short dress and into her moist princess, Alexis was quite certain that Dexter was very interested in women.

It had been a long time since she had felt someone hold and kiss her with so much care as Dexter had. Marc usually started this way, but by the end of the kiss, he was biting on her lips, and she was trying to keep herself from yelling bloody murder.

"Damn, Alexis...maybe we should have kept this at the crib, huh?" Dexter said and kissed Alexis lightly on her cheek.

"Maybe we should have," Alexis said quietly. She took a look around the room and saw a couple of women looking at her with disgust.

Shit, if they knew what I've been getting for the past five years they wouldn't be all in my business! She thought and flipped one of the girls the bird before grabbing onto Dexter's arm and pulling him over to a table that had empty chairs. In the few minutes that she had been made aware of Dexter's sexual orientation, she had enjoyed herself more than she had during the past few years and no one was going to mess that up for her. She didn't want to have sex with him until she figured out what was going on with her and Marc, but she intended to do everything but.

"So, do your friends have a problem with me coming here with you?" Dexter asked after he sat down after pulling out a chair for Alexis.

"They are just being nosy. That's all. There are a lot of things they don't know, but they think they know. I'm doing what I need to, and I don't care what anyone thinks anymore," Alexis said and finished off the rest of her champagne. She grabbed another glass off of the tray of a passing server.. "I really wish I could get something stronger than this!" Alexis said finishing off the second glass.

"It's an open bar here. Want me to get you something?" Dexter asked standing up. Alexis looked him up and down. Dexter was dressed to impress, just as she had remembered him doing years ago. He had on a beige sweater vest with a brown plaid shirt underneath that had subtle flecks of orange. The orange flecks brought out the orange thread in his dark jeans and the orange thread in his brown Doc Martins. His curly hair was cut low, and he had long, neatly trimmed side-burns that framed his caramel face. There was a lot that she would love for him to give her...maybe at another time.

"Yes, something strong, but easy going down. You pick," Alexis said and gave him the sexiest grin that she could muster. Dexter licked his lips slowly and walked away towards the bar.

Alexis looked around the room to find her friends although she didn't wish for them to join her. She wasn't really in the mood to take any of their reprimanding at the time.

I can't really blame them. It's not like I told them what was happening with me and Marc; Alexis thought. *Unfortunately, everyone still thinks he's Saint Marc.* Alexis looked through the crowd and saw Jazmyn standing with Dom. Alexis had only met Dom a few times and was surprised that her friend would invite him to an event. Although she didn't know much about him, she did know that Kaylen was always talking about the fact that he sold drugs and may have killed quite a few people. Either way, Alexis didn't want to judge, but she did know that Dom had involved Jazmyn in a few situations that had almost ruined her life as an attorney and nearly stolen her freedom.

Alexis turned her eyes away from Jazmyn and focused in on Kaylen, who was standing alone, although she looked as if she was searching for someone.

"Must be looking for Salem," Alexis said aloud. Something had been off with those two. Kaylen didn't usually involve her friends all up in her business, but she did like to brag when things were going right. Kaylen hadn't spoken about Salem in a while and to Alexis; that was a signal that something was wrong. Alexis shifted her sight to the left of Kaylen and saw Salem's friend Zo staring at Kaylen. This made Alexis chuckle.

"Those two act like we stupid or something and can't tell they be sweating each other," Alexis muttered as she finished off Dexter's champagne. Kaylen always looked like she was struck by lightning whenever she was looking at Zo. And as slick as he was, he wasn't able to hide the fact that he liked looking at her, as well. Alexis drummed her nails on the countertop of the table and continued to watch as Zo walked over to Kaylen, and they began to talk. Then Alexis turned and looked at the girl that had been hanging onto Zo's arm the entire night. Poor child had so much jealousy in her eyes as she looked at Kaylen that it was a damn shame.

"This is better than TV!" Alexis said to herself.

"What is?" Dexter said as he sat down at the table and handed her one of the drinks he was holding.

"Nothing. What is this?" Alexis said as she picked up the glass and took a whiff of the dark liquor. Whatever it was, it was strong.

"Hen and coke," Dexter said nonchalantly as he began to sip his drink.

"Oh, this that shit that Jaz likes to drink," Alexis said turning up her nose. Then she relaxed her face and decided to take a sip. Jazmyn always seemed to be enjoying life when she drank, so it couldn't be that bad.

"It's not too bad," Dexter said, taking his drink to the head like a pro. Alexis raised her eyebrows and watched him.

"Hard times? Need to drown your sorrow?" Alexis asked as she looked him over.

"Not at all. Quite the opposite. I can't believe my luck this evening." Dexter replied as he pulled Alexis' chair closer to his.

"What do you mean?" Alexis asked as she leaned in to him. She allowed him to reach down and squeeze her ass tightly.

"Well, I've been wanting to get at you for a while. Can't believe that I actually have the chance tonight." Alexis sat up straight and looked Dexter straight in his eyes.

"What do you mean by 'you have been trying to get at me for a while'?" Alexis asked. She had no memory of Dexter ever coming on to her in the time that they had been close friends. This was definitely news to her.

"Don't tell me you didn't notice. That night when you met Marc, I was so jealous and so upset that you two were interested in each other. I was planning on that night being a big night for us...I would take you out, and we would hang out afterwards. But I guess you had other plans." Dexter finished the rest of his drink and sat it down on the table. It was barely there for two seconds before an attractive server scooped it up and gave him a wide smile. Dexter winked at her to show his thanks, but Alexis made sure to give her a death stare that wiped the grin off her face.

"Actually, I didn't notice, Dex. Not at all. I just thought you were...." Alexis allowed her voice to trail off as she realized the truth. She had thought that Dex *wanted Marc,* not her, and that was the reason he was jealous. She was embarrassed to realize how wrong she had really been. "Let's forget about that, Dex. The impor-tant thing is that I'm here now, and we 'bout to have a lil' fun." With that, Alexis grabbed Dexter's hand and led him out of the banquet hall.

"Where are we going?" Dexter asked, obviously amused. Alexis looked back and gave him a look so sexy that Dexter thought he would have an accident in his pants immediately.

"Shhhhhh," Alexis said bringing her finger up to her lips. She took her finger into her tongue and sucked on it a little before turning back to lead Dexter into a small closet that they had walked past before entering the party. Alexis turned the handle, hoping that it would be unlocked and thanked her luck when she heard the *click* as the handled turned.

"Ahhh....you got dirty intentions?" Dexter said as he walked into the room. Alexis looked at him and nodded as she felt her phone begin to vibrate from within her black clutch. She sucked her teeth softly.

Probably Marc calling for the umpteenth time! UGH! Alexis thought to herself. She reached inside to grab her phone and turned it off without bothering to look at the screen.

"Someone want your attention?" Dexter said grabbing Alexis by the hips and pulling her over to him.

"Yes, but that belongs to you now," Alexis replied and wrapped her own arms around Dexter before pulling him into a kiss. She felt him when he placed his hand under her dress and rubbed on her thighs as she pushed her tongue in his mouth to make the kiss deeper.

Dexter ran his hands around the back of her thighs and grabbed onto her ass, squeezing tightly. Alexis said a silent thanks to the universe for the fact that she had decided to wear a G-string tonight. It had been a passive-aggressive way of getting back at Marc although he didn't know, but now it was serving another purpose. She was able to feel the soft, but firm grip of Dexter's hands on her soft, velvety skin as he gripped her tightly and pulled her closer to him. Alexis had to interrupt their deep kiss to let out a breath as she felt Dexter's manhood pressing against her. Her clit began to swell in a way that she had never imagined it could, and she was certain that she had soaked her panties with the waterfall that gushed from within her.

"Ohhh, Dex...." Alexis sighed as Dexter began to unzip her dress while he began kissing on her neck. She began winding her hips on his erection. It seemed to be an automatic action, not something that she willed herself to do...however, her body was beginning to take over, and it wanted more and more. Dexter's body responded as well, and Alexis took note of the heaviness of his breathing as well as the way that Dexter began to push forward, nearly digging into Alexis' skin.

"I want you," Dexter said, and he hastily pulled Alexis' dress down to expose her erect nipples. Alexis had no need for a bra most times and had not bothered to put one on before she left. Dexter was happy about this fact and wasted no time sucking one of her nipples into his mouth.

Alexis moaned loudly as he ran his tongue back and forward over the tip of her nipples. She felt the throbbing of her clit and rubbed herself even quicker and harder over Dexter in an effort to satisfy the throbbing. Dexter responded by sucking harder, taking more and more of her tender breasts into his mouth as he lowered his hand from cupping her ass and instead placed it at the base.

He gripped firmly around her thigh before placing one finger through her panties and swiftly pushing it into her sweetness. Alexis let out a gasp and began grinding her hips in a circular motion on Dexter's fingers. She grabbed the back of his neck and pushed him more forcefully onto his nipples, and he responded by sucking even more hungrily, making loud smacking noises that made Alexis rotate her hips even faster. Dexter bit softly on her nipples and Alexis winced, expecting pain that never came.

He's not Marc. He's not Marc. She thought to herself as she began to will herself to accept this pleasure without expecting pain. Dexter placed another finger inside of her, and Alexis moaned as she heard the wet smacking sounds of her juice making way for him. She leaned back on his fingers and began to bounce up and down slowly on Dexter's hand. She loved the way that her clit tapped on his fingers with each bounce as he continued to suck away at her nipples. She felt her warm juice drip down his hand, and she gripped him harder and harder.

"Damn, you wet as fuck, Alexis!" Dexter said as he pulled his mouth away from Alexis' breasts. Alexis' eyes fluttered open as she felt the cool air run across her nipples.

"Don't stop, baby! Don't stop..." Alexis breathed heavily as she continued to bounce on Dexter's fingers until he slid them out of her. "Noo....baby."

"I gotta taste you, Alexis. I can't wait no longer," Dexter said as he held Alexis' hips and slowly glided her to the floor. There were table-cloths folded atop a table in the room and Dexter grabbed one in order to drop it on the floor beneath Alexis. Alexis lie back on the cloth and allowed Dexter to pull off her panties and let her legs fall open. She watched as Dexter looked between her legs and licked his lips.

"Damn, girl, you got a pretty pussy," Dexter said as he stuck his fingers deep inside her and then pulled them out slowly. Alexis twitched with sheer pleasure as she watched Dexter stick those same fingers into his mouth. "Damn, you taste good too."

Alexis opened her eyes and looked down at Dexter as he dove straight between her legs headfirst. Although he seemed eager to taste her, he did not rush. He seemed to be taking it slow, so that he could savor every moment. Alexis closed her eyes and enjoyed the feeling of Dexter's tongue teasing the opening of her lips before he slipped his tongue slowly through the middle. He used his tongue to open her up, and he licked softly on her inside folds. Alexis felt the waterfall gushing from between her legs, and she released it all as Dexter continued licking. She almost lost her mind when he wrapped his lips around the most sensitive part of her clit and began sucking.

"Ohhhhhhhh, mmmmmmmm....yesssssssss, Dex! Don't stop, baby!" Alexis sighed deeply with pleasure, and began grinding her hips against Dexter's face. He responded by grabbing her ass to pull her in closer. He sucked harder, and Alexis fought the feeling that she felt coming up inside her. She was about to cum, and the feeling was something that she had never felt. She arched her back and pushed her pussy further onto Dexter's face. He began licking and sucking even more furiously; digging his face deeper and deeper until Alexis' juices covered his entire face. Alexis felt the climax start at the tip of her toes and then it rose up through her body and erupted as a loud squeal out of her mouth.

"Ahhhhhhhhhhhhh!" Alexis said as she squeezed her toes under and dug her fingernails into the sheet. She felt the pleasure move all throughout her body, and she continued circling her hips around Dexter's face as the feeling continued washing over her. Dexter moved his mouth lower and began sucking the juice straight out of her as she released it.

"Mmmmmhmmm, so good!" he said and he stuck a finger inside of her to open her wider so he could lick even more out of her.

"Damn, baby…that was so good," Alexis gasped. She was nearly out of breath and didn't know what to do with herself. Marc had never made her feel this way. She had read and heard about other women having orgasms, but had never experienced one on her own. It was amazing, and Alexis knew that she would never be able to go back to how it had been with Marc.

*Marc….*Alexis thought about her husband and immediately grew sad. She would have loved to be able to experience this feeling with him. The feeling of guilt settled on Alexis quickly. *My God…what have I done?* She thought to herself as she looked at Dexter. He was rubbing her juices off of his face and sucking on his fingers. Although the act was making Alexis wet again, she knew it was time to go. She had gone too far this time, and now she would have to tell Marc what happened with Dexter.

"I gotta go, Dex. Shit….I really had too much to drink. This shouldn't have happened. Marc…" Alexis stopped short when she saw the way that Dexter's expression began to change.

"Marc, what? I know you not trying to back out now that you done got yours?" Dexter said frowning up his brows at her.

"No…I mean. I just…I'm married, Dex," Alexis stammered as she tried to grab her clothes from the floor. Dexter reached out and snatched her panties from her hand.

"You weren't married two seconds ago when you were grinding your ass on my tongue! I hate when bitches do this shit. Fuck that shit,

Alexis!" Dexter grabbed her thighs and forced them back open. Alexis panicked immediately and began trying to scoot away.

"Dex!" Alexis shrieked. "Wait....what are you doing?" Alexis began to kick at Dexter, and she reached out over her head, trying to grab anything around her that would assist in her beating him away. She grabbed what felt like a broom handle and tried to ram it as hard as she could towards Dexter's head. He slapped it away and grabbed her by the throat.

"Listen to me, *Alexis*," he sneered right into her face. Dexter had pulled her so close to him that Alexis could feel the heat of his breath and could almost taste the sour smell that escaped through it. "I don't take no shit from no one, not even you. I hate motherfucking women who just wanna take and don't wanna give shit. Spoiled ass!"

Alexis opened her mouth and tried to let out a cry for help, but before she could Dexter began to squeeze harder on her throat. Alexis felt tears burning at the rim of her eyes, and she began to see spots in front of her.

This can't be happening. This can't be happening! She thought. Dexter had been her best friend. *Oh, my God, save me, please!*

Alexis squeezed her eyes closed as she felt Dexter pushed her legs further apart. He positioned himself between her and with one quick motion; he thrust himself inside of her. He began moving deeper and deeper inside of her until Alexis began to feel like she couldn't take anymore. When Dexter finally seemed satisfied with the depth in which he penetrated her, he began quick and sharp thrusting motions.

Alexis let her body go limp as she stared at the ceiling. Tears began to slide from her eyes and down the side of her face. The pain didn't matter. She was used to pain. What she *couldn't* handle was the thumping of the drops of water that were seeping through the roof.

How could a place this grand and this expensive have a leaky roof? Alexis thought as she felt Dexter release her throat and grab one of her breasts.

One drop. Two drops. Three drops....shame, really. Someone must know that the roof is faulty. I wonder how much Salem and Zo paid for this place.

Wait...would Zo pay for his own birthday party? Seems kinda tacky to me....Hmmm...maybe not.

Alexis shifted slightly as Dexter raised one of her legs in the air and continued banging away at her insides. Alexis could feel the grinding of his skin against hers as he continued. The dryness from inside her seemed to be bothering Dexter as he struggled to get deeper inside of her. Alexis watched as he pulled out his member and spit into his hand. He wiped the saliva over the tip and shaft of his dick before driving it back into her. Alexis let out a long breath and continued to count the drops from the ceiling.

*One drop. Two drops. Three drops....*Alexis shuddered as sweat began to drip off of Dexter's body and onto her skin. The moisture began to make her feel dirty, and she squirmed a little with discomfort.

"Yeah, that's right. Throw it back on that dick, baby. Mmmm-mmhhhh just like that!" Dexter grabbed tight on one of Alexis' breasts and squeezed tightly. Dexter's groaning of satisfaction from her movements jarred her back into reality, and Alexis stopped her motion immediately and focused on being as still as possible.

"Yeah, that's it. Make it tight for me," Dexter grunted more as he continued his swift motion.

No, I can't do this! I can't do this anymore! With that thought, Alexis began to fight back. She struggled to push Dexter off of her and began kicking at whatever she could. She reached up and clawed at his face, trying to scrape whatever she could off of it.

WHACK! Dexter punched Alexis so hard that she fell back onto the floor and paused for a while to make sense of the spinning room around her.

This can't be happening. Oh, my God...why is this happening? Alexis let her body go totally limp. She thought that maybe if she let Dexter have his way, it would be over soon. Dexter seemed to be happy at the opportunity to continue with his violation of her. He grabbed at one of her legs and pushed it further open to deepen his reach inside her.

"Uhhhhhhhnnnnn! This shit is good! Uhhhhhhhnnnnnn!" Dexter grunted and began thrusting longer and harder. Alexis felt a strange burning sensation that seemed to come about from their skin rubbing too hard together, but it didn't bother her. She was in another world. She continued to stare at the leaking and count the drops as Dexter continued pounding a hole into her.

"Oh…..my…..gaaaa uuuuuuhhhhhhhnnnnn!" Dexter yelled loudly and then pulled his dick out of her leaving a long line of semen trailing from out of her swollen and sore opening. He lifted up on his knees and continued to squeeze the rest of the sticky matter on the top of her stomach and the pieces of her gown that still remained wrapped around her mid-section.

"Yeaaaaah, shit! There you go, you bitch…take that!" Dexter said with his eyes closed tight as he ran his hand up and down his member to squeeze out the last few drops all over her front.

Alexis' eyes flickered as she felt the drops of the sticky liquid on her skin, but she still didn't move. As he finished, he picked himself up and pulled his clothes back on to his body. Alexis tried to remain focused on the ceiling, but she couldn't stop the emotions that began to flood into her mind. Though she wasn't looking at him directly, she could see the shadow of Dexter as he fixed his clothes and began walking towards the door. He paused for a second to turn back and look at Alexis before opening the door, and walking out.

Alexis let the tears fall as she sat there hoping that sometime soon the dirty feeling would pass away.

JAZMYN

*J*azmyn tried to hide the annoyance that she felt. There was always a downside to inviting Dom out anywhere. He was definitely a "ladies man" and the fact that they had always been clear with each other where they stood, only made it easier for him to grab onto any attractive and available woman that floated by.

She looked over at Dom as he smiled in the face of a young, attractive woman who appeared to be in her early twenties.

"She's cute, but that bitch ain't got nothing on me!" Jazmyn said aloud and brought her glass of champagne to her lips. This party was not turning out the way that she had wanted. She had hoped to be able to rid herself of Kingston's memory, but it seemed that the man was permanently etched in her mind.

Jazmyn felt her cellphone vibrating again and ignored it. The same number had been calling her for the past couple hours, and Jazmyn figured it was someone trying to reach whoever had this number before her. Only a few people knew to call her on this line, and other than her mother, those people were at the party with her.

"Fuck this!" Jazmyn said as she slammed her glass back on the table.

I am not about to sit here and be ignored by this nigga! She thought as she walked over to where Dom stood. When she approached him, she slid her hand into his and tugged slightly to draw his attention. The young woman that he had been speaking with also turned to look at Jazmyn. Jazmyn only paid minor attention to the woman as she looked her up and down quickly, and then rolled her eyes. She let out a short breath and narrowed her eyes to show much attitude.

Jazmyn turned quickly to look at her and gave her the best "Bitch, please!" look that she could muster before turning back to Dom.

"Hey, Dom. I need to speak with you, baby," Jazmyn said as she flicked her thumb back and forth over Dom's hand.

Dom responded by looking at her in a shocked manner for all of about two seconds before pulling his lips into a grin to show a mouth full of gold teeth.

"A'ight, shawty...let's get it then," Dom turned to follow Jazmyn's lead. The woman he had been speaking to, looked on, and her mouth fell open with surprise.

"Dom...wait, a minute..." the woman started as she began walking a few steps behind him.

"Hey...deuces, mama. Holla at me later, a'ight?" Dom replied without looking back.

As they arrived at an empty table, Jazmyn sat down and waited for Dom to take a seat next to her.

Damn, did this nigga just get sexier? She thought to herself. Dom had never been ugly, but Jazmyn just never thought of him as anything more than what he was. He was someone that she could have fun with, have great sex with, and he introduced her to a life that she hadn't experienced in the past. He had a dangerousness air about him that intrigued her, but she would be lying if she said that she ever wanted more from him.

Dom seemed to like it that way also. He had never pressured Jazmyn to be his woman. In fact, he always kept it real with her, and she liked it that way. Jazmyn had seen in the past how he played the women that he dated and she wasn't for all of that. Lil' girl standing across the ballroom with the shit-face was indicative of how much

Dom actually cared about the women that he courted. Jazmyn took a second to look back over at her and felt a small inkling of pity. She was sure that the girl had believed all of the game that Dom had been throwing.

Oh, well....not my problem. Jazmyn thought as she refocused her attention on Dom. He was sitting next to her looking at her with laughter in his eyes. He seemed to be waiting for something, but Jazmyn was clueless on what to say. Unfortunately, she hadn't thought it too much through before approaching him.

"So, what was that all about?" Dom asked with a smile. He seemed to be tickled about what had just occurred, and Jazmyn couldn't blame him. Cock-blocking had never been her role in his life, and she was somewhat embarrassed about it.

"What was what about, Dom?" Jazmyn asked, feigning ignorance.

"I ain't never seen you get at your boy like that, Jay. What you jealous 'bout a nigga now?" Dom asked grinning wider, while stroking his goatee. Nothing seemed to stroke his ego more than having two women vying for his attention.

Shit! Jazmyn thought to herself. This was not her role in life to stroke some man's ego by being one of the many chicken-heads fighting in the street trying to get some dick from him.

Well, fuck it. Time to roll with this shit now. She tossed her hair over her shoulder and leaned in close to Dom. She placed her hand on the back of his chair and looked directly at him. She made sure to lean in close enough that he had a direct line of sight to her breasts and could feel as she rubbed the side of one on his chest.

"It's never too late to change up the game, you know what I mean? You taught me that," Jazmyn whispered, giving him a light kiss on the cheek. Dom had always been magnificent when it came to sex. If nothing else, at least she could get her kitty taken care of tonight.

"Well, let's do that then," Dom said leaning over to grab her thigh. Just then, Jazmyn heard her phone vibrating against the table, and she groaned inwardly.

Dammit! I just can't win tonight!

"Hold on a minute, Dom." she said as she grabbed her phone and pressed the answer button. Obviously it was time to set the record straight and stop this person from calling.

"Hello? Who is this?" Jazmyn asked, making no effort at all to mask her annoyance.

"Jaz....this is Kingston. It's important; I need to speak with you!" The alarm in Kingston's voice made Jazmyn hesitate for a minute before going with her first thought to cuss his ass out.

She placed her finger in the air to motion to Dom to give her one minute, and she got up to walk out the ballroom door.

"How did you get my....," her voice trailed off as she turned and looked to her left. She saw Dexter adjusting the belt on his pants as he stormed out of the room that was adjacent to the ballroom. He scurried quickly away from the room and directly out of the glass doors leading outside of the building. Jazmyn started to yell out to him, but was stopped short when she heard Kingston's next words.

"Jaz, listen. I think you're in danger. I'm not sure, but I think Shanice may be following you or something," Kingston finished.

What the fuuuck?! Jazmyn thought as she willed herself not to hang up the phone in his face.

"See? This is the reason I should have never messed around with your ass! You're such a damn liar, Kingston! I thought this shit was over! Now you telling me this bitch done found out about us and caught feelings so she coming after me?!" Jazmyn spat out.

A few people standing around her at the entrance looked over at her with interest, but Jazmyn did not care. She was livid and could not believe that Kingston had allowed this to happen. How did his wife even know about her? How did she even know where she lived or where she went to be following her?

How this bitch know more about me and my life then I know about her! This shit is whack! Jazmyn thought to herself as she ran her fingers through her hair with frustration.

"Listen, Jazmyn, I can come get you. Where are you?"

"Kingston, are you crazy! How about you take care of your wife and leave me the hell alone. I didn't sign up for this family shit! You claim you love me, and you put me in this situation and now you

149

wanna be captain save a hoe! Lose my number...AGAIN!" Jazmyn slammed her finger against the "end call" button and let out a frustrated growl.

This day was getting worse and worse. Now in addition to her feelings, which were all over the place, she had to deal with a woman on the run. Who knows what the hell Kingston had been telling her to make her want to actually *follow* Jazmyn?

"You gotta be a mad bitch to get your shit and follow someone around!" Jazmyn huffed out. She was so frustrated she began talking to herself. "If anything, I know since I've done the shit myself!"

Jazmyn decided to stop giving the nosy people around her more to talk about, and walked outside to get some fresh air. Before exiting out of the building, she turned to see what Dom was up to.

Guess I shouldn't just leave him alone. But that was not at all the case. As she searched back through the doors to the ballroom, she saw that Dom had not wasted any time waiting for her to return. The young lady that he had been speaking to earlier seemed all too happy to replace Jazmyn at the table and was leaning over so close to Dom that she may as well have been straddling him.

Jazmyn rolled her eyes as she looked at the way Dom grinned at the woman who was desperate enough to forget the way he had just left her in the middle of the room looking stupid.

Once Jazmyn made it out of the building, she took in a deep breath. Times like this made her wish that she smoked cigarettes.

Shit, at least a fat blunt would work. She thought to herself. She needed something to calm her nerves.

On cue, a handsome face walked out of the building holding a freshly poured drink.

"Hey, there...can I have that?" Jazmyn asked throwing on her sexiest smile.

"Sure," the man said and handed her the drink. Just as it seemed like he was about to open his mouth to continue speaking, Jazmyn walked off in the other direction.

Not trying to hear that shit; she thought. Just as Jazmyn was about to take a sip of the mixture, her phone began vibrating again. She ignored it and continued to taste her drink. More than likely it was Kingston again, and she wasn't trying to speak with him at all.

"UUUUGGGGHHH, how in the world did I get in this mess?" Jazmyn groaned to herself as she thought about what was going on. Her mind was telling her not to answer the phone, but she felt her willpower fading. She reached down and grabbed her phone, pressing the button to answer it before the call went to voicemail.

"Yes?" Jazmyn said dryly without checking the caller ID. There was no answer. She could hear light breathing on the other end, but nothing was said.

"HELLO?!" Jazmyn shouted into the phone. No answer. "Listen, I don't like when motherfuckers play on my phone, so you better say something!" Jazmyn said and waited a little while. Nothing. She looked at the screen, promptly hung up the phone, and then downed the rest of her drink. She knew exactly who was playing on her phone, and it just pissed her off even more that the bitch didn't have the guts to speak up.

Jazmyn decided to call the number back that Kingston had called her on. He picked up on the first ring.

"Jaz...," he said breathing heavily.

Must be in the middle of fucking something; Jazmyn thought to herself.

"Am I interrupting?" Jazmyn replied back placing her hand on her hip.

"What? No, Jaz, listen...," he started.

"No, you listen. Your bitch is playing on my phone. You need to handle that." Jazmyn turned to look at a couple that walked outside next to her. She didn't want them in her business, but it didn't seem like they cared. The girl was obviously drunk and was peeling off her clothes as they headed over to the parking lot. Her man was happily following. Jazmyn smirked a little at the sight, and it made her think about when she and Kingston had first started messing around.

The sexual tension was so thick in the beginning that they barely made it out of the office before they started ripping off each other's clothes. Kingston had opened the door and placed her gently inside of the car, making sure to palm her ass and squeeze tightly before he let go. He then ran over to the driver's side and jumped in. He was barely able to turn on the ignition before Jazmyn jumped into his lap and pulled at his belt.

Once she was able to rip open his pants, she reached in and released the bulge that was forming quickly in the seat of his pants. Jazmyn wasted no time reaching under her skirt to pull down her panties. Instead, she decided to pull them to the side before sliding down on him. Her wetness made Kingston suck in a sharp breath, and he immediately relaxed as she began to twerk on top of him.

Jazmyn grabbed onto the back of his neck and kissed him up and down the side of his face as she bounced slowly on his long, thick, and hard erectness. It had the perfect curve to it, and it hit a place in Jazmyn that made her feel absolute pleasure. She was so wet that they could hear the wet smacking sounds as she moved up and down on Kingston's lap. The sound seemed to turn him on even more, and he reached behind her to grab her ass, parting it slightly, which drove Jazmyn crazy.

She bounced faster and harder until Kingston began begging her to stop. But she couldn't. It was getting so good that Jazmyn had lost all willpower to control herself. She clutched at the headrest on the seat and began bouncing even more fiercely with her eyes squeezed tightly shut. Kingston moaned and then grabbed her from underneath. With one quick motion, he pulled her off of him and tossed her back in the passenger seat right before he erupted with pleasure and let go all of the driver's side of the car as well as his designer suit. They looked at each other and laughed as he drove them over to the nearest 5-star hotel.

"Hello? Jaz? You there?" Kingston's voice jarred Jazmyn back into the reality of her current situation, and she immediately began to get back angry.

"Look, just handle your bitch, Kingston!" Jazmyn hung up her phone and turned on her heels to head back into the party. Dom may have been chatting up with that lame hoe that temporarily took her spot, but Jazmyn was pissed, frustrated and ready for something to calm her down.

Shawty gotta go; Jazmyn thought checking her reflection in the glass doors. She was just about to open the door to walk in when she noticed a car heading her way. She couldn't make it out clearly, but she did notice the headlights shining through the glass door. Jazmyn's mouth dropped open as she realized the car was speeding towards her as if the driver were about to plummet directly into the door. She turned around quickly, and her mouth opened in shock as the car swerved to the right and then skid to a complete stop. The driver sneered at her out of the window, and Jazmyn noticed she was looking face to face with Kingston's wife.

"Bitch..." Jazmyn started right before she caught two hard cracks right on the forehead.

What the fuck?! Jazmyn stopped in her tracks and reached up to where she had been hit. She felt a wet substance and pulled her fingers down towards her face. The wet liquid dropped down her forehead, and Jazmyn seethed.

"I know this bitch didn't just throw eggs at me!" Jazmyn said through gritted teeth. She looked back up and saw Shanice smiling back at her. The smug look on her face made Jazmyn see red. She lunged forward in a motion so quick that Shanice couldn't even prepare for it. Shanice struggled to hit the gas and drive off, but she was too slow. Jazmyn had already grabbed her by her throat and started throwing punches square in her face.

"Bitch, you...done...fucked...with...the...wrong...ONE!" Jazmyn said throwing blows between each word. She noticed that people began walking out of the ballroom and were watching the fight, but she didn't care. She was pissed off at Shanice, pissed at Kingston, but even more pissed off at herself for getting into this situation in the first place. She knew that she should have stopped when Shanice started bleeding from her mouth, but she just couldn't. She reached back far and slapped Shanice as hard as she could. Jazmyn smirked as she saw the way that Shanice's head bounced off the headrest.

She stretched down inside the car and unlocked the door as

Shanice aimlessly flung her arms towards Jazmyn trying to divert the blows. It didn't work because Jazmyn was too quick for her, and the punches were coming down with such precision and force that Shanice's attempts to play patty-cake had no effect whatsoever.

"Oh, you ain't know I was hood, huh? Thought I was just some dumb corporate bitch that Kingston was fucking 'round with!" Jazmyn said as she grabbed Shanice by her hair and dragged her out of the car. Shanice's body folded and fell out of the grey BMW sedan like a paperweight. The crowd started rooting and getting louder with anticipation that they were about to see a good beat down happen right in front of their eyes.

It wasn't until Shanice fell onto the dark and gritty asphalt that Jazmyn came to her senses. Shanice rolled around on her back, and all of the voyeurs gasped in unison as they looked at her round belly. It was so quiet that you could hear the bass of the music playing back inside the ballroom. Jazmyn stumbled backwards in shock as she began to fully comprehend what she had just done.

"Damn, she beating up on a pregnant bitch!" One man yelled out, and Jazmyn could hear women sucking their teeth. She looked behind her and saw some people staring at her with utter disgust. She tried to run her hand over her face and was unable to due to the sticky residue that was still left over from the egg. She reached up to try to fluff out her matted hair that had also been victimized by the egg splatter. Just then, someone grabbed on to her arm and pulled her.

"Time to be out now, don't ya think, shawty?" Jazmyn looked to her right and focused her eyes on Dom as he tugged her away from the crowd and out towards the parking lot.

"Dom, I didn't...I mean, I forgot that she was preg...," Jazmyn stuttered as she tried to move her feet fast enough to keep up with Dom's pace. She was still wearing her 6-inch stilettos, so it was proving to be very difficult.

"No, need to explain to me. It's just time to chuck the deuces and be out. Hand me the keys," Dom said once they reached Jazmyn's car. She reached down in her bag and fumbled around for her car keys. She took one second to glance back towards where she had left Shanice. Some of the people standing by had managed to pull her off the ground, and she was sitting in a chair. She was fully conscious and glaring in Jazmyn's direction as another woman dabbed at her bloody lip.

All of the sympathy that Jazmyn had felt oozed out of her as she returned a deadly look of her own in Shanice's direction. She sat down in the car and stared at the pregnant woman as Dom drove off. Just as they turned out onto the main road, Jazmyn raised her middle finger out of the window and waved it at Shanice.

"Sayonara, trick."

KAYLEN

This right here is for the birds; Kaylen thought as she sat down in her chair and downed her fourth glass of Pink Moscato in a row. She had no idea where Salem was and did not care at all. But she did care that she was sitting down looking fine as hell, and no one had even bothered to ask her to dance or stopped by to chat. She looked over to where Alexis and Dexter were sitting. It seemed like Alexis was having the time of her life. Kaylen watched as Alexis rubbed on Dexter's thigh before he rose up from her chair to walk over to the bar.

"At least somebody about to have some fun tonight," Kaylen muttered to herself as she glanced around to find a waiter holding more champagne glasses. She turned a little in her seat to continue her search, but stopped when she locked eyes with Zo. It was such a strange feeling that she got when he stared at her. It was as if the room was moving in fast motion all around her, but he was standing still. She glanced down nervously, breaking the eye contact in order to catch her breath before she looked back up at where he stood. She saw him duck his head a little as a greeting to her before he started walking in her direction.

"Oh, my God, he's heading this way," Kaylen muttered under her breath. She cleared her throat and then flicked her eyes to the right. She noticed that Alexis was looking at her with a coy grin on her face and Kaylen's face heated up with embarrassment. Was it really that obvious how Zo made her feel?

"Kaylen...," Zo started. Kaylen loved the way he always let her name linger on his tongue. It was sexy, and it made her smile. "I hope you are enjoying the party. You look a little...bored." He smiled at her, and Kaylen's stomach started turning. She felt the butterflies beginning in her stomach, and she struggled to keep the anxiety from showing up in her face.

"It's cool. I just...I don't know where Salem is. Actually, I don't even know if I care. We haven't really been getting along and earlier..." Kaylen stopped when she realized that she was babbling, *and* she was talking about Zo's best friend. Probably not a good idea. "I mean...we're cool. I just...don't know where he is."

I'm a complete idiot. That didn't sound ridiculous at all, Kaylen. She looked back at Zo, who had taken a seat next to her, and expected him to be looking at her with utter confusion, but that's not what she saw. Instead, he looked like he was having a hard time trying to tell her something. He was looking down, and had a frown on his face that clearly showed he was thinking about something that he was struggling with. Kaylen felt embarrassed as she assumed that Zo felt awkward about how she was speaking to him about Salem.

"I mean...I'm sorry, Zo. I really shouldn't have said any of that stuff about Salem. I've had a few drinks, if you can't tell." Kaylen laughed lightly in an attempt to make light of the situation.

"No, it's not that, Kaylen. How has everything been with you and Salem? I'm actually interested in that," Zo said looking directly into her eyes. Kaylen noticed that he watched her with so much concern. It was almost as if he knew more about her than he let on. For some reason this didn't make her uncomfortable, it did exactly the opposite. She instantly felt like she could trust him. She looked back at him and let her eyes probe deeply into his. She felt no ill intent within them. His soft brown eyes only showed pure concern.

"Not good, honestly. He's been acting really...strange. Moody...we actually kinda fought before coming here. He slapped me and....," Kaylen stopped when she noticed Zo's jaw clench up. "Well, I hit him first though! I shouldn't have done that."

"Kaylen, Salem has had a lot of shit happen to him in the past. Did he ever speak to you about what he does for a living?" Zo asked just above a whisper. It usually annoyed her when people spoke so low that she could barely hear them. But this time, she used Zo's soft voice as an excuse to lean in closer. "No...well, he told me he was in business with you. You and him own some restaurants." Kaylen was a little confused at where Zo was going with this. What did Salem's work have to do with how he's been acting? Unless he was going broke.

Oh, shit! He's not going broke, is he? What am I going to do with Levi gone? Shit! Kaylen started to panic a little as she waited for Zo's response.

"Yes, Kaylen...He is a part owner of my restaurants. Salem and I grew up together in the hood. That nigga Dom that your home girl vibing with tonight; we grew up with him. Dom got Salem mixed up in that drug shit young. Salem was a young kid in the hood with nothing. He wanted money, and Dom was promising him a lot of it. Salem tried to convince me to join him...sell drugs on Dom's team, but that wasn't my style. I've seen too many of my fam strung out on that shit; no way I could be a part of the problem."

Kaylen hung her head a little in shame. *What would he say if he knew that I had the same experiences and still chose the opposite way? That I chose to be a part of the problem...*

"Salem got caught up, Kaylen. He was selling drugs and making a lot of money. I remember when I left for culinary school; Salem gave me money every month to live on. I never cashed the checks because I had a feeling one day he would need me. I got a call from my mama one day saying that Salem had overdosed on something. When I saw him in the hospital it shook my soul. I never saw my boy that gone," Zo paused shortly as he began to think back to that time. Kaylen felt her eyes tearing up as she listened to his story. It mirrored a few things that had happened to her father.

"Anyways, I was able to send Salem to rehab and he got clean. But I could tell he was only a step away from going back to that life. I could see it in him that he wasn't fully recovered. That's why I told you to be careful with him when I saw you that day after the club...at Jaz's house. I didn't think he was ready to be in a relationship yet. Anyways, Salem got clean.

He had some money saved away, and he invested in my first restaurant. He's my partner in the business, and we make legitimate money. But I noticed a couple months back; he started back fucking with that nigga Dom." Zo stopped his story, and Kaylen waited for him to continue. After a while, she thought that maybe he was done, so she decided to ask the question that had been lingering in her mind.

"He's using again, isn't he?" Kaylen asked although she already knew the truth. Salem's behavior for the past few months told it all.

How could I have not known? Kaylen thought to herself. She saw the way that her father deteriorated once he began messing around with heroin. She didn't suspect that was Salem's drug of choice, but she could tell that there was something going on there.

How could I be so stupid? Kaylen began to get angry with herself. There had been so many signs. From the interaction with her mother to what Nesha had started to tell her at the salon, Salem's clothing, and his change in appearance...she should have known something.

"Where is he?" Kaylen asked Zo with her eyes narrowed. Zo's eyes flicked to the right at a door on the other side of the ballroom. Though the look was very quick, Kaylen caught it and knew that, though unintentional, Zo had just let her know where to find Salem.

"Kaylen, I don't think you should..." Zo began as Kaylen jumped up from her chair.

Kaylen wasn't clear if it were the alcohol that put her in such an emotional state, but she was a combination of angry, sad, as well as, just plain ole embarrassed at the fact that she had been dealing with Salem and had no idea about his background or that he was using while with her.

That motherfucker probably took that baggy of meth that was in my pants! Everything seemed to make sense now, and Kaylen could only feel stupid about how she had allowed it all to happen.

Kaylen had a tough time getting over to the room where she believed Salem was because people were scurrying towards the entrance of the ballroom. Kaylen heard someone mention something about someone fighting a pregnant lady, but she was barely paying any attention. The only thing on her mind was Salem and whether or not he had a different explanation for what was going on.

As soon as Kaylen approached the doors, she burst through as hard as she could. There had been a person leaning on the door, but Kaylen pushed with such force that she propelled him into the wall behind the door.

"What the f.....," the man started.

"Get out," Zo said from behind her. The man obeyed without a word.

Once she entered the room and allowed her eyes to focus on the sight in front of them, she immediately grew faint, and her knees buckled under her as she started to fall. Zo caught her right before she hit the floor, and she closed her eyes as he cradled her. She was trying her hardest to erase the memory of what she had just seen with her own eyes. She felt heat rising up in her cheeks, and she was beginning to feel extremely hot. Memories of her past were coming at her with such force that she was barely able to control her psyche enough to contain the images.

Salem was sitting on a couch in front of her. He was laid back, with his long dreadlocks spread out under his neck, and his eyes were closed. His right arm was outstretched to the side, and a needle was sticking out of it. He seemed to be barely breathing as he sat unconscious in his state of drugged euphoria.

When Kaylen had walked in the room, she hadn't seen Salem at all; she had only seen her father. The way he was lying, and the peaceful look in his eyes reminded her of exactly what her father had looked like when she saw his dead body on the kitchen floor of her home. The sight had brought back feelings and emotions that she had worked so hard to repress, and she could do nothing but cry as Zo held her.

"Kaylen...it will be alright. Listen, it will be ok," Zo said lowly as he rocked her. Although he was not speaking loud at all, the commotion in the room must have been enough to wake Salem from his drug related stupor, and Kaylen noticed that he began to stir.

"What's going...Kaylen, what are you doing here?" Salem asked groggily. His eyes danced around a little in his head as he spoke, and Kaylen noticed that he had spittle collecting in the sides of his mouth. Immediately, her emotions flipped from sad to extremely angry, and she ripped herself out of Zo's embrace.

"What the fuck is going on, Salem? You using now?" Kaylen asked walking over to where he stood. Salem just stared at her with his mouth open. It seemed as if he wanted to answer her question, but was unable to find enough words to string together in order to do so. For some reason, this made Kaylen see red, and she lunged at Salem and slapped him as hard as she could. Zo ran up and grabbed her hand as she prepared to slap him again. Salem didn't even attempt to shield himself or to hit her back. He simply let his head hang down, and his long dreadlocks swooped down over his face.

"How could you, Salem? You know what happened to me! You know about my parents! You know this shit! How could you do this to me....to yourself?!" Kaylen cried out. Zo began shushing her, in an attempt to get her to calm down. He wrapped his hands around her and pulled her back.

"Let me drive you home, Kaylen. You need to get out of here," he said slowly.

"You're right, I do," Kaylen said looking at Salem. Part of her felt sad, but most of her felt disgusted. She couldn't believe what he'd done to himself. How could someone with so much potential and so much intelligence go back to this?

"Wait right here, Kay. Two seconds." Zo peeked his head outside of the door, and Kaylen heard him calling someone over.

"Cash, I need you to take our boy home," Zo said to the man that he'd called to the room. "Make sure he ain't got nothing with him.

Don't let him leave 'til I get there." Cash looked extremely unenthused about the idea of babysitting Salem, but he also seemed to be concerned as well about Salem.

"Shit, Salem…what the hell you been doing in here?" Cash said as he grabbed Salem and hoisted him up on his feet. Zo beckoned towards Kaylen to follow him out of the room.

"Oh, and before I forget," Zo turned back around to look at Cash. "That nigga Tim was in here when we first walked in. Tell him I'm about to see him later on, too."

Kaylen saw Cash's head jerk up as he looked at Zo.

"He was in here with this nigga while he was shooting up?" Cash asked, still struggling to hold up a limp Salem. Zo nodded his head in response.

"Well, yeah, I'mma need to see that nigga, too, then." Cash said, steadying Salem and half dragging him towards the door.

"You do what you gotta do," Zo said and Kaylen followed him out the door.

"You ok?" Zo said looking over at Kaylen as they sat at a traffic light. Kaylen cleared her throat and shot her eyes quickly in Zo's direction.

"Yes. I am," she responded. The crazy thing was that she really was fine. She was pissed more than anything at the fact that she had been so stupid all this time. Kaylen prided herself on being a person that was in command, in control, and incredibly intelligent. But the fact was that she had been dealing with an addict all this time, and she felt like the only person that didn't notice it.

Kaylen groaned out loud as she thought back to the day in the salon when Salem showed up looking like a beggar on Skid Row. She hadn't even thought about why he was changing, why he was having mood swings. Part of her felt guilty, like she may have been partially responsible for him going back to that life since he found the meth baggy in her pants pocket, but she felt that he had still pulled her into a situation that she knew nothing about.

"Shit, I didn't know he was an addict," Kaylen mumbled under her breath as she laid her head on the window as they continued towards her home. Zo turned to look at her and then went back to face the road again. For what seemed like a lifetime, Kaylen heard nothing but the beeping of the GPS as they drove on.

Finally, Zo pulled into Kaylen's driveway and stopped his car right outside of Kaylen's garage door. The soft hum of his car halted once he turned the key in the ignition. Kaylen felt the side of her face heating up, and she knew he was staring at her. She reached for the door handle, but stopped when he began to speak.

"I wanted to tell you, but, you know....that's my nigga though," Zo said slowly. Kaylen turned to look at him. She wasn't upset at him at all. She would have struggled with the same thing. She covered for her girls all the time even when she knew their asses were dead wrong.

"I get it, Zo. It's ok, really. Salem knew some things about me that...anyways, this is no one but Salem's fault. I'm done with it all. I just want to go lie down."

"I will get your door," Zo said before hopping out of the seat and walking over to her side of the car. He opened the door, and grabbed her hand to gently lift her out of the vehicle. Kaylen felt slightly wobbly.

Guess the effects of that champagne have kicked in a little; she thought as she struggled to steady herself. Zo grabbed her around the waist, and she allowed herself to lean into him a little as he walked her around the side of the house and to the front door.

Kaylen stopped to grab her key out of her purse and opened the door quickly. Tiny ran to the door and she dropped down to rub his head and move him out of the way.

"Why don't you come in to get something to drink?" Kaylen asked leaving the door open as she walked in to deactivate the alarm. She looked back at Zo, who was still standing at the entrance of the door. "Something wrong?" Kaylen strolled back over to him slowly, and

Tiny followed behind. She noticed that he had a look of longing, like he wanted to come in, but his feet did not move.

"No, it's cool. I gotta get going, though. I gotta go check on Salem," Zo said quickly.

"Oh," Kaylen responded. She was visibly disappointed, and though she tried to change her facial expression, she was certain that Zo saw it.

"Well, thanks for everything tonight. I really needed to know what was going on," Kaylen said leaning on the front of her door.

Damn, he looks good; Kaylen thought. The way that the light of the moon was shining down on him made him look even sexier than he naturally was. Kaylen took a minute to look him up and down slowly. She didn't know if it was the champagne or the liquor that she downed earlier, but she was feeling bold and ready to let caution go and forget about everything.

Zo quietly stared into her eyes as he watched her look him up and down. He didn't say a word, but Kaylen could tell that he wanted her, and she was ready to see how far that would get her. She leaned over and kissed Zo lightly on the lips. Though subtle, she felt his lips respond to her touch, and he kissed her back. Kaylen pulled back slowly, and her eyes ran over his face as she tried to gauge his reaction. Suddenly, he pulled her in close and kissed her more passionately. He grabbed her and let his hands drop so that they were just barely above her plump, round ass.

Kaylen was surprised, but not caught off guard. She responded by kissing him back, much deeper than before, but it wasn't until Zo pushed his tongue between her lips that she had to catch her breath. He let his hands drop further, and he gripped her ass so tightly that Kaylen could feel her body responding in ways that it never had before. Something about this felt so right, and she wanted more. But suddenly, Zo pulled back.

"Shit! I'm sorry, Kaylen," Zo apologized. Kaylen looked at him confused for a minute as he stared at the ground and clenched his jaw.

What the hell? Shit, I kissed him first!

"I shouldn't have done that. You're Salem's girl. I'm sorry about that," Zo turned on his heels and headed back in the direction of his car. "Lock up. Have a good night," he said without turning to face her.

"Wait, Zo...it's ok," Kaylen replied, but she was sure he didn't even hear her. Kaylen sat staring at the space where she had last seen Zo for a while. She was confused about what had just happened. Obviously, he was feeling her, and she was feeling him. Her and Salem were done...who cared about him at this point? Kaylen decided that this was a topic for another day. She was tired, so she closed her door and headed upstairs to her bedroom.

"YOU KNOW YOUR DADDY'S HOOOOMMMMMMEEE....," KAYLEN GROANED AS she heard her cellphone ringing. *Who the hell is calling me this late?* Kaylen thought to herself. It felt like she had just gotten to sleep, and now someone was interrupting a great dream in process. She had programmed ringtones for all important people so she as soon as she focused; she was able to figure out that it was Caleb calling. She struggled with herself on whether or not to answer. This was the first time he had called in months. Though she wanted to sleep, somehow her willpower failed her, and she pressed the answer button. She placed the phone on speaker so she didn't have to hold it to her ear.

"Hello?" Kaylen answered gruffly.

"Hey there, baby," Caleb responded smoothly. It almost made her laugh that he had the nerve to respond as if they talked like this every day. As if she hadn't hung up on his ass the last time they spoke.

"What do you want, Caleb?" Kaylen said without opening her eyes. If he didn't hurry up, she was ready to hang up on him again.

"I want to see you. I need to see you, Kaylen. I've been missing you. Seriously...I need to be able to see you." That woke Kaylen up a little. Caleb had never said anything about missing her or *needing* to see her. Maybe hanging up on him was the lil' push he needed.

"When?" Kaylen asked. This was the test. If he said "tonight," then she knew it was just a booty call, and he hadn't changed.

"Tomorrow. I want to take you out to dinner and a movie or something. Nothing major. Just that."

What? This nigga must be serious! Kaylen thought to herself.

"Sure, I don't think I'm busy then, Caleb. Call me tomorrow to give me the details. I can't focus at this ungodly hour of the morning."

"Well, I couldn't sleep because you have been on my mind. But I do apologize."

"Hmmm....ok, Caleb. Talk to you tomorrow," Kaylen said and pressed the button to hang up the phone.

Finally, sleep time. Kaylen adjusted her pillows and relaxed her body.

"WHO THE FUCK IS CALEB, KAY?!" Kaylen nearly jumped out of the bed at the loud voice that yelled at her. She tried to focus her eyes in the direction the voice came from, but was unable to see anything. She reached over and flicked the switch for the lamp on her nightstand.

How the hell someone get through my alarm and pass Tiny?! As soon as the light flicked on, she knew how. Standing in front of her was Salem. And he looked like hell on Earth.

"Salem! What are you doing in here?" Kaylen asked. She grabbed the covers on her bed and held them over her. It wasn't like he'd never seen her naked, but something about this man standing in front of her seemed strange and unfamiliar. Kaylen felt like she had no idea who he was.

"Get the fuck outta the bed! How long you been fucking around on me with that nigga?" Kaylen looked back at him confused. Salem's eyes seemed to be dancing around in his head like he had no idea where to aim them. He was pacing back and forth in the room punching at his hand as he spoke. Kaylen reached into her nightstand to grab her .9 millimeter.

"That shit ain't in there! What? You going to *kill* me, Kaylen? *Me?* I'm your man! You wanna *kill your man?*" Salem was able to narrow his eyes at her as he said it. With each word, he jabbed himself in the chest with an incredulous look on his face. Suddenly he charged at Kaylen and grabbed her by the throat. Kaylen felt something pressed between her breasts, and though she couldn't look down, she was positive that it was her .9 millimeter pointed directly at her.

"You're coming with me. I was trying to talk myself outta taking you to help me settle this situation with that nigga, Dom, but now I don't give a shit about you," Salem sneered at her. Kaylen tried to open her mouth to say something, and he slapped her hard in the face.

"Shut up and let's go."

ALEXIS

*A*lexis could hear the noise calm down around her. It should have by now. It had been hours since she heard the soft thumping coming from the DJ booth, the roar of the excited guests, and the casual chatter of the cleanup crew as they placed things where they needed to be, and prepped the ballroom for the next day's festivities. Alexis felt that it was time to get up and go, but her legs were weak. She could hear the roughness of her breathing, and it confused her. Although she was sore, she wasn't tired, but she did feel drained. Maybe that's what it was.

She wiggled her legs a little to see if they would cooperate. Thankfully, they did, so she pulled them up off the floor. She felt a little resistance as her legs pulled away from the stickiness beneath them, but she kept on until she was able to bring up her knees completely and place the bottom of her feet flat on the floor. She then lifted up her back and adjusted herself so that she could attempt to sit up completely. Her back ached as a direct effect of lying too long on the hard concrete floor. She moaned a little once she sat up and rubbed her aching head. Though there was no noise, it was throbbing to the point of great displeasure, and she felt like falling back onto the floor to lie there a little longer.

Her eyes jerked upwards as she heard the door handle jiggling. Alexis backed away quickly into a corner and prayed silently that Dexter had not returned. She reached out to grab something to protect herself, but there wasn't anything but a broom. She snatched it towards her and held it in front, gripping it so hard that her knuckles cracked.

The door swung open, and a short, thin man stood at the opening pulling a stack of ballroom chairs behind him along with a vacuum cleaner. Once he saw Alexis crouched in the corner he stopped abruptly and let go of each. Alexis jumped as the chair hit the floor with a loud *thud.*

"What are you doing in here?" He frowned at first. Then his eyes ran over Alexis, and he took in her tousled hair, torn dress and the dark bruises that were beginning to appear on her arms and face. "Are you ok?"

Alexis didn't say a word. She tried to retreat further back into the closet, but her back was already against the wall. The man started to move in closer to her, and that's when Alexis snapped. She raised the broom and slammed it down on the top of his head.

"HEY!" The man yelled as he crumbled down to the floor. Alexis took the opportunity to run out of the closet as he scrambled to get back on his feet. She was not about to let another man violate her again. She continued to run until she got to the entrance of the ballroom. The door was locked and although she pushed she could not get out. She turned her head behind her and saw that the man from the closet had finally gotten up on his feet and was looking at her from by the closet door.

"Hold on! I'm not going to hurt you!" He said with his hands up above his head, but Alexis did not believe him. She turned around to face him and leaned her back against the glass door. She darted her eyes around at her surroundings to try to find a place to escape.

"Listen...just pull at that latch right there on the corner of the door. It will let you out. The alarm will go off, but it's ok, I will shut it off," the man continued. He still had his arms in the air, but he was taking small steps forward, and Alexis didn't trust him. She turned her head only slightly enough to see the latch he was referring to and she pulled it hurriedly. Once she heard the click; she pushed the door open and ran out into the parking lot. It was dark, and there were no cars out except for a few scattered about. She took off running as fast as she could to the only place she knew to go. Home.

❦

ALEXIS FELT AN ODD FEELING ONCE SHE SAW THE GATE TO HER HOME. Instead of feeling happy to finally reach the estate after running and walking for what felt like hours, she felt disconnected. She walked to the gate and keyed in the code that made the automatic doors swing open, and she continued up the trail to her home. As she stared at the building, she thought about Marc and instead of feeling passion, love or wanting, she felt nothing. Not even anger or frustration as she had earlier. Something about what Dex had put her through had taken something away from her, but she wasn't ready to think on that yet. All she wanted to do was get home and climb into her bed.

Once she got to the porch of her home, she reached down under the plant that lay on the top stoop, and she grabbed the spare key. Thankfully, it was still there where she had left it years ago when they first moved in. She placed it into the door to unlock it and then walked into her home. It was dark and quiet which was pretty much how she expected it. Alexis had no idea what time it was, but she knew that Marc would most likely be asleep. He never stayed awake late. The last thing she had told her husband was not to wait up because she wouldn't be returning. Apparently, he had decided to take her advice.

Alexis stood at the base of the stairs and looked up at the winding staircase. It had been her idea to have one in the house. It had always been her dream. At this point, she wished that she had also selected an elevator. Each step up the stairs made Alexis ache. She'd had no idea that she was so heavily bruised and sore from fighting until this moment. She sucked in her breath as she tried to make it up the stairs without collapsing in pain. She was coming up on the last few steps when she felt the muscles in her leg give out from under her. She landed on the top of the staircase with a loud *thud.*

She looked up when she heard the door to her bedroom open. Marc ran out quickly, and as Alexis looked into his face, she saw a look of surprise and concern staring down at her. She ran her eyes quickly over his body and noticed that he was still wearing his white dress shirt from earlier before she left, but it was torn open, and his chest was showing. His pants were off, and he was wearing nothing but boxers and socks below. Alexis' eyes darted back in the direction of the door as she heard another noise coming from there.

"Oh, my God...baby! What's wrong with you? Are you ok?" Marc asked pulling Alexis up into his arms. He scooped her up with little effort and turned towards the bedroom. Alexis could barely keep her eyes open.

"I'm so tired. I'm sooo...tired, Marc," Alexis said as she let her head fall back onto his arms.

"It's ok, baby. You can go to sleep now. It's ok. Oh, my God, what happened? Do I need to take you to the hospital?" Marc asked placing Alexis onto the bed.

"No...I'm just tired," Alexis mumbled as she turned on her side to close her eyes, and continue on to what she hoped to be blissful sleep. She heard gentle footsteps in front of her, and it made her eyes jerk open. She clutched at her sheets thinking Dexter was lurking somewhere in the corner waiting for her. But it wasn't Dexter that she saw at all. Instead, creeping out of her room was Vanessa. She looked absolutely stunning with a soft, yellow lace negligee and a matching yellow lace thong, and black stilettos. Alexis thought nothing of it and continued to drift on to sleep.

"Lexi! Wake up, baby....Alexis!" Alexis jolted awake with a scream as she reached over to grab the lamp off her nightstand for protection. The cord ripped out of the wall, and something crashed down to the floor as it whipped up from behind the nightstand.

"What are you doing? It's me Lexi! It's Marc!" Alexis blinked in the dark. She couldn't see anything but knew from his voice that it was Marc. Seconds later he flicked on the light, and she blinked quickly, waiting for her eyes to adjust.

"You were screaming in your sleep. And fighting me. What's wrong with you? What's going on?" Marc stared at her with deep concern, but Alexis said nothing. She looked back at him and realized that there was nothing she wanted to say. She closed her eyes and placed her head back down on the pillow.

&

THE NEXT MORNING, ALEXIS WOKE UP TO WHISPERS. SOMEONE WAS talking, and she could hear their voices. She wasn't able to make out the words, but the sound was vibrating in her ears in a way that made it hard for her to ignore it. She tried to squeeze her eyes closed tightly, but it did nothing.

"Wait...hold on. She's awake," Voice #1 said.

"Ok, then...should I do anything? What do you want me to do?" Voice #2 said; it was Marc.

"Nothing. Just wait. And give her some space," Voice #1 sounded familiar. Alexis opened her eyes slowly. Voice #1 was Dr. Barnett. The woman who had been her doctor pretty much all of her life. Alexis groaned inside. She did not want to see Dr. Barnett. Dr. Barnett was also a close friend of Duchess' and was sure to break patient confidentiality if she found out about anything that had happened to Alexis.

"Hi, Alexis. Good morning," Dr. Barnett smiled. The woman was perfectly put together for such an early hour. Her make-up was done as if she had a professional make-up artist in her back pocket.

"Good morning. Why are you here so early, Dr. Barnett?" Alexis asked. She used her hand to shield her eyes from the light. The curtains were pulled open, and the sun showed brightly in the room.

"Lexi, it's not early. It's nearly three in the afternoon. What's wrong with you, baby?" Marc asked with concern. Dr. Barnett shot him a look that told him to keep quiet, and she continued on.

"Alexis, Marc called me here because he was concerned for you. He said that you came home disoriented, tired, and badly bruised. He was worried and called me to check in on you. Is everything ok, Alexis?"

Alexis nodded yes, but her body felt like "no." Her eyes welled up with tears as the memories of what had occurred yesterday replayed in her mind. Her best friend for years had raped her; the one man that she had no problem trusting once he reappeared in her life. She pulled the covers up under her chin to cover her body. She felt dirty and used. She felt disgusting, but most of all there was a smell. She wasn't sure if anyone else could smell it and if they were able to stand in her presence, she guessed they didn't. It smelled like sweat, grime, and dirt mixed together with semen and it made her want to vomit. She was not ready for this, and she wanted to be left alone.

Alexis tried to blink away her tears with no success and turned on her side away from Marc and Dr. Barnett.

"Ok, Alexis. I will give you some space. But you know if you need anything to call me." Alexi heard Dr. Barnett's footsteps as she started to walk towards the door, then she heard them stop.

"Oh, and Alexis, I must say this. If you were attacked….attacked in the way that Marc and I *think* you were attacked, you need to get to the hospital now. AIDS and HIV are real…and so are other diseases. You need to tell the police what happened, and you need to get help. If what I *think* happened to you did happen, you *need* to get help right now. This is not your fault. If this happened, it's because the person who did it is a sick, *sick* person," Dr. Barnett paused and waited for Alexis to respond. "I'm here if you need me, Lexi. C'mon, Marc. Let's let her continue to rest."

WEEKS LATER AND ALEXIS STILL WAS NOT ANY CLOSER TO GETTING OUT of the bed. It had become a safe place for her, and she dreaded the thought of leaving it. Marc had pulled her out each day to allow her to soak in the tub. He even tried to bathe her, but Alexis wasn't having it. She didn't want him to touch her or to look at her. She didn't want him to know how dirty and smelly she had become. No matter how much she scrapped her skin with her loofah, washcloth or body scrubber, she could not get rid of the smell or the feel of funk. Every time she looked at her body; she thought about how Dexter had rubbed her, grabbed her….vandalized her. She couldn't stand to stare too long.

Marc had been trying to bring her food, but she was not interested. Today, however, her stomach had gotten to the point where it no longer growled in pain for wanting nourishment. It seemed that she had gotten used to it.

"Lexi….?" Alexis groaned. She knew this voice and was not in the right mood to deal with it. It was Vanessa. Alexis opened her eyes, grateful that her back was to her younger sister. The last thing that she wanted to do was look at her. She assumed that Vanessa was flawless, as usual, and, therefore, the last person that she wanted to see in her current state. It would be another thing to remind her of why she was inferior, filthy, ugly, and dirty. How could she be anything but nasty with a sister as perfect as Vanessa?

"Hmm?" Alexis grunted. She squeezed her eyes closed; willing Vanessa to leave, but it did not work.

"Lexi…Are you ok? I'm worried about you. I'm thinking I need to talk to Mom and Dad. They are asking questions because no one's heard from you," Vanessa whined. Alexis squeezed her eyes together harder.

This is not what I need right now!

"Get the fuck out of my room," Alexis whispered. She heard Vanessa take in a sharp breath.

"Whaaa…? What did you say?" Vanessa asked. Alexis groaned loudly and turned around to face her sister.

Yep. This bitch looks impeccable, as usual; she thought.

"Why don't you tell them that when I came home from being *raped*, I found you in the room fucking around with my husband? Why don't you share that lil' tidbit with them, Vanessa?" Alexis sneered. She almost chuckled a little at the look on Vanessa's face. It was priceless. Her mouth was wide open, and her eyes were stretched as wide as they could go. She looked absolutely mortified, and that was the reaction that Alexis had wanted.

"If you want to spread some gossip, spread your shit, Vanessa, *not mine*. Now get out!" With that, Alexis flopped back down on the bed and waited for Vanessa to leave. Once she heard the door close, Alexis jumped up out of the bed and ran to the bathroom. This had become a morning ritual for the past few days, but today it seemed like it was going to be an all-day thing. Alexis reached down and slammed the lid of the toilet up and dry heaved into the toilet. Since she had eaten nothing all day, the only thing that came up was fluids. She held her stomach as she struggled to let out everything that was inside of her.

Well, unfortunately, I can't let out everything, Alexis thought wiping her mouth with her sleeve as she leaned over the sink to rinse her mouth. She glanced over to the top of the toilet at the pregnancy test that was still sitting where she had left it five minutes before Vanessa had decided to barge into her room unwanted and uninvited.

After Alexis dried her mouth, she walked over and stood over the test. Finally, she reached down and grabbed it.

Positive. Damn it.

She wrapped the test up with toilet paper and dropped it in the trash. She'd had plenty of unopened pregnancy tests tucked away under her bathroom sink. She and Marc had tried for about the last year to get pregnant. They weren't taking any additional measures for it to happen, but they weren't trying to stop it, and they each had hopes that it would happen naturally one day. Alexis had hopes of getting pregnant because she thought it would change their relationship and change him. She thought it would make him gentler and more caring. Now she was pregnant, and though she couldn't be positive who the father was, her gut told her that it wasn't Marc. Alexis walked over to the mirror and looked at her reflection as she ran her hand over her belly.

What am I going to do?

JAZMYN

*J*azmyn stared open mouth at the package in front of her. It was filled with things that could ruin her life. Things that she thought that no one knew about, and things that she had worked very hard to make sure were buried way back in her past. She was totally confused. She didn't understand how these photos surfaced and how the person whose name was on the box was able to access them. Though she hated her father for neglecting her and leaving her and her mother to pursue a new life, his name carried a lot of weight, and it was the reason she had been able to cover up her own dirty secrets.

When Jazmyn first met Dom it was amazing. He was exactly what she had needed at the time to liven up her life. She had lived a life that consisted of school, studying, and chores. Her mother was adamant about Jazmyn being able to make it out of the hood. But Jazmyn wasn't too concerned with that. Once she got to an age where she was fully aware of how beautiful she was and how much it made the opposite sex adore her, she was only concerned with using that power for pleasure and personal gain.

Meeting Dom had been the start of a new life for her. She rebelled, and she rebelled hard against everything that her mother had wanted for her. Dom introduced her into a fast paced life where drugs were the product, and deceit, murder, and sex was all part of the game. Dom began including Jazmyn in on his business deals as he rose through the ranks from being a small time corner boy to the boss. Once Dom made his ascent, Jazmyn noticed that the room was no longer filled with other teens around their age. The room was filled with cold-hearted killers; men who wouldn't hesitate to pop someone off if they noticed the slightest bit of disloyalty. Instead of scaring Jazmyn, it intrigued her to be around that much power, and she begged Dom to be a part of the team.

It was at that point that Dom introduced Jazmyn to Crimson. Crimson was a bad ass chick and to this day, Jazmyn would do anything that Crimson asked of her. The first time she met Crimson; she was standing over a man who was lying on the floor, belly up. Crimson was wearing a short leather skirt with long leather Christian Louboutin boots. She had on a red corset top, and her hair fell down loosely around her shoulders. She looked incredible.

Crimson was standing directly above him with one leg on either side of the man's body, staring straight down at him. Most men would have been overcome with sexual desire at the sight of a woman like Crimson standing over them with her legs wide open. However, Jazmyn was sure that the long and sharp machete she was holding was keeping that from happening.

That night, Jazmyn found out what happened to people who stole and anyone else that was disloyal to The Disciples, the crew that Dom founded. By the time that Crimson turned her attention to Jazmyn, Jazmyn was shuttering with excitement and eager to learn everything that she saw. From that point, she became Crimson's apprentice, and her job was to take care of the "wet work."

One day she had to take care of someone whom Dom gave her no information at all about. His directions were clear: go to the address left on the sheet of paper that he had given her. Once there, she was to enter the house with the key that was left in the mailbox and head into the living room. She was told that the man was already there, tied up and waiting to meet his maker. Jazmyn was ready to get to work, and she was exceptionally excited about this job. She knew that it was important because that would be the only reason that Dom wouldn't give her details, so she was focused on not fucking up.

Everything went as planned until the police arrived while Jazmyn was setting the scene. She always thought of wet work as a work of art and she liked to leave her jobs with a dramatic flair after she was done. For this guy, she'd decided to remove the light cover from around the light on the ceiling and stuff his severed head in its place. She separated his arms and legs from his body, and was preparing to arrange them in a special way around his torso like she had seen Crimson do one time, but she stopped when she heard the cars pull into the driveway.

Jazmyn panicked and grabbed everything that she brought into the home with her. Unfortunately, she had left her knife. Her father had pulled a lot of strings to get her out of that situation and keep the record sealed. The man that she had killed had been a rising politician who had been a threat to The Disciples operation.

Apparently, a young, up and coming journalist had been on the way to ask for an interview from the politician when she peeked through the curtains and saw what Jazmyn was up to. She snapped a picture and called the police. Thanks to her father, all evidence had been destroyed and wiped clean. That was the one thing that he'd done for her and her mother had to beg him to do that. Jazmyn wanted to return to work, but Dom and Crimson had told her she was through.

Dom had decided that Jazmyn needed to keep her hands clean. He thought it better for her to become an attorney and help his crew on the legal side of things. Crimson had agreed, and Jazmyn threw away her life of crime, murder, and torture to live on the straight and narrow side...or so she thought.

Someway that Jazmyn was quite unsure of; Shanice had sent a package to her home that included the photo of Jazmyn on that night as well as the police report and other evidence that was supposedly buried.

How did she get this? Jazmyn was confused and didn't have any idea of how to react. She hadn't heard from Shanice in weeks, and figured that she had taken her ass whooping and moved on. Jazmyn had no time to even decide the appropriate way to react before she heard the doorbell followed by a knock on her front door.

Jazmyn walked to the front door and looked through the peep hole. What she saw almost chilled her to her bone. It wasn't so much the people that were standing there. It was the fact that she saw them at her front door *together*. Combine that with the package that she'd just received, Jazmyn was ready to pass out. Jazmyn tried to gather herself as much as possible before she opened the door.

"Well, come on in. Long time, no see, Ms. Crimson." Jazmyn slid to the side to allow Dom and Crimson entry into her townhome. She glanced outside to make sure there was no one watching before she closed the door.

"So, what's going on?" Jazmyn asked as she walked behind them into her living room.

"We got shit to talk about," Crimson started.

Leave it to her to get right down to business.

Crimson ran her hand along Jazmyn's fireplace before turning to face her. Dom wasted no time and decided to sit down on Jazmyn's leather sectional. He reached down and pulled the lever to make the seat recline. Jazmyn sat down in one of the chairs near the entrance to the grand room.

"We got a problem. We got an anonymous package stating that someone has some dirt on us and is ready to expose it to the feds. I wouldn't pay too much attention to it, but it was sent to my *home* address; an address that no one should have. It also had some stuff dealing with information that only the three people in this room should know." Crimson paused and stared hard at Jazmyn. "Any thoughts?" She said after a while.

Jazmyn cleared her throat and spoke confidently, "Yes, I know who is doing it. I just got the package right there with evidence about that issue we...I had a while back," Jazmyn nodded her head in the direction of the box. Crimson didn't even flinch or follow Jazmyn's eyes. She already knew what Jazmyn was talking about.

"You know who it is?" Dom asked. Jazmyn nodded her head. "Well, handle it." Jazmyn's mouth dropped suddenly.

"What do you mean...?" she started.

"He means handle it or we will handle you. You feel me?" Crimson stated. With that, she pulled out a machete from behind her. She was so slick with it that Jazmyn had no idea she was even holding a knife so big on her. Jazmyn wondered for a minute how in the world she was able to conceal it. Crimson dropped the knife on the coffee table, and Jazmyn stared at it. It changed something in her; almost like a light switch. The last time she'd held that blade; she was holding it to the politician's throat. Now, here it was in front of her. She felt the anxiety growing in her stomach.

"I know you can do it. Call us when it's finished," Crimson said. Jazmyn didn't respond as they walked out of the door.

I gotta handle this shit.

TWO HOURS LATER, JAZMYN FOUND HERSELF OUTSIDE OF KINGSTON'S home. This time, instead of checking on what Kingston was doing, Jazmyn was on a very different mission. She knew for a fact that he would not be at the large mini-mansion that he and his wife shared. Kingston's activities were like clock-work. She suspected that he would be leaving for the gym when she got there, and when she saw him pull his Range Rover out of the garage over thirty minutes ago, she knew that was exactly where he was headed.

"I don't know why he would still be living with this crazy bitch anyways." Jazmyn thought to herself as she continued watching through the sheer curtains that did an awful job of shielding the activities that went on in the house from the outside world. Jazmyn watched as Shanice slept in what seemed to be a plush, California King-size bed. She had fallen asleep shortly after Kingston left, and Jazmyn had been watching her ever since as she tried to get herself prepared for what she knew she had to do. Crimson had made it seem like this was instinct, and the skill would easily return to her. Jazmyn had thought the same, but what she had not counted on was the fact that she had developed a conscience during her adult years.

The anger that she'd channeled in her youth in order to complete her tasks just wasn't what it used to be. Although she still blamed her father for nearly everything that had gone wrong in her childhood, she wasn't as angry about that anymore. Granted, she was able to dredge up enough anger to beat Shanice's ass the other night, but that was something that hadn't occurred in such a long time in her life.

Jazmyn looked once more through the window at the sleeping Shanice. The woman looked pretty peaceful. She had her hand wrapped around her bulging belly, and Jazmyn watched as she slept. Her breaths seemed to be short and somewhat labored, but all in all she looked nothing like the Queen Bitch that had thrown eggs on her at the party. Jazmyn's eyes moved towards the dresser in the room, and she saw Kingston's gold watch lying on top. The same watch that she had bought him for his last birthday. Her eyes welled up with tears as she looked at it lying there. The last time she had seen it lying on top of a dresser, it was in the hotel room at the W, where they had met to have wonderful, wild, crazy, and lustful sex. Jazmyn wiped the tears from her eyes and turned to walk away.

Just need to accept that I lost out on this one and move the hell on; she thought to herself. Like clock-work, she felt her phone vibrating in her pocket. *Damn! Thought I left it in the car!* Jazmyn thought a second about how this may be a bad sign. She hadn't even gotten to work, and she was already slipping. Jazmyn looked down at the text, and she immediately began to feel her body get cold.

Did it yet? Was all it said, but it was more than enough. Crimson was doing more than simply checking on the progress, and Jazmyn knew all too well that this was not a simple text to check on her status. Jazmyn looked around at her surroundings quickly. She knew Crimson was around; she just wasn't sure where. And if she knew Crimson like she knew she did, she would not find her. The point is that she *was* there. If Jazmyn didn't finish this job, Crimson would do it for her. Then there would be hell to pay after.

Jazmyn turned back towards the house; confidence renewed and her mind on auto-pilot. She grabbed tightly on her bag of tools that contained everything she needed in order to get to work, and she walked over to the window in the bedroom adjacent to where Shanice slept. It was decorated with soft yellow hues. Jazmyn stopped for a second and looked around, but she felt nothing. Then slowly, but surely, she felt her anger begin to come in. This room signified everything that was wrong with her life at the moment, and she was ready to bring an end to it all.

She reached up and popped open the window easily. It wasn't even locked.

Niggas get too comfortable in these ritzy neighborhoods; Jazmyn thought with a smirk. This was about to be pretty easy. Jazmyn rolled her slim body through the small window and placed her feet softly onto the plush carpet. As she stood in the room, she took a second to look around at what she saw. Could this ever be her life anymore? Half of her wanted to say yes….at some point maybe she could be a mother, and settle down with a man and be in love. But the reality of the situation was that Kingston was the only guy that she had ever fallen in love with. And she was about to kill his wife. Somehow, she was sure that this wouldn't end with a proposal and a baby. Jazmyn walked out of the room slowly, dragging her fingertips atop the dark wood of the crib and the dresser. *So pretty.*

She walked into the master bedroom and looked at Shanice. She was still sleeping soundly, and that brought a smile to Jazmyn's face. This would be easy. Jazmyn pulled out her blade slowly, admiring the noise it made as it slid out of the holster. It was sharp, and made the job as easy as possible. Kept her cuts clean.

Suddenly, Shanice rolled over onto her back, and Jazmyn stopped in her tracks. She sucked in her breath and held it in an attempt to be as quiet as possible. Shanice adjusted and moaned a little, but her eyes stayed closed. She rubbed her hand over her belly and then resumed her soft snoring. Jazmyn's eyes stayed concentrated on Shanice's bulging belly.

When the hell is she due? That baby looks like it's about to bust out at any minute! Jazmyn took a minute to count the months in her head.

Damn...she has to be about 8 or 9 months! Jazmyn thought a minute about leaving, but then she remembered Crimson. At this point, there was nothing she could do. It was either her or Shanice and Jazmyn wasn't about to even play with that decision. Shanice brought this on herself and Jazmyn had to do what she had to do.

Time to get to work.

JAZMYN SAT DOWN ON A CHAIR IN THE CORNER AND LOOKED AT THE scene around her. Crimson wouldn't be too happy with how it was done, but Jazmyn did as she was told. Shanice was finished. Jazmyn hadn't wanted her to suffer, so she injected her with something to knock her out before starting the process. The scene around her was gruesome to say the least. There was blood everywhere. The beautiful bedspread was now stained by the deep, dark red of Shanice's blood. Although Jazmyn had tried to keep the scene as neat as she possibly could, it had not worked according to plan. Part of her thought that the scene that she had created seemed to be indicative of all the pain she had been feeling. Jazmyn took a quick look around the room and shuddered.

What is Kingston going to think when he sees this? She couldn't be the one responsible for him going crazy. Jazmyn pulled out the contents of her small tool bag and laid them out on the table and dresser. She'd defended enough criminals to know how to set a scene to look like it had something to do with drugs. Although Shanice's family members may have been able to attest to her not seeming like she did drugs, no one would be able to explain the drugs that would later on be found in her system. Jazmyn knew what to do in order to cover her tracks.

Jazmyn rose up out of her chair and dialed 911 on Shanice's phone. With any hope, the police would find her before Kingston did. She didn't want him to come home to this. Without saying a word, Jazmyn dropped the phone next to Shanice on the bed and walked out of the room. She walked into the adjoining room that she came in from and headed hurriedly to the window. She hesitated for a second once she got to the baby crib and looked in. There, sleeping in the crib so soundly, as if she was not born out of tragedy, was Shanice's baby. Jazmyn had been unable to kill something so innocent, so she decided to spare the child. It had taken forever to get her quiet, but thankfully, there was formula in the cupboards in the kitchen. Jazmyn took one last look before she jumped back out the window and shut it behind her. She was already in her car and headed towards her home when her phone rang.

Kingston.

KAYLEN

I *guess it's about to get worse.*

When Kaylen returned to consciousness, Salem was still standing over her with his blade in hand. The look on his face worried her. His eyes were wild, and it seemed like he no longer cared about himself; which meant that he, of course, could give a shit about her.

Kaylen had been locked in this place for what felt like months, although she wasn't sure that it was that long. Definitely weeks though. She was unable to see outside, so she could only guess about how many days it had been. She really had no clue. The night that Salem showed up in her apartment, he had made her get into the car, and he drove her out to the very same home that he had picked her up at all those months ago when Levi had died. She had told him long ago about the secret door to the basement, and that's where he'd decided to stash her.

Once there, Salem told her this long story about how he had taken the meth that he found in her pants pocket. He was skeptical about using it because it wasn't his drug of choice. He'd only seen white boys use Meth, but he figured it was worth a try. After using that, he wanted more but didn't want his friends to know what was going on,

185

so he started back working with Dom thinking that he could get some from him by pretending that he was selling it. Dom didn't mess around with it, but he had some white guys that worked for him who handled that branch of the business, so Salem worked with them to suffice his addiction.

Unfortunately, the money that he had on hand, what was not mixed up in the business with Zo, started running short, and he wasn't able to pay Dom's crew for it. Dom had told him the night of the party that he had 48 hours to either return the product or bring the cash. It was at that moment that Salem began to think up what he must have believed to be an ingenious plan: he kidnapped Kaylen so she could make more for him. Somehow he was able to gain access to the ingredients and tools necessary, and soon after stashing Kaylen down in the basement; everything was set up and ready for her to begin working.

Kaylen figured she would only need to make enough to cover Salem's debt with Dom; however, Salem had other plans. Kaylen knew that 48 hours were long gone, but Salem still had her cooking for him, and Kaylen began to realize that he was using her to support his personal habit. He left for hours at a time and would return with boxes of pills so that she could get to work. He'd brought more than enough materials to get a low-level lab put together. It wasn't quite as sophisticated as the ones that Levi used to put together for her, but Kaylen couldn't expect much since she was working with an addict.

Kaylen peered through her eyes and stared at Salem as she began to shiver. It wasn't cold in the room, but she hadn't eaten in days, barely had drunken water, and she was beginning to feel sick, and had the chills. Salem was still looking at her wildly, and she had no idea what to expect from him. He had become quite unpredictable the past few days. Months ago, she would have never believed that Salem could lay a hand on her. However, recently, that had become the norm for her.

Salem had hit her with anything that was around in order to get her to comply with his requests. After she was done making the meth, he would take the finished product and leave her to continue making more. Cooking meth took a while, and Kaylen figured Salem liked to have a continuous supply to sell as well as to use. He had to continue selling; if he didn't want Zo getting even more suspicious of his actions, he had to supplement his income in some way.

"Salem," Kaylen said barely above a whisper. It hurt her to talk, and she wouldn't have tried if she didn't feel like something needed to be said in order to salvage her life. "Salem, please....let me go. Please?" She begged again. She had asked this question of Salem every time she'd seen him. Although she felt that it was time to lose faith, she couldn't do that. Kaylen tried to open her eyes wider so that she could take a good look at him, but her swollen lids were proving that to be a difficult task. She paused to allow her eyes to focus on his face, and what she saw gave her a tiny glimmer of hope. Salem was looking at her, and it seemed as if he had tears in his eyes.

Suddenly, Salem sat down on the floor with a loud thump. He raised his knees and let his head fall between his legs as he started to bawl. Kaylen sat completely still because she was unsure of what to expect. She had never seen him get like this the entire time she'd been trapped down in the basement. He had always been angry, irritable, and just plain evil. This crying thing was new.

"I'm so sorry, Kay. I'm so sorry, baby," he said over and over again through his tears. Kaylen could barely understand what he was saying because of the ringing in her ears and his sobs. He lifted his head, and Kaylen watched as he wiped away the tears and mucus that fell down his face. "I'm so sorry. I don't want to do this to you. I love you baby. I don't know what's wrong with me."

Kaylen opened her mouth. She knew that she should use this moment to her advantage and try to talk him into releasing her, but she was struggling with what she should say. She was actually afraid to say anything for fear that he might snap and start beating her ass again.

C'mon, Kaylen. You gotta do this!

"Salem...baby, I love you, too. Please let me go. I will keep cooking for you, I promise. Please...just let me go. I love you, baby." Kaylen's entire body was aching, but she tried her hardest to scoot as close to

Salem as her chains would allow. He looked into her eyes and stopped crying.

"You still love me? You love me, Kay?" he asked. His eyes glistened with hope as he asked the question. Kaylen readily agreed.

"Umhmmm...yes, Salem. I never stopped loving you," Kaylen lied. She hoped that he couldn't see right through her to the truth that lied beneath. She hated Salem for what he'd done to her. It was hard for her to say the opposite to his face and try to seem sincere.

"C'mere, Kay," Salem said as he slid over to where Kaylen was. He held his arms out to embrace her, and Kaylen reluctantly fell forward into them. She held her breath as she laid her head on his shoulder to make the hug feel genuine. She couldn't wrap her arms around him because of the chains, and for the first time since being there, she was grateful for them.

Salem pulled back from the embrace and looked at her. His eyes glistened, and Kaylen wondered if he was high.

Of course, he is. This nigga is always high; she thought. Salem came close to Kaylen's face, and then placed his mouth on top of hers. He began pushing his lips against her face to kiss her and Kaylen's act was beginning to get harder and harder to keep up. Once Salem opened his mouth and forced his tongue into hers, she almost gagged. His breath was horrid, and his tongue tasted like straight boo-boo. Kaylen fought back the instinct to gag and tried to return the kiss as best as she could without throwing up inside his mouth.

Salem's hands slid down to her backside, and he gripped her ass tightly. Kaylen did not feel an ounce of pleasure. She had been stuck down in this basement for so long, and she had not even been able to take a full shower. Salem allowed her enough time to rinse quickly every once in a while, and that was it before making her get back to work. The last thing on her mind, even if she could stomach being intimate with Salem again, was sex. Kaylen fought the urge to scream out and fight as she felt Salem taking off her clothes. He was leaning close to her, and she could smell the sickly sour scent of his breath as he exhaled loudly while tugging at the shredded pieces of clothing that hung loosely off her body.

"Salem...wait!" Kaylen cried out. She was certain that she was not ready for this level of acting. There was no way that she could see herself hiding the repulsion that she was feeling at the thought of having sex with him. He stopped tugging at Kaylen's clothing long enough to cast a confused stare in her direction.

"What, Kay?" Salem asked slowly. "Don't you wanna make love to me again?" The way he asked it, coupled with the way that Salem was staring at her made Kaylen's heart flutter a little. She was reminded for a split second of the old Salem. The way that he was when they had first met; before the drugs, before the abuse and before the craziness took over. Kaylen wanted to go back to those times, but she knew they were long gone. However, she tried to think on those times in order to make Salem believe that she still loved him. She needed him to trust her enough to let her go.

"Yes, baby. But...I think you need to take these handcuffs off. I can't do anything with you as long as you got me locked up in here. Just unlock me and then we can do what we both want to do." Kaylen licked her lips slowly and watched as his eyes followed her tongue. Suddenly Salem snatched back so quickly that Kaylen could feel the rush of air from his movement.

"Wait...if I let you go, how I know you ain't gonna leave me?" he asked. He made a face as if he had busted her, and Kaylen's heart skipped a beat.

Damn it! What the hell am I supposed to say now? Kaylen had always been a quick thinker in the past and, likewise, quick to respond. However, the fear that she had of messing up this opportunity seemed to cripple her somewhat, and she wasn't sure what to do.

"No...um, Salem. Baby, I told you that I loved you. I won't leave," Kaylen stammered. She wanted to punch herself in the face at that exact moment. She didn't sound believable at all, and she could tell by the way Salem's eyebrow rose upwards that he wasn't convinced either.

"I'on know, Kay. You were getting pretty close with my nigga the night that you tried to leave me. How I know you ain't let that nigga hit it? You think I'on know that he was feeling you first? That's the only reason I spotted you...because I saw that nigga sweating you," Salem spoke forcefully, and it made Kaylen worry that she was losing out on the chance to escape. He didn't seem to be in the vulnerable state that he had been in earlier, and instead of pulling her close, he was backing up.

Damn it! Why didn't I just do what I needed to do? It's not like I haven't done it a bunch of times before! Kaylen thought. She was nearing a state of panic, and her brain was racing frantically as she searched for something to say next. She opened her mouth determined to put on the best performance that she could muster up.

"Salem, stop it. If I wanted Zo, I would have gotten with him when I saw him at the club. You approached me, and I chose you. I fell in love with you, and you are the one that I want. Now, come over here and give me something to remind me of the good times," Kaylen waited and watched Salem's facial expressions as she finished.

"I don't know, Kay. I'm not ready to release you yet. Something telling me that you may leave." Kaylen shook her head quickly back and forth as Salem spoke. She scrambled to try to get closer to him to persuade him that she wouldn't go. Suddenly they heard a big thump from upstairs followed by slow footprints.

"Oh, my God! Oh, my God...not again!" Kaylen mumbled as she tried to back away against the wall.

Fucking Feds here again! Kaylen thought. She glanced around at the scattered materials around the large room. It looked like a meth lab. There was no way to deny it. Kaylen hoped that once they saw her fate; they wouldn't suspect her of any current wrongdoing or suspect her of being involved that day when Levi died.

Salem popped up from the floor and ran over to where Kaylen was and grabbed her by the throat, while placing one hand over her mouth. He pulled his hunting knife out and pressed it so hard against her that it drew blood. She stifled a scream and tried to calm herself as he held her tightly. She was afraid to move for fear that it would drive the knife into her throat.

The footsteps continued to walk above them until they stopped right over the door. Kaylen's heart leaped with hope. This couldn't be the Feds because there was only the sound of one person walking around the room. The Feds never traveled alone, and she knew from before that she would have heard something that resembled a stampede if they were actually in the building.

This might be someone that can help me! Kaylen thought with hope. She hadn't realized that she whimpered a little with excitement as she was thinking until Salem responded by pressing the knife even further into her neck. Her eyes welled up with tears as she felt the pain followed by the wet sensation of the blood dripping down her neck. Salem gripped her even tighter as they listened to the opening of the door above being lifted.

Light shined through the opening from the area above. The appearance of the light made Kaylen squint her eyes. It had been so long since she'd been able to see natural sunlight. In the dungeon, she wasn't sure if it was day or night. It was dark all the time unless Salem wanted her to work. Even then, he only gave her just enough light to see what she needed to see.

"Salem!" A voice called out from the opening. "Salem, it's me!" Kaylen's heart began beating hard in her chest.

It's Zo! What is he doing here? I know he isn't helping Salem! What is going on?

"Shit! Zo, what you doing here? How did you find me?" Salem asked. He didn't move, and he didn't loosen his grip on Kaylen. She could hear his breathing get heavier and faster, and she flinched out of habit. Usually when Salem began breathing like this, it was the precursor for an ass whipping, mainly because he was losing his high.

"You took my car to come out here. Something didn't seem right, so I used the GPS to follow you...everything alright? I'm coming down now," Zo said. Kaylen saw feet dangling from the opening in the ceiling, and her heartbeat sped up. She didn't know what to expect.

"No, Zo! Stay up...," Salem began, but he was cut off as Zo landed on the floor of the basement with a loud thud.

"Salem! What the f....Kaylen! Are you alright?" Zo said as he began running towards them.

"STOP! Stop right there, or I will kill her, I swear to God!" Salem yelled as he pressed the knife harder against Kaylen's neck. She yelped out in pain, and Zo stopped in his tracks with his hands up in the air.

"Salem, look! I'm not coming any closer, man. Look!" Zo said.

"I told you not to come down here!" Salem yelled. Kaylen watched as Zo looked around the room with sheer confusion.

"Salem, what the fuck is going on here?" Zo asked once he had a minute to let his eyes adjust to everything that was in the room. Kaylen wanted to yell out to him to tell him what was going on, but she was afraid to speak. "Kaylen, what are you doing here? What is going on?"

"Zo, I think you better go. You were not supposed to come down here," Salem said through gritted teeth. Kaylen glanced in his direction through the side of her eyes. She didn't think that Salem would try to hurt Zo, but she wasn't sure.

Shit, I never thought he would try to hurt me! She thought to herself. The fact is that Zo had seen some shit that he wasn't supposed to and now it was too late for him to *not* see it. Kaylen knew she had to say something to get him to leave. The important thing was that if Zo left; he would be able to get help for her.

"Leave, Zo. Go...please!" Kaylen struggled to say this even though Salem was still gripping her tightly. He had loosened his grip on the knife, so it wasn't piercing her as badly, and she was able to speak.

Listen to me, Zo. Get the hell outta here! Kaylen was trying so hard to send that telepathic message that she felt beads of sweat on her forehead.

"Hell, no, Kay! I'm not leaving you in here with this nigga. I don't know what the fuck he got you doing in here, but this shit is about to end now!"

"I knew it!" Salem yelled. He slung Kaylen to the ground by her neck and walked over to where Zo stood. Kaylen gasped for breath and then watched with fear of what might come next. "I knew you was fucking my bitch!" Salem charged up to Zo and jabbed his finger into his face.

"No, Salem! Baby, I love you! I told you that Zo and I are nothing. Why don't you believe me?" Kaylen yelled out. She was trying to do anything that she could to stop Salem. She knew that he still had his knife on him, and she was afraid of what he would do to Zo. She watched, and waited for Salem to react to her. She got nothing.

"You been fucking her, Zo? Don't bullshit me!" Salem said as he pushed Zo back. Kaylen waited for Zo to respond, but he didn't. He continued to look at Salem directly in his eyes. His stare was long and hard. His eyes seemed to be piercing directly through Salem.

What the fuck is this nigga doing? Why won't he say something? Kaylen thought to herself.

"Salem, listen to me! I don't give a fuck about Zo, baby. If I wanted him, I would have spoken to him when I first saw him at the club. But I wanted you!" Kaylen yelled, trying to sound as sincere as possible. She watched as both men turned their attention towards her. Kaylen let her eyes fall on Zo, and she saw that he had a peculiar look in his eyes. He looked surprised and hurt.

I know he ain't falling for this shit. I guess I'm a better actress than I thought! Salem, on the other hand, had a different expression. He looked towards Kaylen, and she could feel the rage leaking from his glare. He looked at her as if he were about to boil over.

"Shut the fuck up, bitch! I wasn't talking to you!" Salem ran over to her and pulled her up off the floor by her neck and brought her face close to his. "You are the worst thing that ever happened to me. I knew you was a hoe when I met you and I was right. Now I'm about to teach you a lesson since you decided it was cool to go around fucking the homies!" With that, Salem punched her directly in the face. Kaylen fell back onto the ground with a loud grunt. She heard another noise, much louder and a hard thud. When she opened her eyes, she saw Salem sitting on the floor holding his face and Zo was standing directly over him.

"What the hell is wrong with you, Salem?" Zo asked as he stood over where his friend sat. Suddenly, Salem swiped his feet out and tripped Zo causing him to fall hard onto the floor. As soon as Zo's head hit the ground, Salem jumped off the floor and straddled Zo with his knife out. Kaylen watched in horror as Salem pressed the knife against his neck.

"You was my homeboy, Zo! And you betray me for this bitch?! You know we go back way farther than that! How could you do this shit?" Salem yelled as he hovered over Zo's face. He pressed the knife against his neck, and it began to draw deep, red blood.

"Salem, stop! Please! Stop it, please. Don't do it!" Kaylen cried. She knew what Salem was capable of, and she was afraid that neither she nor Zo would be making it out alive.

"Shut up, bitch! After I kill this nigga, you next! Y'all mother-fuckers think you can fuck around on me?!" All of a sudden, Kaylen heard a loud gunshot. She knew the sound and it caused her to back frantically to the corner. Images of Levi's death that had happened in this very same home came back to her, and she could once again see his body as it popped up in the air riddled with bullets. Kaylen let out a blood curdling scream as she fought to distance herself from the origins of the noise.

"Oh, my God! No, Salem! Why did you do it? Why did you kill him?" Kaylen yelled as she fought to free herself from the handcuffs and the chains around her legs. But it wasn't Salem that stood up and began walking towards her. Instead, she watched as Zo pushed Salem's slumped body from off of him and pulled himself slowly from off the floor. Blood was splattered onto his shirt, and Kaylen could see that a little was on his face. Her eyes looked over to Salem, and she watched as the blood continued to spill from his body and onto the floor. Kaylen's mouth opened wide as she took in the sight.

"Oh, my God...he's dead!" she whispered to herself. She watched as Zo stood over Salem and looked down at his body. He seemed to be zoned out; as if his mind had drifted off into another place as he continued to stare in silence.

"Zo, get the keys off the table! Please take these things off of me. We have to go!" Her voice made Zo snap out of his trance, and he walked slowly over to the table near Kaylen where her latest batch of meth sat. He grabbed the keys and walked over to her to begin unlocking the handcuffs. As soon as Kaylen was free, she jumped up and hugged Zo tightly. He didn't return the hug; his arms were limply hanging by his side. Kaylen looked up at him, and saw that he was staring at Salem's body as the blood continued to ooze from it.

"Zo, we have to go now. Where are your keys?" Kaylen watched Zo as he walked over to Salem and knelt down beside him. He reached into his pocket and grabbed Salem's cellphone.

"What are you doing?" Kaylen asked as she ran over and stood over Zo. She watched as he punched in the numbers 9-1-1, wiped his fingerprints off the phone and then dropped the phone on his body.

"Wait...what about my fingerprints?" Kaylen whispered to Zo as she looked around. Her fingerprints had to be on at least some of the things here. She'd worn gloves when making the meth, but other than that, she had not worn any. Her blood was still on the floor in the corner from where Salem had last beaten her. Zo took one look around, and she could see that he was thinking the same thing, as well. He handed her the keys and motioned for her to go up through the door that led out of the basement. Kaylen obeyed without a word and left.

We have to hurry, Zo! Kaylen said once she was seated inside of Zo's car. The police should have been set to arrive any minute. She squinted through the sunlight as she waited for Zo to surface from out of the run-down shack. It seemed it would take forever for her eyes to adjust to the sunlight, but she was happy to finally see it.

Finally after what felt like hours, she saw Zo running from out of the house, holding a large object.

What the hell? Is he holding Salem's body? Kaylen thought as she squinted to steady her focus. She watched as Zo ran behind the car and dropped Salem near a tree. Then he ran over to the car, opened the door and jumped into the driver side.

"Zo...what is going on?" Kaylen yelled. She barely had time to brace herself as Zo slammed the car into reverse and sped hurriedly out of the driveway. Kaylen's head fell backwards onto the headrest and then sideways onto the window as he whipped the car to the right to turn out towards a side road. Kaylen moaned in pain and rubbed her head. She opened her eyes at the exact moment that she heard a loud banging noise that resembled an explosion.

"Whaaaaa...?" Kaylen said as she flipped around in her seat to look out the back of the car. The portion of the shack that she could see was totally engulfed in flames. Kaylen flipped around in her seat to look at Zo, but he continued to stare straight ahead. He didn't look at her or say anything the entire way to her home.

EPILOGUE

𝒦aylen stared at the man in front of her as he knelt on bended knee. This could not be what she thought it was. There was no way. But it was. She had heard the words as he proclaimed his love. A love that she was confused as to *how* it existed. There was no way. This person in front of her was so different from who she initially thought he was, and he'd shown that to her because never in forever had she thought that she would be where she was now.

Kaylen had to sit down to stop her head from spinning. Everything seemed so surreal…almost as if it were a dream. Not a good dream though. A good dream would not have taken her through the love-struck torture of one man to the proposal of another.

How can he love me? I don't understand? LOVE?! Kaylen pressed the palm of her hand against her forehead, and waited for the room to stop spinning around her.

"Baby? Are you alright?" he said standing up from kneeling only to lean over and hold her.

Baby??? *When did I become his baby?* Kaylen was confused. Never had she dreamed that this would be her. It hadn't even been two weeks since Salem's death. How could she...how could *anyone* move that fast?

"Give me a minute. I need time to get my thoughts together," Kaylen said motioning him away from her. She needed air...and space.

"I will go grab you some water. Stay right there!"

Where the hell does he think I'm going? Kaylen felt beads of sweat bubbling up on her forehead. She felt like she was having a hot flash. Her breathing quickened, and it felt like she couldn't breathe as fast as her body wanted. She started sucking in quick bursts of air, faster and faster and instead of making her feel better, she felt light-headed. It was all too much. She thought she might have been having an anxiety attack.

Or worse. Maybe I'm dying! Kaylen fell backwards on the couch and tried to ground herself.

"Here baby. Here is some water." Kaylen grabbed the glass of water and guzzled it down as fast as she could. The cold liquid chilled her insides, and it seemed to calm her. She felt her body temperature begin to normalize, and her breathing slowed some.

"Oh, my God. Thank you!" Kaylen gasped between gulps. She still wasn't ready to continue the topic of conversation, but she was thrilled to be feeling her panic attack subsiding.

"Now, baby, about that pro....." he was cut off as they turned their attention to the front door where someone was banging loudly.

"Open up! Police!" Kaylen felt herself getting dizzy again.

"The police? Why are the police here?" Caleb asked looking Kaylen directly in the eyes. The confusion was expected...who would expect a police presence in the middle of his proposal? Kaylen felt her body returning to panic mode and her breathing began to increase.

"Open up! This is the police!" Kaylen took a deep breath, and reached up to smooth down her hair and wipe her face. She didn't do anything wrong, so there was no need to panic.

As she swung open the door, she looked up at two tall officers standing at her door with their hands on their hips to make sure they had direct access to their gun holsters.

"Yes?" Kaylen asked quietly. She tried to force as much confidence as she could into the one word as not to appear guilty.

"Hi, are you Kaylen Washington?" the male officer asked her. He leaned back on his legs which threw Kaylen off quite a bit because it seemed as if he were pushing his pelvis towards her. As a natural reflex, Kaylen's eyes swooped down at his crotch before she looked up to meet his stare.

"Uh...yes, I'm Kaylen. Is there a problem, officers?' Kaylen asked crossing her arms in front of her.

"Yes, is there a problem?" Caleb piped up from behind her. Kaylen groaned inwardly as he stepped up and stood behind her at the door.

"And you are?" the officer asked Caleb with a smirk. He looked over to his partner and gave her a knowing glance. Kaylen could have sworn that he saw her wink back.

"I'm the man that was in the middle of a proposal when you all decided to show up. Now what's going on with my fiancé?"

Kaylen suppressed the desire to roll her eyes, and she tried her hardest to hold her hands at her side and not smack him in the face for his comment. She had an idea why the police were here, and she knew that what he'd said would not help.

"Well, sorry – I didn't know that." The officer looked at Caleb mockingly before turning his attention towards Kaylen. "Kaylen Washington, you are under arrest for the murder of Salem Hunte. You have the right to remain silent. Anything you say or do...."

"Wait...what?!" Kaylen yelled. Kaylen pushed the officer's hand away from her as he reached out to grab her arm.

"Ma'am, I don't want to have to use force!" the male officer gave her a look that made Kaylen believe that he would only be too happy to use force on her.

Oh, my God. Under arrest? I thought they may question me about it, but that's it! Kaylen felt her breathing speed up, and she fell down to the floor as she felt her legs give out underneath her. She bent over on the floor and held herself up with her arms as she struggled to steady herself.

"Baby? Are you ok?" Caleb said as he knelt down beside her.

Kaylen tried to answer him, but she felt too light-headed to respond. Suddenly, she felt herself falling into darkness as she fell all the way down to the floor.

You could read part 2 for FREE! Click here and join my mailing list to find out how. If you can't click the link, text PORSCHA to 25827 to join.

NOTE FROM PORSCHA STERLING

Thank you for reading! Please join my mailing list to stay up-to-date on my next releases! If you can't click the link, text PORSCHA to 25827 to join.

I truly do hope that you enjoyed learning about the 3 Queens. Kaylen, Alexis and Jazmyn are characters very close to my heart and they have a lot more in store for them.

Please make sure to leave a review! I love reading them!

I would love it if you reach out to me on Facebook, Instagram or Twitter! Search 'Porscha Sterling's VIP Readers' on Facebook to join my reading group!

Peace, love & blessings to everyone. I love allllll of you!

ABOUT THE AUTHOR

PORSCHA STERLING is an influencer, publisher, and national best-selling author who is widely considered the exemplar of self-publishing success in the digital age. Winner of the SHEEN Magazine Literary Excellence Award, she's best known for her book series Bad Boys Do It Better.

Sterling holds an MBA, which helped her in the development of her publishing company, Royalty Publishing House, a stronghold in the African-American literary community, publishing many top-selling novels in the urban, contemporary romance, interracial romance, and women's fiction genres. Sterling has also partnered with fellow best-selling author and publisher, Leo Sullivan, on the launch of a mobile app, known as the LiT Reading App, which connects readers with exclusive material from independent authors. To find out more information about Porscha Sterling, visit all of the social media outlets at @Porscha_Sterling and her website, Porscha-Sterling.com.

Join Porscha Sterling's Mailing List
To find out more about her, visit her website

JOIN MY MAILING LIST!

Join my mailing list to stay up to date on my blog posts, news and my new releases. I also run many contests that are only mentioned to my mailing list subscribers.

Click this link to join or text PORSCHA to 25827

To submit a manuscript for my review, go here or visit www. royaltypublishinghouse.com and visit the 'submissions' tab.

READ MORE ON THE LIT READING APP!

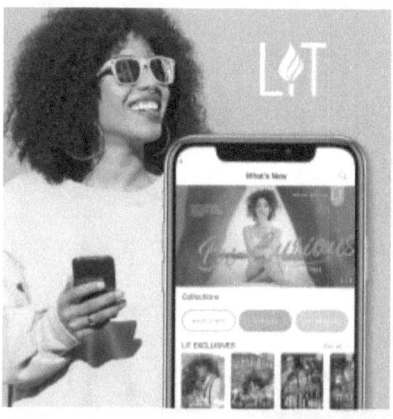

Read more books like this one **for less**! Check out some other new releases on the LiT Reading App. Go to www.litreadingapp.com to learn more!

www.ingramcontent.com/pod-product-compliance
Lightning Source LLC
Chambersburg PA
CBHW051250250626
47155CB00009B/3246